ACT OF NEGLIGENCE

Also by John Bishop

ACT OF MURDER
ACT OF DECEPTION
ACT OF REVENGE

ACT OF NEGLIGENCE

A DOC BRADY MYSTERY

John Bishop, MD

MANTID PRESS

Act of Negligence
A Doc Brady Mystery
Copyright © 2021 by John Bishop. All rights reserved.

ISBN: 978-1-7342511-6-6 (paperback)
ISBN: 978-1-7342511-7-3 (eBook)
Published by Mantid Press

For information about this title, contact:
Attention: Permissions Department
legalquestions@codedenver.com

CONTENTS

1. BEATRICE ADAMS......................1
2. LEOPARD LEOTARD....................12
3. MILDRED BLAND......................23
4. AUTHOR DINNER......................33
5. DEATH..............................41
6. FLOOD..............................51
7. OFFICE.............................61
8. EMERGENCIES........................72
9. AUTOPSIES..........................81
10. RESCUE............................93
11. MORGENSTERN......................104
12. DEATH............................116
13. BONHOFFER........................126
14. BELLADONNA.......................137
15. HOME.............................148

16. REGENERATION.....................157
17. THYROID..........................167
18. JEFF CLARKE......................176
19. STELLA...........................183
20. PLEASANT VIEW....................192
21. CRIME SCENE......................203
22. PROWLERS.........................212
23. PATCHES..........................219
24. CYNTHIA..........................227
25. RECORDS..........................236
26. FRAZIER..........................243
27. PRISONER.........................251
28. RESCUE...........................259
29. OTHERS...........................268

ABOUT THE AUTHOR....................275

CHAPTER 1

BEATRICE ADAMS

Monday, May 15, 2000

"**M**orning, Mrs. Adams. I'm Dr. Brady."

There was no response from the patient in Room 823 of University Hospital. She was crouched on the bed, in position to leap toward the end of the bed in the direction of yours truly. I could not determine her age, but she definitely appeared to be a wild woman. Her hair was a combination of gray and silver, long and uncombed and in total disarray. She had a deeply lined face, leathery, with no makeup. Her brown eyes were frantic, and her head moved constantly to the right and left. She was clad only in an untied hospital gown which dwarfed her small frame. My guess? She wasn't over five feet tall.

"Ms. Adams? Dr. Morgenstern asked me to stop by and see about your knee?"

She did not move or speak; she just continued squatting there in the hospital bed, bouncing slightly on her haunches, and staring at me while her head moved slowly to and fro.

I looked around the drab private room with thin out-of-date drapes and faded green-tinted walls. There were no flowers. I judged the patient to most likely be a nursing-home transfer.

I made the safe move by backing out of the patient's room, and I walked the twenty yards to the nurses' station. The white-tiled floors were freshly waxed, but the medicinal smell was distinctly different from the surgical wing. There was an unpleasant pine scent in the air that could not hide the odor of decaying human beings and leaking body fluids. It was the smell of chronic illness and disease.

"Cynthia?" I asked the head nurse on the medical ward, or so announced her name tag. She was sitting at the far side of the long nursing station desk performing the primary duty of a nursing supervisor: paperwork. She was an attractive Black woman in her mid-forties, I estimated.

"Yes, sir?"

"Dr. Morgenstern asked me to see Mrs. Adams in consultation. Room 823? What's the matter with her? She won't answer me. She just stares, sitting up in the bed on her haunches, bouncing."

She smiled and shook her head. "You must be a surgeon."

"Yes, ma'am. Orthopedic. Dr. Jim Brady."

"Cynthia Dumond. Mrs. Adams has Alzheimer's. Sometimes she gets confused. Want me to come in the room with you? Maybe protect you?" she said with a smile.

"Well, I wouldn't mind the company," I said, a little sheepishly. "Not that I was afraid or anything."

"She's harmless, Doctor. She's just old and confused."

We walked back to the hospital room together. The patient seemed to relax the moment she saw the head nurse, a familiar face.

"Hello, Ms. Adams," Cynthia said. "This is Dr. Brady. He needs to examine your . . ." She gazed at me, smiling again. "Your what?"

"Her knee."

"Dr. Brady needs to look at your knee. Okay?"

The patient had ceased shaking and bouncing, leaned back, slowly extended her legs, laid down, and became somewhat still.

"Very good, Ms. Adams. Very good," Cynthia said, grasping the elderly woman's hand and holding it while she looked at me. "Go ahead, Doctor."

The woman's right knee was quite swollen, with redness extending up and down her leg for about six inches in each direction. When I applied anything but gentle skin pressure, her leg seemed to spasm involuntarily. How in the world she had managed to crouch on the bed with her knee bent to that degree was mystifying.

"Sorry, Ms. Adams," I said, but continued my exam. The knee looked and felt infected, but those signs could also have represented a fracture or an acute arthritic inflammation such as gout, pseudo-gout, or rheumatoid arthritis, not to mention an array of exotic diseases. I tried to flex and extend the knee, but she resisted, either due to pain—although I wasn't certain she had a normal discomfort threshold—or from a mechanical block due to swelling or some type of joint pathology.

"What's she in the hospital for?" I asked Nurse Cynthia.

"Dehydration, malnutrition, and failure to thrive, the usual diagnoses for folks we get from the nursing home. The doctor who runs her particular facility sent her in."

"Who is it?"

"Dr. Frazier. Know him?"

"Nope. Should I?"

"No. It's just that he sends his patients here in the end stages. Most of the folks that get admitted from his nursing home die soon after they arrive."

"Most of them are old and sick, aren't they?"

"Yes."

I looked at her expression while she continued to hold Mrs. Adams's hand.

"Were you trying to make a point?"

"Not really." She glanced at her watch. "Are you about through, Doctor Brady? I have quite a bit of work to do."

"Follow that paper trail, huh?"

"Yes. That's about all I have time for these days. Seems to get worse every month. Some new form to fill out, some new administrative directive to analyze. Whatever."

"I know the feeling. There isn't much time to see the patients and take care of whatever ails them these days. If my secretary can't justify to an insurance clerk why a patient needs an operation, then I have to waste my time on the phone explaining a revision hip replacement to someone without adequate training or experience. One of my partners told me yesterday about an insurance clerk that was giving him a bunch of—well, giving him a hard time—about performing a bunionectomy. He found out during the course of a fifteen-minute conversation that the woman didn't know a bunion was on the foot. Her insurance code indicated it was a cyst on the back and she couldn't find the criteria for removal in the hospital. She was insisting it had to be an office procedure, and only under a local anesthetic. Crazy, huh?"

"Yes, sir. It's a brave new world."

"Sounds like a good book title, Nurse Cynthia."

"I think it's been done, Doctor."

"Well, thanks for your help. I do appreciate it. Not every day the head nurse on a medical floor accompanies me on a consultation."

"My pleasure. You seem to be a concerned physician, an advocate for the patient, at least. As I remember, that's why we all went into the healing arts."

She turned to Mrs. Adams. "I'll see you later, dear," she said, patting the elderly woman's forehead. Still holding the nurse's other hand with her own wrinkled hand, Mrs. Adams kissed Cynthia's fingers lightly, probably holding on for her life.

I poured a cup of hospital-fresh coffee, also known as crankcase oil, and reviewed Beatrice Adams's chart. I sat in a doctor's dictation area behind the nursing station and looked at the face sheet first, being a curious sort. Her residence was listed as Pleasant View

Nursing Home, Conroe, Texas. Conroe is a community of fifty thousand or so, about an hour north of Houston. I noticed that a Kenneth Adams was listed as next of kin and was to be notified in case of emergency. His phone number was prefixed by a "409" exchange, and I therefore assumed that he was a son or a brother and lived in Conroe as well.

Mrs. Adams was fifty-seven years old, which was young to have a flagrant case of Alzheimer's disease, a commonly-diagnosed malady that was due to atrophy of the brain's cortical matter. That's the tissue that allows one to recognize friends and relatives, to know the difference between going to the bathroom in the toilet versus in your underwear, and to know when it's appropriate to wear clothes and when it isn't. Alzheimer's causes a patient to gradually become a mental vegetable but doesn't affect the vital organs until the very end stages of the disease. In other words, the disease doesn't kill you quickly, but it makes you worse than a small child—unfortunately, a very large and unruly child.

It can, and often does, destroy the family unit, sons and daughters especially, who are caught between their own children and whichever parent is affected with the disease, which makes it in some ways worse than death. You can get over death, through grief, prayer, catharsis, and tincture of time. Taking care of an Alzheimer's-affected parent can be a living hell, until they are bad enough that the patient must go to a nursing home. Then the abandonment guilt is hell, or so my friends and patients tell me.

Mrs. Adams had been admitted to University Hospital one week before by my friend and personal physician, Dr. James Morgenstern. I guessed that either he had taken care of the patient or a family member in the past, or that Dr. Frazier, physician-owner or medical director of Pleasant View Nursing Home, had a referral relationship with Jimmy.

Mrs. Adams's initial blood work revealed hyponatremia (low sodium), hyperkalemia (high potassium), and a low hematocrit (anemia). Clinically, hypotension (low blood pressure), decreased skin turgor, and oliguria (reduced urine output) suggested a dehydration-like syndrome. For a nursing-home patient, that could either mean poor custodial care or failure of the patient to cooperate— refusing to drink, refusing to eat—or some combination of the two. Neither scenario was atypical of the plight of the elderly with a dementia-like illness.

According to Dr. Morgenstern's history, the patient had been diagnosed with Alzheimer's disease six years before, at age fifty-one, which by most standards was very young for brain deterioration without a tumor.

"Dr. Brady?" head nurse Cynthia asked, appearing beside my less-than-comfortable dictating chair.

"Yes?"

"I'm sorry to bother you, but might I have one of your business cards?"

"Sure," I said, handing her one from the top left pocket of my white clinical jacket. "Don't ever apologize for bothering me if you're trying to send me a patient."

She laughed. "It's for my mother. She has terrible arthritis." She paused and read the card. "You're with the University Orthopedic Group?"

"Yes. Twenty-two years."

"If I might ask, where did you do your training?"

"I went to med school at Baylor, then did general and orthopedic surgery training here at the University Hospital. I then traveled to New York and spent a year studying hip and knee replacement surgery, then came back to Houston to the land of the free and the home of the brave."

"Is your practice limited to a certain area? I mean, do you just see patients with hip and knee arthritis?"

"Yes. Unless, of course, it's an emergency situation, like one of those rare weekends when I can't find a young, hungry surgeon with six kids to cover emergency room call for me."

"Well, thanks," she said, smiling. "I'll be seeing you. I'll bring my mother in."

"Thank YOU, Cynthia. By the way, I'm curious. Why me? I would think you see quite a few docs up here, and I would imagine that your mother has had arthritis for years. Why now?"

Cynthia was an attractive, full-figured woman with close-cropped jet-black hair, a woman who made the required pantsuit nursing uniform look like a fashion statement. She looked me up and down as I sat there with Mrs. Adams's chart in my lap, my legs crossed, holding the strong black cooling coffee.

"You're wearing cowboy boots. I figure that all you need is a white hat," she said, turning and walking away.

Not my sharp wit, nor my kind demeanor with her patient, nor my vast training and experience.

My boots.

I returned to the University Orthopedic surgical suite after ordering knee X-rays and an MRI study on Mrs. Beatrice Adams. Jim Morgenstern had ordered a second battery of laboratory tests subsequent to his display of great medical acumen in regard to his identification of her right knee problem. *Right knee swelling* was his chart diagnosis. The Medicare Physician Quality Review Committee would be incensed at a diagnosis that simple and would question the patient's need to be hospitalized for that disorder, not to mention the problems that it would create with reimbursement. So, I changed the diagnosis to *synovitis, right knee, R/O tuberculosis*. That would get their attention. I mean after all, TB was a dreaded disease and a rare occurrence, but it was a possibility nonetheless.

I started my third case of the day, a high tibial osteotomy (HTO). That is an operation designed to straighten a crooked knee joint. We orthopedic surgeons do it for varus of the knee, which in patient-speak is a bowleg deformity. If the knee joint isn't too arthritic and a replacement of the surface isn't indicated, we go in just below the knee joint, break the larger leg bone, the tibia, and straighten it out. We fix it with screws, staples, or a plate. Then, after about five years, the knee joint would have to be replaced. Since in those days an artificial knee joint lasted only five to ten years before requiring revision, the HTO bought the patient joint recycling time.

I sawed and hammered on my patient, feinting and dancing with my feet while my hands did the work, to the raucous music of Miss Etta James. Loretta, the head nurse in orthopedics, coordinator extraordinaire and keeper of the proverbial crying towels for those days when surgery just didn't go like it was supposed to, sat across the room, filling in the blanks in the morass of the required paperwork and swinging her crossed leg in time with the music.

Loretta Birdwell was in her late thirties and had worked her way up the political ladder from staff nurse to head nurse. She was attractive, with deep-brown skin and a perpetual smile. I knew she had to have hair, but I had never seen it. In fact, I had never seen her outside the operating room, where she always wore her light-blue bonnet with pink flowers.

"So how much longer, Dr. Brady?"

"Half an hour, Loretta."

"I love that song."

"Which one?"

"'The Right Time.' I wish I had my old man up here right now. Man, I'd take him right home."

That brought oohs and aahs from the crowd, which included the anesthetist, the anesthesiologist, the scrub nurse, and the medical student and resident who were assisting me in the operation.

"Go ahead, Loretta. Call him. I'll cover for you," I said.

"Uh-huh. Sure. Right. I've known you too long, Jim Bob Brady. Soon as I'm outta here, you'd be whining about the paperwork not getting done to anyone who'd listen."

"Aw, Loretta. You're no fun. I can't believe you don't trust me. And after all the time we've spent together."

"That's exactly why I don't trust you."

Before I left the operating room, I asked Loretta to page Dr. James Morgenstern and have him call me in the surgeon's lounge. That's where I went after operations to dictate reports, make calls, eat, and most importantly . . . to schmooze. At two thirty, I found myself alone with the hospital volunteer assigned to the doctor's snack bar.

"Dr. Brady, line 6. Dr. Brady, line 6," the page operator called through the overhead speaker in the lounge, interrupting my vegetable soup and tuna on white toast.

"Brady," I answered.

"Jim Bob. You call me?" asked Dr. Morgenstern.

"Hey, Jimmy. I saw your Mrs. Adams. She has a hot right knee. I ordered X-rays and an MRI. Should have some kind of diagnosis for you in the morning."

"Thanks. Some case, huh? Alzheimer's at fifty-seven and already in a nursing home."

"Yeah. What about this Dr. Frazier that sent her in? He a friend of yours?"

"Not really. Well, we have a business relationship. When he has a patient with a problem, he calls me, asks me what to do. He's a

GP. Well, he was. Now, he's medical director of a nursing home in Conroe. Anyway, I transfer the patient here, do a workup, get whatever tests are necessary, and call in consultants. Like you."

"So he works full-time at the nursing home?"

"Don't really know, Jim Bob. I just treat the patients that he refers to me. Why? Does it matter?"

"No. Just curious. The head nurse on Med-8 said that the patients that come in from Pleasant View usually die."

"Cynthia Dumond? Don't listen to her. She's as bewildered as some of the patients I see, man. She's a classic example of the Peter principle, promoted to her level of incompetence."

"Huh. She seemed, well, maybe not competent—I have no basis to judge her competence—but at least kind, caring, concerned."

"You goin' soft on me, Brady? Have you forgotten that this is a business, not a nursery school? Man, you start acting like you have the patients' best interests at heart, and the Quality Management Committee will nail you! Medicare and the insurance companies want these people in, diagnosed, operated on unless there's a way around it, and out of here! Are you losin' it, boy? And thinkin' that Dumond is good?"

"No, Jimmy. It's just that, well, Mrs. Adams seemed so pitiful, and—"

"I know what it is! You're still reeling from that plastic surgeon you got involved with. You're getting suspicious of all doctors, after what you went through with Edwards a few years ago! You're starting to think that all doctors are bad men. You're starting to think that the nurses are the ones who have the patients' best interests at heart, and WE'RE all arrogant, greedy bastards. That's it, isn't it?"

"Jimmy, I think that's stretching it a bit too far. I just think . . . I don't know what I think anymore. I'm not always sure who the bad guy is and who's the good guy."

"Well, if you would stick to medicine and play golf or go hunting or get drunk in your spare time like the rest of us do, you'd be a whole lot better off."

"You're probably right. Unfortunately, it's my nature to be curious."

"You need to get Mary Louise to break you of that habit. How is the wife, by the way?"

"Gorgeous as ever. And still sticking with me, bless her."

"If she ever gets tired of you, I want to be first in line for her attention."

"You have a wonderful wife, Jimmy."

"I know that, but she's no Mary Louise. I don't know why she stays with you and how she tolerates all that nosing around you do, poking into other people's business. You're going to get yourself killed one of these days, Jim Bob. Remember that concussion? And the subdural hematoma? And the brain surgery? Do you?"

"Hard to forget, Jimmy."

"Then take my advice. Stick to medicine. Be miserable like the rest of us."

CHAPTER 2

LEOPARD LEOTARD

Monday, May 15, 2000

By the time I completed my hospital rounds, it was after four o'clock. I headed across the second-floor sky bridge toward University Towers, a four-building office complex housing over a thousand physicians and their staff. I stopped halfway across the bridge, atop Fannin Street, and gazed north and south. New construction was visible throughout the medical center, dotted with mammoth cranes shuffling I-beams from their storage facilities on the ground to various levels of skyscrapers in progress.

The medical center was impressive, extending five or six city blocks along Fannin, South Main, Holcombe, and Hermann Park Drive. The entire complex covered several square miles, housed ten thousand or so hospital beds, and employed in excess of one hundred thousand people, making it Houston's largest employer.

University Hospital System housed three thousand beds under one roof, and consisted of the Cardiovascular Institute of Texas, the Neurological Institute, Harris County Trauma Center, Orthopedic Hospital, the Cancer Institute, and University Hospital Central. And in spite of all the insurance changes, managed-care companies, and government interference and regulation, a steady flow of new doctors and new patients arrived daily.

"How was your day, Pop?" asked Fran Makowski, my secretary, as I arrived in my office on the twenty-second floor of Tower 2.

"Good. Yours?"

"Same old, same old. Too much work for too little pay."

"Oh, you know you love it, Fran. Did you hear from Rae?"

My nurse, indispensable to me, had the flu. It was a bad case, with no known antidote other than time and rest.

"Yes. She's going to try to come in tomorrow, since it's a patient day."

"Thank you, Lord."

"Thank Rae. She's the one that's coming to work sick, Pop."

"I will. Are you going home?"

"Yes, if it's all right with you. I've already signed our phones out to the front desk. Nicky has a baseball game tonight, provided it doesn't get rained out."

"On Monday?"

"Junior varsity."

"Oh. Guess I'm a little out of touch. Go ahead and leave. I'm going to check my messages and hit the road."

I scanned her five-foot-nine-inch frame. "You've lost weight?"

"Nope. Still 110 pounds."

"You're too thin. How many cigarettes are you smoking a day?"

"You should talk!"

"I'm serious, Fran. How many?"

"Too damn many," she said, patting my cheek. "See you tomorrow."

"Okay. Be careful on the way home."

"People get out of my way when I'm driving the pickup. Road hog, you know."

"Right. Well, be careful anyway. And don't smoke so much!"

"Yeah, yeah," she said, waved goodbye, and lit up in our non-smoking building.

My desk was, as usual, a mess. There were phone messages to return, insurance forms to be dictated or signed, files for narrative reports to be dictated and sent to attorneys on the status of various patient-clients, other files for operative reports to be redictated that had been missed by the hospital transcriptionists, since I always complete one as soon as a procedure has ended, and mail to be opened. Letters to me rarely had any good news. Mostly, they consisted of advertisements, lawyer hate mail, patient complaint mail, and insurance company correspondence that explained their newest "reduction in benefits" policies. Not to mention the recertification applications I had to fill out every year for each managed-care payor.

I sorted through the bulk of the messages, files, and mail, organized it into piles on my pine desk that used to be someone's farm table, then put the mail in the center. I took a lingering gaze at my southern view of the city of Houston, the center of which was the Astrodome. The Houston Oilers had played their last game there in 1996, and the Astros had recently moved into Minute Maid Park. The Astrodome had been built in 1965 and at the time was nicknamed the "Eighth Wonder of the World." It was sad to think of the Houston mainstay as empty and abandoned. I had attended many Houston Livestock Show and Rodeos there.

I was about to prepare myself a short single-malt scotch and call my dear wife, Mary Louise, to inform her I would be on the way home soon, when my beeper exploded with its shrill, irritating fire-engine-like sound, startling me from my indecisive reverie. It's interesting how the beeper sound varies between shrill and melodic, depending on the time of day or circumstances when it goes off. The readout declared that University Radiology was calling and reported the number. I picked up my desk phone and called.

"This is Dr. Brady. Did someone there call me?"

"Hold on, Doctor."

"Brady. Where are you?" asked one of the long-term radiologists, Jackson Pierce, whom I thought surely would be on the golf course by that time of day. It was four-thirty or five, after all.

"In my office, wondering what a radiologist is still doing at work."

"I'm on call tonight, so I'm reading films. Damn twenty-four-hour call comes around every forty days and nights, just like the Flood."

"Jack, it rained for forty days and nights. It didn't—"

"Whatever. I have no time for an Old Testament lecture from the likes of you. I want to show you a knee x-ray you ordered this morning. Name of the patient is . . . Adams. B. Adams."

"Now? It can't wait until morning?"

He was silent for a moment. "Want to see it or not?"

"Okay. I'll be over in a minute." I put my thoughts of a drink and of going home aside. I gathered up the mail and charts, placed them in my briefcase, switched off the lights, and headed back down the elevator to the crosswalk.

"So, what do you think, Jim Bob?" asked Jack Pierce, a bespectacled gray-haired man in his sixties.

"Damn weird film. Looks like a healing fracture of the distal femoral condyle, just above the knee joint, that extends into the articular cartilage. What are all those bone fragments in the joint space, though? Loose bodies?"

"Looks like it. They're either from a severe untreated injury or due to repeated trauma to the knee, as in a neuropathic joint. That's an insensitive joint, like in diabetes, in case you've—"

"I know what it is, Jack. Repeated trauma from simply walking on a foot, ankle, or leg with reduced sensation can produce traumatic changes in the bones or the affected joint, causing arthritis, fractures, and loose bodies. This woman has Alzheimer's disease, not diabetic neuropathy, at least according to Jimmy Morgenstern's notations in the chart. Can you get those x-rays with AD?"

"If the patient has lost enough cortical matter in the brain, a relative neurological insensitivity can develop and mimic neuropathic joint disease. Of course, when I first looked at the film, I thought maybe it was a case of TB or syphilis. Has that been ruled out?"

"Man, I don't know. I just saw her this morning. I entered her diagnosis as possible TB just to get the attention of the Quality Management people. I don't think she really has it, though. I've ordered an MRI."

"How cooperative is she?"

I just stared at him.

"That bad, huh?"

"Let me just say that this woman, the one with the fractured knee joint and all the loose pieces of bone in the joint, was sitting up in bed, crouched on both feet, knees bent at least 125 degrees of flexion when I saw her this morning. It appeared to me she was feeling no pain and looked like she was ready to launch right at me."

"So, we'll have to sedate her?"

"Uh, yes. I think 'sedation' will be an understatement."

"Super. Just super. Thanks for another great case, Brady."

"No problem. I do everything possible to make sure you x-ray kids earn your keep, just like we surgeons do."

"I appreciate your thoughtfulness, Brady."

"Any time."

"Hey, sweetie," I said to Mary Louise via the cellular on the way home.

"Hello, my darlin'. You calling from the car?"

"From the truck, remember?"

"Ah, yes. So how is the new ride?"

"It's been a long time since I had a pickup truck, Mary Louise. I've missed being high above the road, watching folks in compact cars try to steer clear of the path of a midnight-blue Silverado. The stereo system is to die for, and, with this incredible ten-disc CD changer you had installed for me . . . well, what can I say? It's the best!"

"You don't miss the diesel fumes from the old Mercedes?"

"Hardly. How was your day?"

"Good. I rode my horse for about two hours. He was all get-up-and-go, what with this late-spring cool weather. I had to run him for about twenty minutes before he finally calmed down. Then I attended a luncheon and signed invitations for the upcoming charity dinner-dance for the Houston Blues Society. Etta James is entertaining that night, you know."

"How could I forget? I can't wait for that event! So, what's for dinner?"

"Turkey burritos, with those tomato-based flour tortillas you like so much."

"Turkey?" I whined. "Low fat again?"

"You won't be able to tell the difference, with all the condiments I've prepared. I have grilled onions, red and green peppers, radishes, mushrooms, and homemade salsa. Trust me, you'll love it."

"I trust you implicitly, but I promise you, no matter how good it is, and no matter how well you prepare it, the dish won't pass the Jim Bob Brady Taste Test."

"I'll bet you."

"You'll bet me what?"

"Hm-m-m-m. You realize this is for your own good, don't you? That I'm simply trying to help you lose a little weight and keep you healthy, so you won't leave me a mourning widow?"

"Yes, I do."

"Anyway, if you can decipher the fat grams within twenty percent or so, I'll put on that leopard leotard after dinner, play a Charles Brown CD, and make myself available to you. How does that sound?"

I thought real hard for a few seconds. "How about thirty percent?"

"Twenty. That's the deal. See you in a few!"

God, I loved that leopard leotard.

I pulled into the driveway of the Post Oak Tower, corner of San Felipe and Post Oak Road, gathered up my white jacket and briefcase, and entered our high-rise apartment building.

"Good evening, Dr. Brady, sir. And how was your day?" asked Raj Nowarden, chief of security.

"Hello, Raj. What are you doing on the evening shift?"

"The three-to-eleven man is ill, so I'm pulling a double, as you people call it. I am working sixteen hours straight. Not a pleasant day, Dr. Brady. Not a pleasant day, indeed."

"Sorry to hear it, Raj. You can have the valet park the car—the truck, that is."

"Very good, sir. Very good. Have a pleasant evening."

"Thank you, Raj," I said, wondering as usual if repetition in phrasing was a Delhi tradition, or just Raj's way of speaking.

The viewing of the city from the twenty-seventh floor, Apartment 271, seemed to be a new event each time I entered the foyer of our condominium. The sixty-foot expanse of the combined dining room, living room, and sunroom offered a spectacular view of downtown Houston to the east and the Galleria and Transco Tower to the west. Daylight Savings Time had not been instituted yet, so at six o'clock in the evening, there was just enough sunlight to cast a reddish-orange glow over our town. By seven, the sparkling night lights of Houston would become visible and transform our apartment into a visual wonderland. It wasn't New York's World Trade Center, but it was still one of the best views in Houston.

Tip, my Golden Retriever, *ruff*ed and greeted me shortly after my arrival. He quickly returned to the kitchen, site of intriguing smells from food preparation, in hopes of a treat. I wondered if he could differentiate diet-food aromas from that of standard fare.

"I thought that was you," Mary Louise said, exiting the kitchen and coming to greet me. There had been no need to wager with her. She looked irresistible, with long blond naturally curled hair to her shoulders, gold hoop earrings, and a black "housedress" that scooped low in the front and was quite revealing of her beautifully ample chest. She was barefoot, with pedicured scarlet toenails.

"Don't you look good enough to eat," I said, wrapping my arms around her trim waist and pulling her toward me.

"I missed you," she said, planting her matching scarlet-colored lips on mine. "You have time for a quick shower, if you like, in case you win the bet." She winked and departed for last-minute meal preparation, Tip in tow, of course. He was my dog, except at mealtime.

After my shower, we sat in our sunroom and watched the end of sunset. The sight of the orange ball melting over the flatlands to the west never ceased to delight me. I was tempted to applaud, as the Californians do at the ocean. We dined on wooden TV trays from Crate and Barrel, a far cry from the aluminum ones my parents had used as I was growing up in a small town outside Waco, Texas.

"Great dinner, Mary Louise. If this is low fat, I'll eat my hat — but not one of my Stetsons, mind you."

"I'm glad you like it. So, it's time for the $64,000 question. What's the fat content?"

"Total grams, or grams per serving?"

"Whatever suits your fancy."

"My guess is . . . one hundred."

My wife of twenty-seven years was pensive, looked about the room, moved her TV tray, crossed those long legs that supported her five-foot-ten-inch frame, and swung her right foot slowly up and down.

"Mind cleaning up?" she asked.

"No. Why?"

"I'm going to shower again. I smell like the kitchen."

"Well, did I get close? I really would love to see you in that leotard."

"We'll see. We'll see."

She must have been hanging around Raj.

My beeper started its sing-song routine while I was washing the dishes in order to place them in the dishwasher. It had never made sense to me, washing dishes by hand prior to the automated washing, but I did what I had been trained to do. The number on the beeper was one I knew by heart—the University Hospital emergency room. I called immediately.

"Dr. Brady," I said into the receiver.

"Hold, please." Then, "Dr. Brady's on the—" the ward clerk yelled before she put me on hold.

Mary Louise's cookbook was open to the turkey burrito page. I checked the fat grams. Twenty! I had missed it by a mile. Hopes of seeing my favorite foreplay costume started to fade.

"Dr. Brady? This is Dr. Stiller, second-year ortho resident?"

"Sure, Tom. What's goin' on?"

"Got a broken hip for you. Intertrochanteric fracture. It's pretty badly displaced and needs to be nailed. Dr. Morgenstern referred the patient to you. What do you want me to do with her?"

"Has Dr. Morgenstern been there?"

"Yes, sir. He admitted her, and the medical resident ordered some blood work to be drawn. She came from a nursing home and looks to be dehydrated. He said it would take a day or two to work her up and get her ready for surgery. Want me to put her in five pounds of Buck's traction?"

"Sounds fine, Tom. What's her diagnosis, besides the fractured hip?"

"Alzheimer's, but she's pretty damn combative. Either she hasn't entered her passive phase of the disease yet, or she's having one of those spikes of clarity the neurologists talk about. Dr. Morgenstern sedated her, but she's still pretty wild."

"Say, do you have the chart handy?"

"Yes, sir."

"What's her name, age, and what nursing home did she come from?"

"Hang on a minute," he said. "Mildred Bland, fifty-six, from Pleasant View."

"Thanks, Tom. I'll see her in the morning. And don't make her NPO tonight, unless Morgenstern wrote that order. I'll be in clinic all day tomorrow, so I couldn't do her until late in the day. Sounds like she won't be ready for surgery until Wednesday, anyway."

"Yes, sir. That's the impression I got from the medical resident."

"Thanks, Tom."

"Yes, sir."

Pleasant View Nursing Home. Alzheimer's disease. Broken hip. Dehydrated. Referred to Jimmy Morgenstern. That made two of those kind of patients in one week.

As I was completing prewashing the dishes, I felt a presence to my left, and turned to see Mary Louise in her leopard leotard. She was leaning against the kitchen entry, arms folded, which pushed her cleavage skyward, almost out of the low-cut fabric of her faux animal skin.

"You mean, I won the bet?"

"Yep."

"Really?"

"Yep. Are you complaining?"

"Oh, no. Not at all. It's just . . . well, when I was using the phone to call the ER, I couldn't help but see the recipe."

"Did you check out the fat grams?"

"Yes. It said—"

"Doesn't matter what it said. I've decided to reward you for simply being an ideal '90s kind of guy, even though it's now the year 2000. You're kind, considerate, and helpful, and you know how to enjoy a home-cooked low-fat meal. And I appreciate you for your obvious lust for me, in spite of all the time we've spent together. We've been married almost thirty years, you know."

"Yes, I know. And you continue to look better all the time. Wish I did."

She walked over to me, put her arms around my neck.

"You might have to get a haircut soon. It's a little over your collar. And your mustache . . . you're starting to look like . . . Yosemite Sam."

"Wish the hair was still brown."

"It's mostly brown. Just the right amount of gray in your sideburns and around the edges. Enough to make you look . . . distinguished."

"Ah-h-h-h. I'm distinguished now. What an achievement."

She pulled me in close.

"I feel that you're achieving quite well. As Mae West would say, is that a rocket in your pocket, or are you just glad to see me?"

She kissed me full on the mouth, tongue darting. Her breath was hot.

"Something strange happened at work today. I saw two patients with—"

"Jim Bob. Shut up and take me to bed. If you're feeling an urge to play Doctor Detective, you're going to have to begin here. At home. With me. Doing undercover work."

"Yes, ma'am," I said.

CHAPTER 3

MILDRED BLAND

Tuesday, May 16, 2000

I went to work early Tuesday morning in order to get patient hospital rounds out of the way prior to an all-day marathon office. After seeing forty or fifty clinic patients, I normally had very little energy left, especially the kind it took to walk the corridors and stairwells of the University Hospitals, so morning rounds always worked out better.

I stopped by x-ray first, a little before six o'clock, to view the hip films on Mildred Bland, my new patient. There were two radiologists reading films: a woman I did not know, and Dr. Jackson Pierce.

The reading room, which had nothing to do with Christian Science, was lined with a built-in shelf used for desk space. Three or four radiologists could fit along each of the four walls covered with fluorescent-lit view boxes. Dr. Pierce operated a foot pedal to employ the automated x-ray "Rolodex," enabling him to view consecutive films of the inpatients. He paused when he brought up Mildred Bland's radiographs from the previous evening.

"You look a little beat, Jack."

"Brady, you don't know the half of it. I've been up all night. All fucking night! Not a wink of shut-eye! The ER drove me nuts.

It seems the residents can no longer read films independently. They have to have staff interpretation on each and every x-ray."

"Jack, that's a medical–legal problem, a liability issue. In case of a misdiagnosis, there's staff back-up—"

"I know what the hell it's for, Brady, but that doesn't make it any more palatable. What was the patient's name, again? My mind has gone to hell. I can't function without sleep anymore."

"Bland. Mildred Bland."

Jack did not look good. His skin was a gray color, and his hands were trembling.

"Jack? Are you sure you're all right?"

"I'm fine. Just need some sleep. There are your films. Bad break."

"Looks like an intertrochanteric fracture, with a subtrochanteric component."

"Yep. And God, look at the osteoporosis in those bones. You can almost see through them. The hip must have snapped like a twig. How is she doing?"

"I haven't seen her yet. She's from a nursing home, same one as Beatrice Adams. Remember her? The one whose films we looked at last night? With the fracture in the knee joint, with the scattered bone fragments?"

"Yeah, yeah, yeah. So?"

"Well, don't you think it's a little coincidental? Two women, from the same nursing home, each with a fracture, admitted the same day?"

He looked up at me from his viewing chair, rolled it over to the next reading area, and tapped the female radiologist on the shoulder. They both stared at me, leaning back in their semi-reclining radiology chairs.

"Brady. Do you know Dr. Peterson? Camille Peterson, Jim Brady."

I nodded hello, as did she. Camille had brown hair, large rim-less glasses, a nice smile, and appeared to be in her early thirties. I estimated she was five foot one, as she was dwarfed by the long white lab coat. She wore black pumps, an unusual style for the reading room.

"Camille, Dr. Brady has a reputation around the hospital. Do you know about him?"

"Just that I've heard him called 'Jim Bob Spillane,' or something like that."

"Very good, Dr. Peterson, very good. Especially for having been on the staff for only—what—eighteen months?"

"More like two years, Jack. Bill's been out for a year, now."

"That's right. Husband's a cardiologist, Brady, with the University Cardiac Institute. So anyway, Camille, Dr. Brady here thinks it's mighty strange to have two old ladies in the hospital with broken bones, especially since they came from a nursing home."

"The SAME nursing home, Jack," I interjected.

"That's right. The SAME nursing home. Camille, you have any idea what the predominant diagnosis is for nursing home transfer patients in this institution?"

She thought for a moment. "A fracture?"

"Excellent! And what percentage of nursing home patients would you presume had marked osteoporotic conditions?"

"Ninety percent?"

"Right again! Who says radiologists just read x-rays? We know all that medicine shit, we just don't practice it. So, Brady, my point is this. Old people go to nursing homes, old people get thin bones, old people break bones. Get it?"

"Adams is, I think, fifty-seven. How old is Bland, Jack? And don't tell me you don't know, because the birthdate is on the identification plate at the upper left corner of the x-ray."

"Fifty-six. Still—"

"I don't think osteoporosis with a subsequent fracture, in a nursing home patient, is unusual, either. I do think it's odd at the respective ages of fifty-six and fifty-seven, especially if you consider that both women had admitting diagnoses of Alzheimer's disease. That's a little young, in my experience, for all those concomitant medical problems. I wasn't accusing anyone of anything. I just think it's odd. A coincidence, maybe, but odd nonetheless."

"I'd have to agree with him, Jack," said Camille Peterson.

He gave his co-worker a look, then shook his head. "God, what is medicine coming to? Bleeding hearts and suspicious minds every-where. Whatever happened to just treating the patient? Or just read-ing the radiographs? Or just doing the autopsy or completing the operation? Whatever happened to just doing your work and going home?"

Before I could answer, Camille Peterson spoke up.

"We're in the 2000s, Jack. The sensitive, caring, and concerned 2000s. Not the wham, bam, thank you ma'am '80s and '90s. We're not in this business just for the money. We want to do the right thing. Make a difference. Know what I mean?"

Jack looked at her, then at me. "I think I'm going to be sick."

I extracted my patient list from the left pocket of my white coat and planned my rounding route. There were only six patients to see, but in three separate hospital wings, on five different floors. I would be in a big rush to get to the office by my standard seven fifteen start-up.

I saw Beatrice Adams first. She was quiet, almost fully sedated, and breathing heavily. Cynthia Dumond accompanied me into her room.

"She's pretty still, Cynthia. She all right?"

"She's going for her MRI at seven."

"How much medication did you give her?"

"I believe it was 75 mg. of Demerol and 25 mg. of Phenergan. Dr. Pierce ordered it. I thought it might be a little much, for her size and all, so I called Dr. Morgenstern. He said fine, that she needed it to keep her still. He assured me she wouldn't stop breathing. I must say, though, I was a little worried. But her pulse and respiration rate have been stable. I left one of the nurse's aides in here to keep an eye on her until a few minutes ago, when we started morning report."

"Huh. Well, thanks much for checking on her, Cynthia. And please call me, or my nurse, Rae, when she's back from radiology, so we can get a report from whichever radiologist reads the films."

"Yes, Doctor."

Once again, I thought that Jimmy Morgenstern had Cynthia Dumond all wrong. She seemed anything but incompetent.

I took the stairs down to the seventh floor, walked a football-field distance to the general hospital wing of University Hospital, and entered Room 743. Two nurses were in the room, attempting to restrain the patient.

"Y'all need some help?" I asked.

"Do we! This woman's a maniac! She's taken herself out of traction four times during the night, so we had to restrain her. She got out of both the arm and leg restraints once and tried to crawl over the railing!"

Mildred Bland was a thin woman who looked much older than her purported fifty-six years. She had a blank look to her face but managed to slap one of the nurse's hands away as she tried to restrain her. Her left leg was in Buck's, or skin traction, with a cable attached to it. The cable traversed a pulley, then disappeared over the end of the bed and connected to a five-pound weight. The purpose of traction is to stabilize the hip and keep muscle spasms in the thigh to a minimum until the fracture is surgically fixated. Although surgery needs to be performed as soon as possible on a hip fracture, traction is standard procedure to reduce the pain until the patient can be medically stabilized and operated upon.

"Doctor, can you hold her good foot, please?" asked a struggling nurse.

"Sure," I said, grabbing my newest patient's kicking right foot, the cloth restraints flapping in the breeze.

The two exhausted nurses finally secured each of Mrs. Bland's arms and wrists to the bed rails with the padded restraints, then did the same to the right ankle while I held the combative patient's left foot steady.

"Thank you so much," said one.

"My God, I'm worn out," said the other. "How in the world this frail little woman can fight like a banshee is beyond me!"

"Guess I won't be getting her to sign her own op permit, huh, ladies?"

They laughed.

"No, sir, don't believe so," said one.

"Have you seen any family up here?"

"No, sir," said the other. "Just another poor elderly woman with no one to take care of her."

After they left, I checked Mildred Bland's left foot for pulses, making sure that the skin traction had not cut off her circulation. I didn't need to check for signs of motor deficits or partial paralysis. No, that woman's muscles and tendons were operating just fine. When I left, she was still writhing against the restraints, shaking her head back and forth, mumbling something unintelligible toward the ceiling.

I was able to see the three post-ops from Monday's surgery schedule fairly quickly once I got back over to the orthopedic wing. None were exactly smiling the day after a hip replacement, a knee replacement, and a tibial osteotomy, but all was orthopedically well.

I wound my way to the rehab unit, on the fourth floor of the neuro wing, to see a man whose hip I had repaired after a hospital

fall. Mr. Purcell was in University undergoing a state-of-the-art reha-
bilitation program after suffering from a massive stroke. Patients are
never allowed to walk solo in the rehab unit, at least until the lower extremity muscles on the nonparalyzed side have regained some
degree of supportive function. Mr. Purcell had achieved just that and
was in the process of showing off to the physical therapists when his
good leg gave out. He fell, right there, in front of three physical therapists, and broke his hip . . . on the good leg.

I had repaired the fracture with a titanium plate and screws, and
since the fracture was theoretically stable, Mr. Purcell was soon able
to be mobilized and continue in the rehab program for his stroke.
Still, the therapists said they were waiting for the lawyers to show up
any day with a summons.

"So, Doc, do you know how linoleum is like a man?" asked a seventy-
two-year-old patient of mine, sometime mid-morning, during office
hours.

"No, ma'am. But I bet you're going to tell me."

"Yer dern tootin'! Ready?"

"Yes, ma'am."

"If you lay it right the first time, you can walk all over it for the
rest of your life!"

And that's how the day went. Sweet elderly petite ladies telling
me cute, but dirty, little jokes. Used to be, it was elderly men telling
those same stories. It seemed to me that many of the husbands had
died, leaving spry widows cackling at their own jokes while goosing
their doctors with a cane that they didn't really need.

It was midafternoon when my colleague Jimmy Morgenstern
called.

"So, how goes it, Jim Bob?"

"Okay, my friend. I'm glad you called. I needed a break from answering another question about an operation I've performed ten thousand times. It's tough some days, going over and over and over the technicalities of the same procedure, its potential risks, expected results, and possible complications. I feel like a recording today, just spewing out the same tired old information to a new face who's all bright-eyed about hearing details of an operation they know very little about. Know what I mean?"

"At least you're not an internist. I have to listen to the same complaints day in and day out, put out the same spiel, give out the same prescriptions, to the SAME patients! At least you have new faces to talk to when you're in the office, and you don't have to go there every day like I do. You're in surgery, what—three days a week? That must be a wonderful place to hang out, where the patients are asleep and can't talk to you. Be thankful you don't have my job."

"I am. I couldn't do it. I like the mechanics involved in my job, especially the carpentry."

"That's it, Jim Bob. You're a carpenter. Just like . . . Jesus."

"I don't think so."

"Well, true. I haven't seen you walk on water or raise the dead, and you don't wear sandals. I've seen you do some good surgery, though."

"Jimmy? Why did you call?"

"Fine. Bland is cleared for surgery, pending an echocardiogram. Can you do her tomorrow if her heart is reasonably normal?"

"I'm sure I can. I'll have Fran add her on to the schedule. I'll be operating all day tomorrow anyway, and there's always room for one more. You want to pre-op her for me? Have anesthesia see her, type and crossmatch her, all that jazz?"

"No problem. I'm up here anyway."

"What about the operative permit? She have any family?"

"No idea. If not, we'll three-doctor her. I'll sign the permit, and I'll have the anesthesiologist sign it as well. Stop by here after clinic, and you sign it, too."

"You will try to find a family member if possible, won't you?"

"Of course! Why don't you quit being such a worrywart and just let me handle things like I always do?"

"Sure. Sorry. By the way, the Bland woman came from Pleasant View Nursing Home. Just like Adams."

"Yeah?"

"Well, I don't want them to die."

"Why would they die?"

"Remember, Cynthia Dumond told me yesterday—"

Click.

"Jimmy? Are you there?"

Dr. Camille Peterson, radiologist, called about 4:00.

"Dr. Brady, I have the MRI report on General-852. Adams?"

"Great. I was starting to wonder, since the test was done at seven this morning. What did you find?"

"Sorry, we've been swamped down here. I just finished reading the films. The femoral condyle fracture is healed. Well, healed enough to be stable. The bone fragments we'd seen in the joint and in the periarticular tissues represent signs of myositis ossificans. As you well know, that's calcification in the muscle, and in the joint lining, due to—"

"Lack of immobilization of the fracture. She's been walking on the leg and bending it to impossible angles. In general, she's been traumatizing it, probably due to lack of care and supervision. How old do you think the fracture is?"

"Hm-m-m. Best guess?"

"I'll take it."

"Three to four months."

"I'll tell you, Camille, that's some pain tolerance she must have. Do you know of any link between Alzheimer's disease and a lack of sensation that would allow a patient to walk on a broken leg without recognizing pain? Like diabetic patients can experience?"

"No, sir, I don't."

"I thought that Jack Pierce told me this morning that you radiologists know all that—how did he put it?"

"Jack said we know all that medical shit, we just don't use it. If you ask me, Jack is full of it. But, please, don't tell him I said that. I've only been on staff for two years. I've got to kiss the asses of all these testosterone-laden children in the radiology department for another year until I make partner."

"You're the first female in radiology, aren't you?"

"Yep. One Jewish female against thirty-four Anglo-Saxon rednecks. The male chauvinist capital of the world is right here in the radiology department of University Hospital, the world's largest health care institution, in the world's largest medical center. Not to mention that most of them wear cowboy boots, drive pickup trucks, and spend most of their free time fishing, or hunting, or golfing. Please tell me you're not one of those."

"Well, I wear boots and drive a pickup truck. Listen, I need to finish seeing patients. Thanks again for your help."

"Sure. And by the way, I'll check into radiological manifestations of Alzheimer's disease for you and see what I can find out. Jack doesn't need to know this, but . . . I like solving mysteries."

CHAPTER 4

AUTHOR DINNER

Tuesday, May 16, 2000

"**H**ow was your day?" asked Mary Louise as I entered our apartment. She was dressed in a black cocktail dress with matching pumps. Her hair was piled high atop her head in a professionally constructed, and probably expensive, coiffure. I sat my briefcase down and held her close.

"Pretty good. You look fabulous! Where are you going?" I asked, pressing my overly bushy mustache against her freshly painted ruby lips.

"Careful. Don't start something you can't finish. And the question should be, 'Where are WE going?'"

I held my gorgeous wife in my arms, studied her scant laugh lines, smelled her delectable fragrance, my large hands against her small, well-worked-out waist, and felt somewhat undeserving of her affection at that moment. I wore wrinkled scrubs, a stained white clinic jacket, and faded anteater boots with dried, forgotten goo on the tips. I savored her scent, which permeated my hospital smell.

"Why are you pulling away, husband?"

"Frankly, I stink."

"You never stink, Jim Bob. You might be a little ripe, but it's manly. Quite manly."

"Right. Where are WE supposed to go tonight, anyway?"

"The *Houston Chronicle*'s Book and Author Dinner, benefitting the Houston Public Library? You've been looking forward to it for weeks!"

"Tonight? I thought it was Wednesday!"

"Nope. It's tonight, baby cakes. So, you'd better shower. Robert Parker and Lawrence Block are signing their new novels at seven. It's now six ten," she said, checking her grandmother's watch, an antique she had rescued from a "jewelry store," where it had been pawned by a ne'er-do-well cousin.

I showered and dressed in record time. My bride had kindly laid out my clothes for the evening on our bed. I found a double-breasted Italian suit, black with a faint gray stripe; a white starched shirt; and a brightly patterned red-and-black tie. My dress ostrich boots stood handsomely at the foot of the bed.

"Well, don't you look dashing and debonair, Dr. Brady," she said, as I stepped back into the living room.

"Thank you, my dear. Of course, I owe it all to you, seeing as how you selected my clothes for me."

She faced me, held me close, and placed her thin but strong arms around my neck. "Have I told you today that I love you?"

"Let me think. No."

"I love you."

"God, you're beautiful."

I stood in line with the rest of the thrill seekers in the foyer of the Doubletree Hotel main ballroom and finally, after almost an hour, managed to get Mr. Parker and Mr. Block to sign recent works of fiction.

Parker's recent novel was called *Hugger Mugger*. I complimented him on his ability to consistently, for twenty years, entertain his readers with fresh new adventures of his famous protagonist, Spenser, Boston private detective. I wondered aloud if he ever tired of writing about the same character and if that was why he had deviated from the Spenser series with other non-Spenser novels, such as *All Our Yesterdays*.

He smiled, signed my copy, and said something to the effect that he didn't intend to become bored with Spenser as long as his readers continued to buy books.

In the five or ten seconds of my interchange with Lawrence Block, as he signed his latest Matthew Scudder novel, I asked if there was an Elaine in his life. His real life. He winked and laughed. He was still laughing as I walked away. Unfortunately, I had no idea what that meant, but would have loved to know.

All in all, the evening was delightful. In addition to Parker and Block, the *Chronicle* had managed to attract Texas's own Liz Carpenter, Peter Maas, author of *Serpico* and *The Valachi Papers*, Barbara Bush, and Kinky Friedman. Each author had ten or fifteen minutes with which to plug their latest book and entertain the crowd, a diffuse mix of socially prominent fundraisers, literary types, doctors, lawyers, and bookstore owners and employees.

I especially enjoyed a story told by Liz Carpenter— press secretary to Lady Bird Johnson and co-founder of the National Women's Political Caucus—that she said she had borrowed from a colleague.

"It seems," she said, "that when the good Lord was making the world, he called man aside and bestowed upon him twenty years of normal sex life. Man was horrified, but the Creator refused to budge.

"Then the Lord called the monkey and gave him twenty years.

"'But I don't need twenty years,' the monkey said. 'Ten years is plenty.'

"Then man spoke up and said, 'May I have the other ten years?' The monkey agreed.

"The Lord then called on the lion and also gave him twenty years. The lion only wanted ten years. Again, man spoke up.

"'May I have the other ten years?'

"'Of course,' said the lion.

"Then came the donkey, who was also given twenty years. Like the others, ten years was enough for him. And man again asked for the spare ten years, and he got them.

"This explains why man has twenty years of normal sex life, ten years of monkeying around, ten years of lion about it, and ten years of making a jackass out of himself."

As the crowd dispersed after a standing ovation, a man came up to me while I was bidding various and sundry goodbyes to acquaintances in attendance.

"Dr. Brady? I'm Theodore Frazier. It's good to see you," he said.

"I'm sorry, I don't think we've met."

"That's certainly possible, but I believe you have two of my patients under your care from Pleasant View Nursing Home?"

Dr. Frazier appeared to be in his sixties, an inch or two shorter than my six-foot frame. He was bald, save a gray rim of well-trimmed hair over his ears and the back of his pate, with what appeared to be an athletic physique. He was immaculately dressed in a single-breasted suit of an Italian light-wool fabric, appropriate for the Houston spring weather.

"Yes, sir. Happy to meet you," I said, extending my hand.

"Dr. Morgenstern keeps me informed as to my patients' progress while at University. Since you are now treating two of them as well, I thought it would be appropriate to meet you and perhaps suggest that you might do the same. When you have the time, of course."

"Certainly, Dr. Frazier. My pleasure."

"Call me Ted, please. And your first name?"

"Jim."

"Fine, Jim."

"You've been in charge of the nursing home for . . .?"

"About six years now. I spent twenty-eight years in general practice, then was offered this opportunity to become a part-time administrator and part-time practitioner. It's a wonderful job for a sixty-four-year-old man. The care of the patients is mostly custodial, or maintenance care, if you prefer. When someone becomes ill, I call Morgenstern, or one of the other specialists to whom I refer, and have the patient transferred immediately to University or one of the other medical center facilities. And yes, I do enjoy the work."

"I believe both of the patients currently under our care have Alzheimer's disease. One, Ms. Adams, has a three- or four-month-old fracture in her knee. It's healed, so there is nothing I can do at this point. The other, Ms. Bland, has an intertrochanteric hip fracture. She's scheduled for surgery tomorrow."

"Very good, Jim," he said, glancing around the room, apparently bored with my rendition of the status report on his two nursing-home patients. "Listen, I must run. I see my wife at the exit. A pleasure. A real pleasure," he said, pumping my hand like a politician running for reelection.

"Nice to meet you," I said, as he hurried toward the ballroom doors.

"Who was that?" asked Mary Louise, sliding up beside me, putting her left arm through my right arm. I could feel her ample breasts as she wedged my elbow between them.

"Name's Ted Frazier. He runs a nursing home up in Conroe called Pleasant View. I have two of his—you know, when you do that, my mind doesn't function."

"Do what?"

"You know damn well what I'm talking about. See where my elbow is? Next thing you'll be doing is biting my earlobe."

"Really? So I'm that predictable?"

"Not that predictability is bad, you understand. Are you . . . Mary Louise! What in the world are you doing?"

"Being less predictable."

"Your hand is on my butt, under my jacket, with your fingers . . . Mary Louise?"

"Yes, Jim Bob?"

"You'd better take me home."

"Are you sick?"

"Hardly. But I'm about to embarrass myself in front of all these people."

"Ah-h-h. Vasodilation of the corpora cavernosa."

"How do you know about that?"

"I'm married to a doctor, aren't I?"

"I'm an orthopedic doctor, not a urologist."

"Yes, and you have a bone and joint problem that I need to fix."

We were lying in bed, comforted by the glow of Houston's night lights clearly visible through our bedroom windows on the twenty-seventh floor of the Post Oak Tower. Trisha Yearwood softly crooned a love song on our compact disc player.

Mary Louise snuggled against me, her perfumed hair unfurled, a pedicured foot with brightly painted nails thrown over my bare legs.

"So tell me again who that man was you were talking to before I turned you on?"

"Huh?" I asked, somewhere between heaven and earth.

"That man? The distinguished-looking gentleman? You were speaking with him before I walked up to you at the end of the party."

"Oh. That was Ted Frazier. He's a GP. Well, he used to be, maybe still is. He runs a nursing home in town. Actually, it's in Conroe. Called Pleasant View. I have two of his patients in the hospital. Didn't I tell you this at the party?"

"The party was eons ago. Frazier . . . I wonder if he's related to Stephanie Frazier."

"Who's she?"

"She and I served on the invitation committee for the Book and Author Dinner tonight."

"Don't know."

"She's barely thirty. He looked to be, what? Sixty?"

"He told me he was sixty-four. Could be his daughter."

"Could be. But this is Houston, so she's probably his wife."

"Now why do you say that?"

"A lot of older men take on younger wives here. You should know that. Remember what's-her-name? She was in one of the sequels to *Naked Gun*."

"Anna Nicole Smith?"

"That's the one. She married a man in his eighties, and I think she was in her late twenties."

"I have no idea, Mary Louise. It's a non-issue for me at this moment. Most everything is, thanks to you," I said sleepily.

"So, what's wrong with the patients he referred to you?"

"They both have Alzheimer's. One has a broken femur, just above the knee. The other has a fractured hip, which I'm going to fix tomorrow. And besides, Frazier didn't refer them to me. Jimmy did."

"Morgenstern?"

"Yep."

"So how is the old reprobate?"

"He's my age."

"He's still a reprobate."

"Mary Louise, he's not a bad guy. It's just that his jokes may offend certain—"

"Everyone."

She rubbed my shin with her foot, then rubbed my stomach with her left hand, lying as she was with my left arm around her, tilting her up on her right side. She moved her searching fingers down, stimulating me again.

"Sweetie, it's late. I set the alarm for five thirty. And you know—"

She rolled over on top of me, kissed me with her open mouth, tongue pressing hard against mine.

"Mary Louise," I said, moving my head to the side for air, "I have to get up—"

"Yes, you do."

CHAPTER 5

DEATH

Wednesday, May 17, 2000

Wednesday morning found me extremely tired but in a great mood. I tried to figure out if I was still in my twenty-year sexual allotment or if I was on "borrowed" time. I lost count on the way to make hospital rounds. If Mary Louise's responses the previous evening were any indication, I was in good shape. Of course, there was that restaurant scene with Meg Ryan in *When Harry Met Sally*, one most men would never forget. My friends talked about that for months, all wondering how many truly satisfying sexual experiences they had provided their partner over the years . . . or not.

Unfortunately, no matter how stimulating I found that conversation with myself, it was not getting my work done, which was, at that time of the morning, hospital rounds. Rounds might not be as interesting as the topic I had chosen to mull about while traversing the walkways of University Hospital, but making rounds on one's patients was a necessity, nonetheless. And rounds were part of the duties that eventuated a salary for myself, which in turn allowed me time to daydream and ponder such weighty subjects as those I was perusing that morning.

The same six patients that were on my list the day before were still there, although the three post-ops from Monday were in a little less pain, and therefore not as cantankerous. I wasn't offended, since it was only a matter of time before improvement set in.

Mr. Purcell, the stroke-hip-fracture patient, was feeling better as well, but the physical therapists were taking him slowly. Very slowly, and still on lawyer alert.

I discovered that Mildred Bland was over in the cardiology lab having an echocardiogram. That was to be her last test prior to surgical clearance, so I went on to Mrs. Adams just to see if she was all right and to write a consultation note.

As I penned my barely legible scribblings on the permanent record in the hospital chart, housed in a small wall rack outside the patient's room, Head Nurse Cynthia Dumond approached from the direction of the nurses' station.

"I made an appointment for my mother to see you, Doctor," she said.

"Good, Cynthia. I'll look forward to it."

"Maybe not, after you meet my mother. She's a little . . . shall I say, difficult?"

"She'll just be another in a long line. Don't worry about it."

When we entered the room of Beatrice Adams, the ceiling, bedside, and bathroom lights were all on.

"Good morning, nurse. Doctor," she said clearly and distinctly from her position in a bedside chair normally reserved for visitors.

"Good morning, Mrs. Adams," I said, having some difficulty containing my surprise—my shock, even—to see her lucid.

She had made her face up with rouge and lipstick and had attempted to rearrange her wiry gray hair into a bun. Bless her heart, she had used large, brightly colored paper clips instead of hair pins. Her hospital gown appeared to be fresh, and she wore pink fuzzy slippers.

"We got all fixed up for you, Dr. Brady, didn't we dear?" Cynthia asked. Nurse Dumond had elevated herself to "Saint" status in my book.

"So, how's the knee, ma'am?" I asked.

"Not sore at all, Doctor. I'm ready to go home. Have you seen my son?"

I looked at Cynthia. She shook her head.

"I'm afraid not, Mrs. Adams." I paused. "I'm what is called a consulting doctor—in your case, the orthopedic doctor. Your primary doctor, Dr. Morgenstern, asked me to see you because your right knee was so swollen. It looks like you had a fracture, maybe three or four months ago, but it's healing fine. You do have some calcification in the soft tissues, though, from walking on the break. You should have some physical therapy to try and loosen that up. If Dr. Morgenstern plans to keep you in the hospital a few more days, I'll be happy to see to it that the therapists start treating you, today if you like."

"Whatever, Doctor. Have you seen my son?"

"No, ma'am. His name is . . .?"

"Don't you know?"

I tried like hell to think of the man's name listed as the responsible party on her admission sheet but could not.

"No, ma'am, I don't. But I'll bet your nurse can help you with that."

"Don't worry, dear, we'll find him," Cynthia said, kindly.

"I want to go home, Nurse. To MY home."

Cynthia walked to the bedside chair, patted Mrs. Adams's shoulder, and gave her a hug.

"We'll see. Let me speak to all your doctors first. And I'll try to find that son of yours. Okay?"

Mrs. Adams nodded pitifully.

Back at the nursing station, I asked Cynthia if it was common in Alzheimer's patients to have periods of lucidity, such as the dramatic transformation I had just witnessed with Beatrice Adams.

"It's not unusual, Dr. Brady. As the disease progresses, though, the moments of clear thinking become overshadowed by confusion.

She's pretty good this morning, but by afternoon, she probably won't remember who you are, or who I am, for that matter."

"I guess I don't know much about this disease process."

"Few of us know much about AD. We have a large number of cases admitted to our floor. Since this is a medical floor, and the patients tend to be older and have chronic disease problems, AD is a fairly common diagnosis.

"There are three stages. In the first, the patient notices their increasing forgetfulness and may try to compensate by making lists or asking for help from friends and relatives. Memory problems may cause the patient to feel anxious and depressed. Oftentimes, however, these early symptoms may go unnoticed.

"The second phase is characterized by a more severe memory loss, especially of recent events. Patients can remember what they wore to their high school prom but can't recall what they saw on television the day before, or if anyone visited them that day. Sometimes the coffee pot gets left on, the iron doesn't get turned off, or the non-affected husband or wife finds the morning paper in the refrigerator. The patient may become disoriented as to time and place and forget the way home while driving a car. They may become dysphasic and unable to remember a simple word or phrase. We had a patient here a few weeks ago who could not for the life of her remember the word for the color red. This produces increased frustration and anxiety, which brings about sudden and unpredictable mood swings.

"In the third stage, patients become severely disoriented and confused. They may become psychotic and experience hallucinations or paranoid delusions. Symptoms tend to be worse at night. Patients may become incontinent. Some become very demanding, some are docile. They tend to neglect personal hygiene and may wander aimlessly, with or without clothes on. Full-time nursing care is usually required in this stage."

"Sounds pretty bad. So, what's the deal on Mrs. Adams's son?"

"There is no son, Dr. Brady. Her younger brother is the only family she has. Her husband died of a myocardial infarction a couple of
years ago. Her son died some time ago, of what I'm not sure."

"How did you find all this out?"

"Her brother came in Monday evening after she was admitted.
We had a nice chat. I was confused at first because her brother had
the same last name as Mrs. Adams, even though she was married. But
I guess it's a common enough name.

"By the way, Mrs. Bland can go directly to the operating room
from the cardio lab if you're ready for her by the time the test is
complete. Dr. Morgenstern told me to be sure and tell you. He made
rounds quite early this morning."

I finally looked at my watch, having lost track of time listening
to the nurse's dissertation.

"Oh, man! It's seven fifteen. I have to go, Cynthia."

Loretta Birdwell was standing at my first patient's bedside, in the pre-
op identification area, arms crossed, and foot tapping.

"Where you been? At the IHOP?"

"No pancakes for me this morning, Loretta. No time and not on
my diet. Sorry, I was delayed with a patient upstairs."

I turned to my patient. "Morning, Mr. Fleming. You ready for
that new hip, old buddy?" I asked.

"Yes, sir, I am. Remember Mrs. Fleming?"

"Yes, ma'am, how are you?" I said, and extended my hand to a
tall, attractive silver-haired woman. My patient was sixty-eight years
old, and I suspected his wife to be about the same age.

"Take good care of my man, Doctor Brady. He's promised to go
square dancing with me in a few months."

"No, I did not, Margaret. I said—"

"Oh, hush up, you old poot!"

Mrs. Fleming kissed her husband, and Loretta and the nursing assistant wheeled the patient off to surgery. I went into the surgeon's lounge, scarfed a quick egg sandwich with half a cup of black coffee, and went to work.

After Mr. Fleming's hip replacement, two other cases followed. One, a core decompression of the femoral head, or "ball" side of the ball-and-socket hip joint, for avascular necrosis. "Dead head" syndrome, we call it. The blood supply to the hip joint is precarious and can be disrupted by a fracture or dislocation, metabolic problems, or alcoholism. The purpose of the surgery was, by coring out the center of the hip-joint bone, to increase the microcirculation and thereby attempt to reverse the lack of local blood supply. Excessive alcohol consumption was the cause of that particular patient's problem. I do not know how much ethanol intake, or over what time span, it takes to cause the hip circulation to shut down. I have always, hoped, however, that it was at least slightly more than I consumed.

My third case was an above-the-knee amputation in a twenty-two-year-old man for osteosarcoma of the proximal end of the tibia, just below the knee joint. The five-year survival prediction for his disease, even with amputation, chemotherapy, and radiation therapy to the stump of his leg was about 15 percent, optimistically. Operations like that always made me thankful for having bypassed the Grim Reaper for yet another day.

I went back to the pre-op area to identify Mrs. Bland. She had no family present, so I had to sign the permit, along with Dr. Jimmy Morgenstern and the anesthesiologist. I wondered how the patient had managed to be admitted to the hospital, or more importantly, to the nursing home, if she had no family. She was still restrained, still muttering at the ceiling, still darting her eyes from side to side uncontrollably.

The anesthesiologist assigned to my room that day felt that Mildred Bland was a significant enough surgical risk to avoid a general anesthetic. He opted for a spinal. The nurses, with assistance from Dr. Tim Kelly, resident-in training, tilted my patient up onto her right side. Considering that her hip was fractured and painful, not to mention unstable, the procedure took some effort. I held her leg as carefully as possible while the anesthetist deftly inserted the spinal needle. On the first stick, he drew clear cerebrospinal fluid and then inserted a small catheter attached to plastic tubing, which would be used for the anesthetic as well as for postoperative pain control. The technique is termed an epidural, one especially familiar to postpartum females, it being the anesthetic procedure of choice for delivering babies.

With Mrs. Bland's lower extremities satisfactorily numb, I popped in a Waylon Jennings CD called *Waymore's Blues (Part II)* and left the operating room with the resident to scrub. I made small talk with my young assistant as we washed. All the while, however, through the window placed strategically over the scrub sink, I kept my eye on the prep proceedings taking place inside the green-tiled room.

"How's she doing, Fred?" I asked the anesthesiologist, Dr. Green, as I entered the operating room.

"All right so far, Brady. She's a little unstable, though. Her echo showed a 50 percent ejection fraction, about half the normal pumping capability of the heart. If you can manage not to lose much blood and I can keep her hydrated, we may be all right. You did order two units, didn't you?"

"Yes. But packed cells, not whole blood, Fred."

"That's fine, but let's hurry it up. And I'd appreciate it if you would do this one yourself. I don't think we have the time to play around while you teach the resident how to nail a hip."

"Just make sure she gets transferred to Med-8 after she gets out of ICU. We don't want sick folks on the orthopedic floor."

I donned a heavy green water-resistant surgical gown, pushed my hands forcibly into my size-nine gloves and, with Tim Kelly's and the surgical tech's assistance, draped the patient with sterile disposable sheets.

I made a lateral hip incision along the "saddle bag" area, cut through the fascia and muscle, and exposed the fracture. Much to his dismay, I made resident Kelly hold retractors and suction the wound of blood and debris. I agreed with Dr. Green; the patient was too sick and unstable to employ her as a teaching case, although most fractures were resident cases—supervised of course, but an integral part of their training.

I worked quickly, applied the external jig, and reduced the pieces. Unfortunately, Mrs. Bland's bone was soft, which had allowed the fracture to extend down the femoral shaft, or thigh bone, several inches.

I drilled a pin into the femoral head, reamed over it with a calibrated drill bit, measured the depth, and screwed in a large stainless-steel screw. I then selected a six-hole side plate, hammered the flange at the top end of the plate into the receptacle in the hip screw, and tightened a locking screw into position, in order to marry the side plate to the large-bore hip screw.

Kelly and I then manipulated the fractures with the jig and brought the side plate into contact with the series of femoral fracture components. We then started drilling and placing screws into the plate in order to secure the pieces to the remainder of the intact femur below the fracture. On about the third screw, thirty minutes into the procedure, and about fifteen minutes from completion, Mrs. Bland started moaning—and moving.

"What the hell? She's moving, Fred!"

"I know. Give me a minute. Let me give her some muscle relaxant. Just hold on, Brady."

I waited for a minute or two, after which she seemed to relax, and Kelly and I started working again. Then the patient started a low-pitched moan, which turned into a yelling and screaming crescendo.

"Dammit, Fred. The epidural's not working! She feels what we're doing down here. Loretta? You're going to have to get under those sheets and see if the catheter's come out."

I stopped working again, and Nurse Birdwell, with the help of a circulating nurse, lifted the opposite hip and prowled under the drapes, trying to maintain a sterile field.

"It's out, Boss Man. The Sensorcaine is dripping all over the sheets. What do you want me to do?"

"Fred, we have a problem here! I'm about fifteen minutes out, but I can't finish this case with her awake and feeling the operation! What are you going to do?"

"Shit! I'm going to have to put her under. Give me a minute. Loretta, any allergies on her chart?"

"No sir, but there's very little medical history. Only a physical exam by Morgenstern and an echo report," Loretta said, studying the notes. "The chart says she's a nursing home patient with Alzheimer's, and—"

"I know all that!" he thundered. "I'm just going to have to go with my gut, Brady, and do what I think is right so you can complete the operation. Any problem with that?"

"No, not as long as you don't fuck up!"

The room was silent as Fred Green injected various drugs into Mrs. Bland's peripheral IV line, and once she was anesthetized and paralyzed, he intubated her. He then attached her endotracheal tube to the automated respirator and told me to go ahead and finish the surgery.

Kelly and I inserted the last three screws, washed out the gaping wound with saline and antibiotic solution, and started the closure. As we were suturing the last of the muscle and fascia, prior to closing the skin, Fred Green spoke yet again.

"How much longer, Brady?"

"A few minutes, Fred. We're hurrying as fast as we can."

"She's into a bradycardia pattern. I can't get her heart rate above forty. And her oxygen saturation is down to 60 percent. I've got to cut back on the anesthesia, try to let her rebound. I think we ought to get the cardiology service in here, maybe consider an emergency pacemaker."

"That's fine. Whatever it takes. We'll be finished—"

I was interrupted by the rhythmic beeping of the pulse oximeter, showing the patient's oxygen saturation had fallen below 50 percent. Tim Kelly and I quickly closed the skin with an unattractive continuous stitch and watched Fred Green frantically administer various drugs to increase the patient's heart rate, and thereby increase her blood oxygen level. He had Loretta call for another anesthesiologist stat, which brought two more docs into the room.

I dressed the wound, stood back, and watched the experts work in hushed tones in a valiant effort to stimulate the patient's cardiac function. Her heart rate continued to fall, as did the oxygen saturation. An irregular pattern suddenly appeared on the electrocardiogram, followed by a flat line. Asystole. Bells originating from the EKG monitor began to ring. One of the anesthesiologists immediately hit the CODE-BLUE alarm. I stood further back as the emergency team arrived, administered more drugs, and intermittently tried to restart Mrs. Bland's heart with shock paddles. The cardiac team inserted an emergency pacemaker as well. But the efforts were to no avail.

As I sat helplessly on an operating stool in a corner of the room, with Waylon Jennings singing "If you want to get to heaven, gotta D-I-E," Mildred Bland was pronounced dead at three forty-three p.m.

CHAPTER 6

FLOOD

Wednesday, May 17, 2000

"Pleasant View Nursing Home. May I help you?"

"Yes, ma'am. I'm Dr. Jim Bob Brady. May I please speak with Dr. Ted Frazier?"

"One moment, please."

I listened with disinterest to the prerecorded strains of an orchestra playing a melodic version of Beethoven's Ninth Symphony. It was depressing.

"Dr. Frazier's office. Dr. Brady?"

"Yes?"

"Dr. Frazier is on another line. Would you mind holding for a moment?"

"No problem."

I sipped my single-malt scotch as I leaned back in my red-leather desk chair and propped my cowhide Justin boots on the pine table-cum-desk. Fran, my secretary, and Rae, my nurse, had left for the day. Rain was coming down in torrents and was predicted to continue through the night and on into Thursday. Both my employees lived twenty miles outside of Houston, so, kind and benevolent soul that I am, I suggested that they leave early. All in all, it was mostly a selfish maneuver, since I wanted to be alone and brood in private about the death of Mildred Bland an hour earlier.

Dr. Frazier's somewhat raspy voice interrupted my reverie.

"Well, hello there, Jim. Nice of you to call. What can I do for you?"

"I wanted to give you a follow-up on two of your patients here at University. First, the good news. Beatrice Adams has a three- to four-month-old fracture of the distal femoral condyle. It's healing, but she's developed a fair amount of myositis ossificans. We've started her on some physical therapy, but I think Morgenstern plans to send her back to you fairly soon. I think you should continue her program in order to loosen that knee up."

"Sounds fine, Jim. We have excellent physical therapists here at our facility."

"Good. Secondly, Mildred Bland. I took her to surgery this afternoon to fix her broken hip. We did her under a spinal, since the anesthesiologist thought she was too much of a risk to be put to sleep. Her echo showed an ejection fraction of just under 50 percent. Anyway, we lost the epidural catheter during the procedure, and she started moving around, so we had no choice except to convert her to a general anesthetic."

"And?" he asked, during my pause.

"We lost her."

He was silent.

"She developed bradycardia. Once her heart rate got down below thirty, she developed asystole. The anesthesiologists tried everything. We even had cardiology insert a temporary emergency pacemaker. The code-blue team was there as well. We pulled out all the stops, but she just didn't respond. I'm very sorry."

"Brady, you're taking this much too hard. She was old, she had Alzheimer's, and she had a broken hip. Mortality rate after a hip fracture has to be high, doesn't it?"

"About 50 percent in the old days, when we used to treat the patients in traction for two or three months, which predisposed them to develop pulmonary emboli from blood clots in the legs. It's quite a bit lower these days with operative treatment, which as you know is designed to get the patient up and moving quickly to try and prevent vein thrombosis. It's just that . . . well, I don't get very many deaths on my service, and I don't like it one damn bit. Besides, she was only fifty-six or fifty-seven."

"Jim, your attitude is admirable but very impractical. I'm sure everything was done completely in accordance with standard medical procedure. I have the utmost confidence in your abilities and the abilities of your colleagues at University Hospital. This is an old cliché, but death is part of living. As you might imagine, the death rate over here at my place is 100 percent and is virtually independent of the treatment rendered to these elderly and disabled people."

"Well, I appreciate your comments, but I can't say you've made me feel all that much better. What about family? There's no one listed on the chart, so I have no idea whom to notify."

"You've notified me, Jim, and that's all you need to do. To my knowledge Mildred has no immediate family. Don't worry, I'll take care of the arrangements. By the way, will there be an autopsy?"

"I believe there has to be, considering she died in the operating room. That's hospital policy, I think."

"Just make sure I receive a copy of the findings at post, okay?"

"Sure. Well, I guess I'll be talking to you. And I hope this . . . event . . . doesn't cause you to lose confidence in me and my staff."

"I told you, Jim, this happens every day in my world. Don't give it another thought. Talk to you soon."

I finished my drink in silence and stared at the Houston rush-hour traffic through the windows behind my desk. I gathered my phone messages, ignored the "needs dictation" and "signature please" reminders on the yellow adhesive notes affixed to the charts in question, and dejectedly left my office.

On the way home, I thought about calling Cynthia Dumond to give her the bad news. However, she probably didn't come on duty until a half-hour before the eleven-to-seven shift, so I reasoned I could talk with her on rounds Thursday morning. Once in traffic, I realized that relating the unfortunate events of the afternoon to the head nurse on Med-8 was not my most pressing problem. Getting home was the problem. Rain was coming down in sheets, and the intersection of University Boulevard and South Main Street was already underwater.

Fortunately, my pickup truck had four-wheel drive and rode high above the ground. I knew it would take a tremendous flood to slow her down. My main problem was dodging all the sedans who underestimated the depth of the water in the street. I passed five cars, emergency lights flashing, floating helter-skelter either into the yards of residences on the south side of University Boulevard or into one of the adjacent parking lots on the Rice University campus. I shifted into four-wheel drive and made steady progress, feinting and cruising through rising water and around stranded and sputtering autos, until I reached an entrance onto the Southwest Freeway, which would intersect the 610 Loop and lead me to Post Oak Tower, and home.

The lateness of the hour, the darkened sky, and the torrential rain combined to reduce visibility to no more than fifty yards. All I could see was a sea of red taillights both on the feeder road and on the freeway. The prospect of a significant delay brought pangs of hunger and the almost irrepressible need to empty my bladder. I supplanted those desires by lighting a cigarette. I cracked my window to let the smoke out, but the south wind blew rain through the small crevice. As a result, I had to suffer my own secondhand smoke, which meant a doubling of the noxious fumes.

"I hope you have an ark hidden somewhere, Mary Louise, because it looks like I'll need it to get home," I said, calling her from the cellular phone amidst the colossal traffic jam.

"My God, Jim Bob, I was beginning to worry. Where are you?"

"In the parking lot next to the freeway."

"Which parking lot?"

"THE parking lot! The one full of cars trying to get up the Kirby entrance ramp onto the Southwest Freeway and higher ground. It looks like a disaster area to me. Has it been raining like this all day?"

"Yes, and if you'd paid attention to the weather forecast, you would have known to come home early. You can make it, can't you?"

"If I can get past some of these smaller cars stalled out everywhere, maybe. I couldn't get away early anyway, even if I had known we had weather trouble. I had a patient die in surgery."

"What!?"

I briefly related the events of the day to my wife, who worried about the patients and their situations as much as I did.

"Was the family upset?"

"There is no family, according to the chart and Ted Frazier."

"Who?"

"Frazier. The nursing-home director? From the party last night?"

"Oh. Stephanie's husband. I'm so very sorry. I know how upset you must be, since I know how badly you hate death and dying."

"Yeah."

A comfortable silence ensued.

"Well, I guess I'll keep plugging along. Any advice about the best route to get home?"

"Slowly, Jim Bob. Slowly and carefully. Stop in a drive-through and get a grilled-chicken sandwich if you're starving. Just don't sit in that truck and smoke your lungs out."

Was she watching?

"I won't."

"I can hear you inhaling even as we speak. Get something to eat. Not too much, since I'll have dinner waiting when you get home. Are you listening?"

"Yep. I see a window of opportunity around some of these cars, so I'm going to concentrate on driving. I'll keep you posted."

"Love you."

"Me too."

I jumped the curb adjacent to a taco joint and entered the empty drive-through lane. Service was quick, since no one else was apparently smart enough to know that you need to fuel the brain and body while trying to get through the rising water and sinking cars. I ordered a ten-pack of mini-tacos and a large coffee. I exited the drive-through lane, turned the truck around, got back onto Kirby Drive, and headed north, turning on the radio to keep abreast of Houston's latest disaster. As far as I was concerned, the baseball strike in 1994–95 was still the worst thing that had happened in the city. The World Series had been canceled! The pundits on the radio suggested the rainstorm was Houston's biggest disaster since the last hurricane. How quickly they forget.

The fifteen-minute drive took two hours, but I was lucky to get home at all. It wasn't so much the flooded streets, but the myriad of either stalled cars or cars creeping along and trying to assess the water depth before taking the straightaway plunge. The radio announcers kept saying that we motorists could not tell how deep the water was once it crested the curb and not to chance it. Problem was, once one's car was in the street, just where did those radio personalities think it was going to go? Unless you were lucky enough to have helicopter blades attached to the roof, it was either take a chance through the water or turn the engine off and sit.

Thus it was that after dodging floaters, stallers, and creepers, a few other fortunate souls and I managed to reach our destinations. I felt guilty that I did not stop and help anyone. Had I opened my door, the interior of the truck would have been full of water. So I kept on trudging along, trying to ignore folks walking toward the closest service station in waist-deep water.

The Tipster was thrilled to see me. I would swear that on certain days, he forgets I live with him during the eight or ten hours I'm at work. Tip is a beautiful golden retriever, friendly and loving, and except for the constant shedding, he is the world's greatest pet. But not the world's smartest pet. He had succumbed to the old "three strikes and you're out" rule of Retriever School, which is why I had received him as a gift from a grateful patient and dog breeder. Grateful for the good job I had done on his hip operation, and probably grateful for taking Tip off his hands.

"I'm so glad you're home," said the lovely Mary Louise, dressed in an ankle-length floral cotton housedress. It fitted her shapely form tightly and was cut very low in the chest. She pulled me up against her, put her arms around my neck, and almost squeezed the life out of me. I ran my hands down her back, across her waist, and onto her firm cheeks. I pulled her against me.

"I see the storm didn't let the wind out of your sails," she said.

"Nope. I'm tacking right along, thank you."

"Hungry?"

"Sure."

"Did you stop and get something?"

"A few tacos."

She eyed me with her deep blues, peered into my irises, through my brain, and into my soul.

"Not that ten-pack of cholesterol?"

"Well, you said—"

"You could have had a chicken sandwich."

"The situation called for tacos, with all the stress."

"And a few smokes, or so your breath would indicate."

"Maybe one or two." I pulled away. "Think I'll shower before dinner and brush the old teeth. Then I'll feel presentable. Okay?"

"Sure. And I'm sorry about your patient. You can tell me more about it while we eat."

"C'mon, Tip. You can watch me shower." I watched him eye me for a second, never lifting his haunches from the floor. His soulful brown eyes then followed Mary Louise into the kitchen. He whined, looked at me, then looked toward the mistress of the house. He carefully lifted his thick, sandy-haired body, stretched, and calmly strolled in the direction of the food smells.

"Traitor."

He barked once and went into the kitchen.

Like I said, he's my dog until suppertime.

After I related the events leading up to the death of Mildred Bland, I told Mary Louise how upset I thought the head nurse on the floor would be.

"Cynthia seems to be an extraordinarily compassionate person. She even applied makeup on one of the other Alzheimer's patients on the floor this morning, another woman I'm seeing from the same nursing home as the one who died. Jimmy Morgenstern thinks Cynthia is incompetent, but I totally disagree."

"This other patient, what's wrong with her?"

"Alzheimer's as well. Also, she has a fracture just above her knee that's about three months old."

"Why is she so late in getting medical attention? Doesn't Dr. Frazier see the patients every day?"

"Well, that's a good question. I don't really know his rounding habits. He may be mostly an administrator and may have nurses, or other doctors even, that see the patients on a daily basis. Besides, this patient—Beatrice Adams is her name—has some kind of bizarre pain tolerance. The first time I saw her, which was Monday, she was squatting in bed with the injured knee bent at greater than a right angle. That normally is just not possible.

"When I reviewed her films with two of the radiologists yesterday morning, I asked if either of them knew of any neurological problem that Alzheimer's patients get that would reduce their sensation, like diabetics get. It's called peripheral neuropathy, which means nerve deterioration. They lose the feeling in their lower extremities, primarily in the feet and ankles. Neither radiologist knew of any such phenomenon, but the younger one, a woman—the only one on the University Radiology staff—said she would check into it."

"What's the woman's name?"

"Camille Peterson."

"That's a coincidence. I know her."

"You're kidding."

"No. She joined our Professional Women's Breakfast Club last year. Short woman, brunette, with glasses?"

"Seems to be the same one. I liked her. She's married to a cardiologist. Richard is his name, I think."

"Interesting. I'll have them for dinner one night next week."

"Good. How would you like them cooked?"

"What? Oh, you silly boy. You know what I meant. I'll have them OVER for dinner or invite them out."

I resumed my eating, slowly enjoying fresh turnip greens, a baked potato with real butter, sour cream, chives, and bacon bits, and a roasted chicken basted with an almond-based marinade. Tip studied each bite we took, turning his head from Mary Louise to me in hopes one of us would share. He was out of luck.

As we were cleaning up the dishes and feeding Tip his regular food, laced with just a touch of the marinade used to flavor our main course—and just a wee bit of leftover chicken—my beeper signaled its loud, shrill command. The number was a 790 prefix, making it more than likely a hospital call.

"Med-8," the ward clerk answered when I called the number.

"This is Dr. Brady. Someone there call me?"

"Hold please, Doctor. Dr. Morgenstern wants to speak with you."

I washed off a dish or two while I waited.

"Jim Bob. Jimmy here."

"Hey. I tried to call you this afternoon, but your office said you were making rounds. I wanted to let you know that Mildred Bland died—"

"Yeah, I know all about it. Tough break. She had a bad heart, you know. That's not why I'm calling. Looks like we're two for two today."

"What do you mean?"

"Beatrice Adams bit the dust about an hour ago. She apparently had a cardiac arrest in the bed after they brought her back from the bathroom. The code-blue team worked on her for a while but to no avail. She's dead."

He waited for a response, but none was forthcoming.

"Anyway, I thought I'd save you a trip up here on your morning rounds. You don't have any patients on Med-8 anymore. Like I said, you're two for two."

I hung up the phone. I could not shake from my mind the image from the early morning of that sweet woman, sitting in her bedside chair, lips and cheeks red, with colored paper clips in her hair.

So far, Cynthia Dumond had been right with respect to her comment about Pleasant View patients admitted to University Hospital. Both patients I had seen in consultation had, in fact, died. It was my turn to wonder if they all did.

CHAPTER 7

OFFICE

Wednesday, May 17, 2000

Fatigue enveloped me, but sleep would not come. Rain continued to pelt the windows of our apartment, interspersed with flashes of lightning. Thunder seemed a distant partner.

Mary Louise softly snored—or rather, in her words, purred. Women did not "snore," as she had pointed out too many times to count over the years. The lights were out, and only the flickering of the television brightened the room, casting animated shadows on the white walls.

I put the sound on mute, then activated the closed caption function, and finally settled on *The Tonight Show* and the *Late Show with David Letterman*, alternating between the two depending on the interviewee. After all, I didn't want to miss Jay Leno glean Miranda Richardson's comments about her movie with Sly Stallone. Neither did I want to miss Tim Allen's explanations to Dave about his adventures in prison during his errant twenties.

After both shows had ended, I still couldn't sleep, so I quietly left the bedroom, padded in my bare feet through the tiled foyer, passed through the dining area, and prowled the refrigerator for something. I settled on a light beer, hoping it would help me rest.

I strolled into the living room, opened the sliding glass door onto the veranda, pulled one of our all-weather chairs under the awning, and smoked a cigarette. The rain was still pummeling the concrete, but the wind was minimal, so I managed to stay dry.

As I was lighting another smoke, the sliding door opened, startling me from my reverie as I watched the rain distort the high-rise lights of the adjacent Galleria shopping mall, with its stately office buildings and luxury hotels.

"What are you doing out here? You'll catch your death of cold," Mary Louise said, in a rare chastising manner.

"Couldn't sleep. Thought a beer might relax me."

"It might if you weren't smoking."

"I guess."

"You have a phone call. The answering service is on the line."

"At this hour? Must be something terribly important, or just terrible."

"Want me to bring you the portable?"

"No, I'll come in. Sorry, I didn't want to wake you, so I got out of bed. I had no idea the service would be calling me at this hour."

"It's okay," she said, patting my shoulder. She was barefooted and wore an extra-long tee shirt that hung down to her knees. It was her favorite nightshirt, a soft, white, cotton one that read in large red letters I LOVE MY ATTITUDE PROBLEM.

"Dr. Brady," I said into the telephone extension in the kitchen.

"Doctor, I'm very sorry to bother you at this late hour, but the family of a patient of yours is insisting on speaking to you. He's holding on the other line. May I put him through?"

"Sure."

"Go ahead, sir," I heard the page operator say to a third party.

"Is this Dr. Brady?"

"Yes, it is. Who am I speaking to?"

"Kenneth Adams," he said, "What the hell happened to my sister?"

I knew exactly whom he was talking about. Beatrice Adams, one of the two reasons I had been unable to sleep.

"I'm very sorry about your sister, Mr. Adams. Have you spoken to Dr. Morgenstern, the internist who admitted her, or to Dr. Frazier at the nursing home?"

"I called Frazier's office, but it was closed. He doesn't have an answering service, or so the operator at Pleasant View told me. I wrote down the name of the doctor that admitted her on Monday night when I was up at the hospital, so I called him. He just told me she had a heart attack and died. When I questioned him about whether it had anything to do with her leg, he said he didn't know, that I'd have to talk with you."

Great. Morgenstern knew exactly what Mrs. Adams had died from, and that it probably had nothing whatsoever to do with her leg, but I guessed he wanted me to share in the late-night conversation.

"Well, Mr. Adams, she had a fracture—a break—in her right leg, just above the knee. It was about three months old, and I doubt it had anything to do with her demise."

"Her what?"

"With her dying."

He was quiet for too long, breathing deeply. He had sounded somewhat inebriated, but not to the extent his words were unintelligible. So, I just waited, since it seemed the polite thing to do.

"I didn't know she had a bad heart."

"Well, to be honest, I didn't either. Since she didn't have a surgical problem and therefore did not require an anesthetic, I really didn't note her medical status, except for the Alzheimer's. I have to tell you, this morning on rounds, she was clear as a bell."

"What do you mean?"

"I mean that she was lucid. She wanted to go home. HER home, she said. She asked where her son was. We had a conversation—your sister, me, and Cynthia Dumond, the head nurse on the night shift. Cynthia had helped her put on makeup, lipstick, and rouge, even put her hair in a bun. Having seen her so . . . so normal, it's especially hard for me to believe that she's gone. Again, I'm truly sorry."

I waited.

"I'm sorry too, Doc. Real sorry," he said, choking back the tears. I heard him sniffle, blow his nose. I got a little misty-eyed myself, which was, I don't know, excessively emotional I guess, having known the woman for three days. Events such as sudden deaths, and especially postoperative deaths, were not my cup of tea. If I had wanted that type of practice, I could have entered the field of cardiovascular surgery, or oncologic surgery.

"Mr. Adams, it's very late. If there's nothing else I can do for you . . ."

"No, Doc. Nothing else. Thanks for talking to me. She was all the family I had, except . . . well, she was all the family I had. I'm sorry to have bothered you. I was just so upset when I got home and found that message on my answering machine. That's a helluva way to find out a loved one has died, don't you think?"

"Yes, sir, I do. Which of the hospital personnel called you?"

"I think it was a clerk, either on the floor where she was admitted, or in the administrative offices at your hospital. She was indifferent, if you ask me. In my business, we always try to bring bad news in person. Psychologists say it softens the blow. We have to take those classes, you know, in social awareness."

"Just what is it you do, Mr. Adams?"

"Sergeant with the Montgomery County Sheriff's Department. We're headquartered here in Conroe. I was working on a murder case in the north part of the county, got back late, and met some of the boys at Tut's for a couple of beers to sort of unwind. I'm sure you can appreciate that."

If he could have only seen my beer.

"And then, all I needed was to hear Bea had died on the fucking—sorry—on the answering machine. I knew about the Alzheimer's, of course, but I had no idea she had a bad heart."

"I can appreciate your being disturbed about the way it was handled. It was not done in a very professional manner. I'm curious, Sheriff; how long had your sister been a resident of the nursing home?"

"About two years, give or take."

"Nurse Cynthia told me you and your sister had the same last name, and she was confused because according to the chart Mrs. Adams had been married. Did she marry someone named Adams?"

Ken Adams laughed. "Yes, my sister was quite the vamp in her younger days. She was very proud of her monogrammed towels, and she was insistent that she marry a man who had the same last initial as she did. He just happened to be another Adams."

Another silence ensued. I sipped my beer, not knowing what else to say.

"Doctor, you've been very kind," he said abruptly. "Thanks again."

"If there's anything I can do, please let me know."

"Yeah. I'll see you."

The alarm went off at its usual five a.m. I stumbled into the shower, made myself presentable, and sleepily went for coffee. The timer had fortunately functioned normally in spite of the storm, and I poured myself a steaming mug of Seville Orange. I stepped to the foyer door and opened it, retrieved the morning paper, and returned to the kitchen, where I sat at one of the two barstools and read the headlines on the front page: CONTINUED FLOODING LIKELY. STAY HOME! The gutters and sewers were overflowing, and the local rivers—the Trinity, the San Jacinto, and the Brazos—were dangerously high. Persons living in outlying areas to the east and south of Houston were being instructed to evacuate low-lying and flood-prone areas.

The warnings failed to deter me, since, in my twenty-two years of practice, neither rain, nor sleet, nor snow, nor hurricane had ever kept me, or my patients, from the office. There were always plenty of people who wanted to complain about their ailments to someone, and I had always been available.

I poured my second cup of coffee into a large Styrofoam container, went back into the bedroom, kissed my sleeping bride goodbye, petted man's best friend, still sleeping himself, and called down to the security desk on my way out.

"Morning, this is Dr. Brady. Can you bring my truck around to the front, please?"

"Uh, are you sure? The water's pretty high out there, Doc," the night-shift security man told me.

"Well, I've got to get in to work. My truck should have three or four feet of clearance. Did it rain all night?"

"Yes, sir, sure did."

"Huh. Bring it around. I'm sure I'll be fine."

One of the first things I learned as a young surgical resident was an adage that should permeate the minds of all surgeons each and every time they pick up the scalpel to start an operation. If, either during or at the end of an operation, you or your assistant feel the need to say the words, "I think it will be all right," trust me when I tell you that it won't. Start over, repair it, do whatever you have to do right then, because whatever procedure you've done is not going to work. I know from experience.

I repeated the familiar phrase that morning as I drove out of the high and dry parking area in front of the Post Oak Tower and descended onto San Felipe, heading east. Water was immediately up to my bumper. Cars were strewn about the street, in yards, and in parking lots of the upscale shopping centers along Post Oak Boulevard, abandoned to the vagaries of the freshly formed lake in the middle of town.

I tried to get up onto the 610 Loop, but the water on the feeder road and the entry ramp had already swallowed a truck larger than mine. I continued on in the three-foot-deep water, feeling quite the Ancient Mariner, but fording a faux ocean.

There were no other fools on the road, which meant my only obstacles were moving water and stalled vehicles. As a result, I was able to drive where I pleased. I couldn't see where the street stopped and the curbs started, so I hoped angry homeowners couldn't identify the deep tire tracks they would find in their yards when land resurfaced.

It took me over an hour to get to the University Medical Center, where standing and flowing water covered the streets and sidewalks along Fannin, Main, and University. I turned into the employee–doctor's parking garage and inserted my key card into the identification slot. The B level was dry, except for splotches of water standing in puddles due to leakage through the inadequately sealed concrete driveways. I drove slowly down to the B-1 level, which had about a foot of water standing throughout the parking floor. I continued to the next level down, B-2, which was my level, and found it submerged. I noted the rooftops of two prized automobiles belonging to colleagues of mine, stored, as usual, in the parking garage on the B-2 level for "safety reasons"—a Rolls Royce Silver Shadow and a Bentley. They were no longer safe, as both were completely submerged. I hoped for their owners' sakes that the British were experts in waterproof sealants.

I drove back up the ramp to the B level and parked in a slot with no name on the ID label affixed to the concrete slab directly in front of my bumper.

The garage elevator functioned normally, implying that the building's electricity was intact. Some years before, a major hurricane had interrupted electrical power. Emergency generators functioned well enough to provide power to critical areas such as the ICU, emergency room, operating room, and recovery room. However, I remembered clearly trying to repair a broken hip in an elderly heart patient, with minimal staff assistance, when the lights and the anesthetic equipment, including the respirator which was breathing for the patient, all malfunctioned, signified by a loud BANG. It was a tense ten seconds before the emergency power kicked in. My personal reaction at the time could best be described as fear laced with an impending loss of sphincter control. That is not an event I wanted to experience again.

"My God, I can't believe somebody made it in!" said Raul, the middle-aged night-shift security guard, to whom I had been saying "good morning" for a couple of years.

"Well, it wasn't too bad, if you drive a tank. No one else has made it here, then, Raul?"

"No, sir. The operating room crew for the eleven-to-seven shift called me a few minutes ago and said that administration had canceled all elective surgery, not that the patients could get here anyway. Are you supposed to be in surgery today, Doc, or in the office?"

"Office."

"Looks like you'll be all by yourself."

"Well, I can make rounds and catch up on some paperwork. I clean off my desk at least once every year, when the weather's bad and there's nothing else to do."

All his phone lines seemed to suddenly ring at the same time, so we waved farewell, and I took the elevator to the twenty-first floor. After two key-card security entry clearances, I entered the offices of the University Orthopedic Group.

It was six thirty in the morning but still dark as night under the immense cloud cover and the continuing rain. Through my office window, all I could see were sheets of water, with only a few glimmering headlights crawling slowly down the medical center streets.

I picked up messages on my private line and found that neither Rae nor Fran would be in. River bridges in their respective communities were closed, and while their houses were still dry, the situation was not good. Schools were closed, the kids had to be looked after—especially to avoid their playing in the flooded streets where snakes of the water moccasin variety were the major nemesis—and they had to be available to move their furniture, even themselves, to higher ground if the need arose. I was destined to have a great day all by myself, since nobody in their right mind would attempt to see a doctor on such a day unless they were very sick or very crazy.

I made a pot of coffee, turned on the radio, and sipped the hot Panamanian brew while I listened to the news of our town's latest disaster. Schools closed, businesses closed, major medical clinics closed. Residents were instructed to leave their homes only under absolute emergency conditions and were advised to call 911, the police department, or the fire department for assistance.

My private phone line rang, startling me.

"Are you okay?"

"Yes, Mary Louise, I made it fine. It took me an hour, even though there was nobody else on the road. Except for all the stranded cars without drivers, I was the only fool I saw."

"Anybody else make it in to work yet?"

"Nope, I'm the first. Fran and Rae left messages saying they couldn't get in."

"Yes, I know. They both called here a little while ago. Are you safe up there?"

"I think so. The power's on, and I surely do not want to walk down twenty-one flights of stairs. What I thought I would do is to catch up on paperwork, make rounds at the hospital, and hang out up here for a while to see if anyone shows up for clinic. With the weather this bad, I'm doubtful that even our ancillary personnel can get here. It would be impossible to run an orthopedic clinic without x-ray techs, cast room techs, patient reps, and nurses. We docs might actually have to work for a living, and I, for one, don't know that we could handle it."

She laughed. "Don't kid yourself. You work for a living. I've lived with you for . . . what, twenty-eight years? You've worked as hard as any man I know."

"I love you. You're my greatest fan."

"Yes I am, and I'd like to keep it that way. Be careful, and as soon as you feel you can safely leave, I want you to come home. I have something in mind to while away the rainy day."

She made me an offer I could hardly refuse. I vowed to complete my duties as soon as possible and join her for lunch and her proposed afternoon escapades.

I got so worked up thinking about stealing an afternoon away from work with Mary Louise that I decided the paperwork could wait. I poured a second cup of the dark, flavorful coffee into yet another Styrofoam cup and prepared to leave the office to make rounds when the phone rang again.

"I've decided to forego paperwork in order to delight you even sooner than you anticipated," I said into the receiver.

"I'm not your type, Brady," responded Jimmy Morgenstern.

"Shit. I thought you were—"

"If it was somebody besides Mary Louise, don't tell me."

"Not to worry. What's going on? And by the way, thanks for having Mrs. Adams's brother call me in the middle of the night."

"Anytime, Jim Bob. I figured that if I had to be awake, you might as well be awake too. That's old news, anyway. I have two patients in the ER for you. Get here now!"

"What's wrong with them?"

"Broken wrist and a broken ankle."

"Jimmy, I do hip and knee work, as you well know. Get one of the other guys."

"First of all, you're probably the only idiot at work, and these two folks need immediate attention. I'm right, aren't I? You're the only bone doc up there?"

"Looks like it."

"Just as I suspected. Secondly, both patients are referrals from Frazier, and he insisted on you. I tried to explain to him that you preferred to deal only with your sub-specialty area, but he wouldn't hear of it."

"Aw, Jimmy. If both patients are referred from Frazier, then they're from his damn nursing home!"

"You got it. Prime rib from Pleasant View."

"What kind of shape are they in?"

"I can't wait for you to see for yourself," he laughed. "Frazier wants you, and the patients do too, although they don't know it. And so do I, big boy. I'll be waiting," he said mimicking Mary Louise.

I felt my chances of afternoon delights dwindling.

CHAPTER 8

EMERGENCIES

Thursday, May 18, 2000

University Hospital Emergency Room is a cavernous facility covering at least a city block, serving six separate hospitals under one roof. Located on the ground floor, it is divided into sections relative to the patients' diagnoses. There is an orthopedic section, a multiple-trauma unit complete with two fully equipped "shock" rooms, a pediatric ward, an OB-GYN section, a general medical holding area, and so on.

I came through the Staff Only entrance and found the place, for all practical purposes, deserted. In the orthopedic area, the few employees who were there looked to be bone tired.

"Hey, guys and dolls."

"Hello, Dr. Brady," most said in unison, like school children— Morning, Teacher.

"Are you all coming or going?"

There were half a dozen nurses and technicians sprawled in chairs, in various states of repose, behind the chest-high counter of the nurses' station.

Most just stared at me. The female ward clerk finally spoke up.

"Nobody can get in. We've been here all night, and since our replacements aren't coming, and since we probably can't get home anyway, it looks like we're all stuck here for, I don't know, at least another shift. Isn't that some shit!?"

"Yep. It's pretty bad out there. You need a truck or an SUV of some kind to get through the water. I passed through some areas around the Med Center, in fact just west of here, that had water up to four feet deep."

I heard and saw muttering, mumbling, head shaking, and numerous expletives.

"Where's Morgenstern?" I asked.

One of the male nurses looked at the chalkboard behind the ER desk.

"Treatment Room 11 or 12. He's got a patient in each room. 'Course, I guess they're yours now," he said, and started to laugh.

"Yeah, Doc, you've got your work cut out for you," said a female nurse, laughing with her colleague.

"Thanks so much. I'm really glad I could make it in this morning."

"Yeah, Doc. Early bird catches the worm. Or catches something," said yet another nurse, who then broke out laughing as well. "Better use gloves before you touch the one with the broken wrist. You don't want what he's got!"

"What in the hell are you all talking about?"

They were all laughing too hard to respond but, almost in unison, used their thumbs to direct me to the appropriate treatment area.

I wished I hadn't been so damn compulsive about getting to work that morning. The only sound I heard was the clumping of the heels of my boots as I walked down the gleaming tiled corridor toward God only knew what awaited me.

"Hold still! Hold still, Mr. Jeffries! I need to draw some blood from you!" shrieked the lab technician as I opened the double aluminum doors and stepped into Treatment Room 11.

"Jim Bob! Top of the mornin' to you! Hold this guy's feet, but put some gloves on first. Looks like he has scabies," Jim Morgenstern shouted to me, as he tried to hold the patient's left arm still while the tech drew the required blood samples.

"Scabies? Isn't that some kind of skin infection?"

"Yes, and very contagious. Hurry up and put gloves on and hold his damn feet still!"

I quickly slipped on a pair of disposable latex gloves and held the man's feet as I had been instructed. I noticed that his right arm was tied down and splinted. Morgenstern held his upper left arm with one hand and had the man's forehead pinned down with the other. An ER nurse was lying across the patient's chest, trying to keep him from getting up.

"What in the hell is wrong with this guy? He's strong as an ox!"

"Alzheimer's disease, Brady. He's in a combative phase right now. These AD patients possess incredible strength sometimes, like their metabolism is supercharged. Pretty fuckin' amazing, huh?"

I wanted to talk more, but I was struggling with the man's feet, which were kicking so rigorously that I had to save my strength for holding, not talking. Finally, the lab tech got her six or seven tubes— red tops, blue tops, purple tops. A second nurse entered the treatment room and deftly started a peripheral IV line while we three continued to hold the patient as steady as possible.

"Give him 5 mg of Versed, IV push," Jimmy shouted to the nurse.

"Won't be enough," she responded. "He'll take 10 to 15 mg, Dr. M."

"I just want to relax him, I don't want to kill him." He paused. "So give him 10 mg."

She pulled a syringe from her pocket, calibrated to 20 mg, and quickly pushed half of its contents into the small rubber stopper just behind the 18-gauge IV line.

Almost immediately, I felt the tension go out of the patient's legs. We all started to relax and stretch ourselves to relieve our own tensions when, suddenly, the man bolted upright. We resumed our positions while the nurse injected an additional 5 mg. We waited until our problem patient was still before we moved. Morgenstern checked the man's respiratory rate and his pulse rate to make sure he hadn't been overdosed.

"Take a look at his films, Jim Bob. They're on the view box."

I looked. "Radius bone fracture in the wrist but comminuted into the joint. It's collapsed down about 30 degrees. I can set it and cast it, but it probably won't hold, since his bone is so osteoporotic. The fracture should be pinned and put into an external fixator. How old is he, and what kind of shape is he in?"

"According to the nursing-home sheet, which was sent along with him, he's sixty-two. Has some heart problems, history of prostate cancer which is in remission, and the usual Alzheimer's."

"Do all of Frazier's patients have AD?"

Jimmy Morgenstern looked thoughtful, or at least as thoughtful as he could pretend to be. About five-foot nine-inches tall, no more than 150 pounds (a runner, of course), with salt-and-pepper short-cropped hair and matching beard, he could always be a stand-up comic, should the medical business go under. Jimmy closed his black eyes, distorted behind bottle-thick lenses, crossed his arms, then put his right fist under his hairy chin. His classic pose: The Thinker.

"I would say yes to that," he said.

"How did you get tied in with Frazier in the first place?"

"He and his wife bought season tickets to the Rockets two or three years ago, and their seats are right behind mine. We got to talking, and one thing led to another."

"Jimmy, if you've been accepting his nursing-home referrals for that long, I'm just curious why you haven't called me in for consultations before. Not that it matters, or that I'm resentful or anything."

"The truth?"

"That would be nice for a change."

"We're good friends, right? I mean, we went to med school together, trained in the University residency programs, and have been doing business for what—twenty-one, maybe twenty-two years? And you and Mary Louise and my wife and I see each other socially, right?"

"Yes, that's all true."

"Well, I wanted to maintain that friendship. Frazier's patients are, in a word, horrible. I've been sending them to guys I don't particularly like, or guys who just started out in practice who really need the business."

"So why all of a sudden did I get two referrals this week—both have died by the way, so thank you very much—and now two more today?"

"No one else in your group will accept orthopedic consults on Frazier's nursing-home patients any longer."

"So you finally called me, huh?"

"At the risk of our friendship, yes."

"Does this mean that Cynthia Dumond is correct? That most of the patients from Pleasant View die?"

"Most of them are old and sick. Dying is . . . a way of life."

"That's an oxymoron, and I heard that same phrase yesterday."

"Maybe so, but you're a moron for coming to work today. You should have spent the day in bed with Mary Louise, fool!"

"Thanks for reminding me."

"I hate to interrupt your erudite conversation, Doctors, but I'd like to get Mr. Jeffries out of the emergency room," the charge nurse said. "If he's going to surgery soon, then I can keep him in a holding area. Otherwise, I want him up on the orthopedic wing and out of my hair."

I stepped back over to take a good look at my newest patient. He looked much older than sixty-two. He was emaciated, with the ribs on his bare chest pushed tightly against the skin. He had a so-called barrel chest, indicative of him having been a heavy smoker, now with chronic bronchitis or emphysema. His white hair was long, thin, and unruly. His beard was a white stubble. And he was covered with red, inflamed skin lesions, each one of which appeared to be excoriated due to constant scratching. I checked the radial pulse in his fractured right wrist, and its presence, combined with prompt capillary refill in the fingertips, assured me that his circulation was adequate. He was in no immediate danger of losing his hand as a result of the break.

"How did he get scabies?" I asked of my internal medicine friend and colleague.

"How else? Not keeping himself clean."

"I can't remember if scabies is a bacterial lesion or—"

"It's a parasite. The little critters bore a hole into very dirty skin and set up shop in the subcutaneous tissue. Hard to get rid of."

"You'd think that the nursing home would at least keep the patient's clean, for God's sake!"

"Jim Bob, if Jeffries here puts up the kind of fight you witnessed while the tech was trying to draw his blood, what would you do when it's time to get his bath at the old homestead?"

I shrugged.

"Exactly. Leave him the hell alone."

He had a point, but it didn't set well with me.

I had posted both ER cases for the operating room and was sitting in the surgeon's lounge, drinking coffee and watching a local newscaster report the current status of Houston's streets and surrounding highways. Were it not for the Houston Fire Department's custom-made four-wheel-drive emergency vehicles, I would be on my way home. Of course, someone had to take care of the injured and infirm, but it was surprising to me that the ambulance hadn't taken the two patients I had seen to a hospital facility nearer to Pleasant View Nursing Home. After all, it was in Conroe, sixty miles away. There had to be at least four hospitals in that area. Why take a chance coming through flood waters just to get to the Medical Center for a wrist fracture and an

ankle fracture? I could understand if the problems had been complicated or life-threatening. Maybe Dr. Ted Frazier simply insisted on
what he thought was the best possible care for all of his patients, no
matter how inconvenient it might be.

I had scheduled Rufus Jeffries for an open reduction, with internal or external fixation, of his right wrist fracture. The second patient,
sixty-three-year-old Agnes Cutkelvin, also with Alzheimer's, was
scheduled for an open reduction and internal fixation of a left-ankle
fracture. She had been in Treatment Room 12 in the ER. She was an
enormous woman with massive rolls of fat covering her legs, right
down to her ankles. Her ankles were disproportionately thin, which
is probably why her left ankle shattered when she fell off her walker
at the nursing home. Fortunately for me, the tissue over the ankle
was thin enough to allow an easy entrance and exit from a surgical wound. The fracture was, however, displaced, her circulation was
compromised, and she was to be done before Mr. Jeffries.

I called Mary Louise while I waited.

"Hello?"

"Hi."

"Oh boy, oh boy, oh boy. You're coming home, right?"

"I've got good news and bad news. Which do you want first?"

"I want only the good news."

"Okay, the good news is that I'm not going out of business."

"Translated, that means you have to operate on somebody,
doesn't it? Which is the bad news. Right?"

"Yep. Two cases." I described them both to her.

"I feel sorry for them, and really sorry for you, seeing as how I
had some very special plans for you, young man."

"Can I have a rain check?"

"You mean for later in the day?"

"You bet! It won't take me that long to do these two cases and
finish rounds. I'm still figuring, oh, about noon or so. It's not even
eight o'clock yet."

"Oh! Then everything's fine. Call me when you're on your way, cutie."

I wanted to call Cynthia Dumond and express my condolences over the loss of patients Adams and Bland, but I didn't know what to say. Besides, Morgenstern had agreed to put both of the fracture patients I was to operate on up on Med-8 postoperatively, rather than on one of the orthopedic floors—those nurses don't like sick people—so I would have a chance to visit the nurse in person. Like Sergeant Kenneth Adams had said to me the night before, bad news is best delivered and discussed in person.

I poured myself another cup of coffee, and since no one else had bothered to make it into work, and since I had the lounge all to myself, I committed the unpardonable hospital sin. It was against all regulations, including the City of Houston's Fire Department Code. I lit a cigarette.

As I puffed, I wondered if Ted Frazier's nursing-home patients were snake-bit or if, like he and Jimmy said, old people simply got sick, broke bones, and died. Dying was a way of life. Part of the cycle. Ashes to ashes, dust to dust. A death, a rebirth.

I really didn't want those two new people to die under my care, especially during surgery, as Mrs. Bland had. If they were going to pass away, let them pass away calmly and peacefully in their sleep, not while under my knife.

I called the main switchboard number for University Orthopedic Group. The answering service picked up.

"Hey, it's Dr. Brady. I was calling to see if anyone from the clinic's front desk made it in. I guess not, huh?"

"No, sir. Your administrator called. She said to keep the phone lines with the service. Since the employees can't get in, she doubts that the patients can get in either."

"Fine. I'll be in surgery for a few hours. I have my beeper on if you need anything. I would think that if any patients have an emergency, they should go directly to the ER. I can't see anyone in the clinic without staff support."

"Yes sir, that's what we've been told."

"Okay, thanks. See you."

I should have known that the able and efficient Peggy Peterson, clinic administrator extraordinaire, would have made arrangements to take care of the patients.

"Dr. Brady? You in there?" the on-duty surgical nurse yelled over the intercom.

"Yep."

"Then get your butt in here."

Ah, yes. Another respectful nurse, speaking with customary awe to the captain of the ship.

"On my way," I responded.

I stubbed out the smoke in my coffee and said a little prayer to the Great Physician to let those two sick people make it out of surgery alive.

CHAPTER 9

AUTOPSIES

Thursday, May 18, 2000

Having been at the hospital all night with little hope of relief by the day shift, the surgical personnel were not in the most stellar of moods.

The radio was set to the only station that came in reasonably clear through the leaded operating room walls, an AM station that played country music interspersed with frequent reports of the weather conditions in Houston and the surrounding counties. According to the DJ, the rain was still coming down in sheets, and water continued to rise in the streets, the bayous, and more importantly, the rivers. Dams were being washed away, bridges had become impassable, and homes—yes, homes—were seen floating down the San Jacinto River, which borders the eastern boundary of Harris County.

Folks living in low-lying areas were being evacuated by helicopter, by boat, and by emergency vehicles that had at least five feet of ground clearance. Five feet? That brought to mind those large trucks with enormous balloon-like tires with six-inch-deep threads that compete in tractor pull contests. I was beginning to get concerned that even I, the great obsessive-compulsive have-to-get-to-work surgeon, might be stranded at, of all places, the hospital.

"Can you suck in that hole for me, Tim?"

"Sorry, I'm not real sharp this morning, Dr. Brady. I was up all night working on a multiple-trauma patient." Dr. Tim Kelly looked beat, despite the blue hood and blue surgical mask. Only his eyes showed, but they had dark circles surrounding them. Raccoon eyes, we called them back in training.

"Shit. Please suck, Tim. I still can't see what I'm doing. She's bleeding like a stuck pig. Fred, can you do something?"

"Like what? Make her clot?"

Fred Green, the anesthesiologist during Mildred Bland's surgery the day before, was still on duty. He told me he had come on duty at seven a.m. Wednesday for his twenty-four-hour on-call shift. He had received no relief yet, and it was already nine a.m. Thursday. There was a good chance he might have to continue working on through Thursday and possibly into Friday. He wasn't happy.

"How much longer you have in there, Jim Bob?" he asked.

"I don't know. I've reduced the fibular part of the ankle fracture, and I've put in what, Lucy, four screws?"

"Yes, Doctor."

"So, I've got four screw holes left to fill. Then I have to close this side, open the tibial side, and put a couple of screws in the malleolus. Give me at least thirty minutes. She's not having a problem, is she?" I said, suddenly panicking and reliving the events of the day before.

"No. Everything is fine. She has a nice steady heart rate, good oxygen saturation. What I thought I'd do is to get one of the nurse anesthetists to relieve me in here while I set up the room next door and get a Bier block into your next patient's arm. That way, I won't have to give him a general anesthetic. The arm block, plus a little sedation, should get him through the case. When you finish in this room, you can let the resident close, waltz next door, get the wrist fixed, and be on your way. Then, maybe I can get some rest. Deal?"

"Sounds good to me. I'd like to get out of here before I can't get out of here."

"And I'd like to get some shut-eye. This is a somewhat selfish maneuver on my part. You with me?"

"I am indeed."

I finally completed the repair of the ankle fracture around ten o'clock and stepped next door, where the circulating nurse removed my gown and gloves, reapplied a fresh sterile gown, and re-gloved me. Mr. Jeffries's arm and hand were already prepped and draped, so I sat, opened the wrist, and reduced the fractures. His bone density was a little better than Mrs. Cutkelvin's—more like Wheat Thins than Saltines—and I started the application process to attach the external fixator. I put two pins through the metacarpal bones just distal to the wrist, and two pins through the radius just above the fracture, and connected all four to an outrigger. I tightened all the various screws, nuts, and bolts that allowed the contraption to hold the fractures stable without a cast. Supposedly, the device allowed for early finger movement to prevent them from stiffening. I managed to get through the case without any significant movement from the patient. Dr. Green had done an admirable job.

I briefly eyed the cardiac monitor and the pulse oximeter. Both appeared normal.

As I was bandaging the arm, the intercom, or squawk box, activated, and a familiar yet irritating voice boomed through the speaker.

"Brady? Are you in there?"

Oh, God. "Yes?"

"Clarke here, your friendly pathologist and grave robber. Looks like you've been at it again, you bad boy. Got a couple of stiffs down here in the morgue, and they both have your name on their big toe as physician. Want to come play with Jeffie, maybe sniff some formaldehyde?"

"Jeff, does this mean you're performing the autopsies on Mrs. Adams and Mrs. Bland today?"

"That's right, Jim Bobby. Want to come watch, see if you did them both in, or if they were already doomed before you got 'em?"

Jeff Clarke, of all people to be assigned to autopsies that day. Considering the number of people who couldn't manage to get through the storm, and all the people who probably couldn't get hold of me that really needed to, it would have to be Jeff who would have been persistent enough to get to work and make my life just a little more miserable. Not that he really meant to make me miserable. It was just his nature to be obnoxious.

"I'll be down shortly, Jeff. I can't believe you were able to get to the hospital today. You drive a truck?"

"Nope. I paddled over from Southampton in my pirogue."

A New Orleans native, Jeff was right at home in Houston's duck weather.

I waited for the x-ray technician, still on duty from the night before, to shoot some portable films on my two patients, just to make sure that there was proof for the permanent record that I had done as good a job as I had thought. Once my success was confirmed, I headed down to the pathology department.

The section of University Hospital that contained Harris County General Hospital was, in part, run by the city. Although primarily for emergency and indigent care, city employees, such as the Houston Police Department and Houston Fire Department, received medical care at that facility via a longstanding contract. The enormous basement of the "General" contained the anatomical pathology lab, where autopsies were performed, as well as the city/county morgue. Murders and "suspicious deaths" were cordoned off from the "regular" deceased by folding aluminum doors in an attempt to keep the look-ie-loos and the rubberneckers away from the official business of Harris County. What the chief medical examiner didn't know was that the privacy measures didn't work, since he was a politician first and a pathologist second.

The entrance to the cool, dank corridor that led to the autopsy suite was adjacent to the housekeeping department. There were only a few employees milling about, probably staff left over from the night shift. As usual, they wore surgical masks to try and deter the formaldehyde stench, which was almost unbearable to casual visitors such as myself.

The secretary's desk was empty, so I pushed open the heavy insulated double doors and entered the huge room, which had high open ceilings with exposed electrical and plumbing fixtures. There were thirty or forty thick aluminum tables ready to receive the newly dead, but it appeared only three were occupied. My former medical-school anatomy lab and cadaver partner was hunched over one of those tables. A bright light hung from the ceiling, suspended by a cable and covered partially by a silvery metal shade. Most of the light seemed to be concentrated on the back of Jeff Clarke's head.

He still had flaming-red curly hair that looked as though it had never been combed. He had a matching red beard and wore thick black glasses. He had on a previously white full-length smock that showed numerous stains, the remainders of many dissections, leftovers from his occupational plate.

"Brady! Long time no see!" Jeff said, extending a hand covered by a bloody glove.

"I'll shake your hand later, when I'm protected, Jeff. Where are the gloves and gowns?"

"Where they've always been. By the front door. Get dressed and let's play."

I wandered back to the entrance to the path lab, donned a surgical hat, a mask, and an oversized white apron, one that appeared to have been freshly laundered.

"So, what you got, Jeff?"

"I'm doing the hip fracture first. What's the story?"

"She had a name. Mildred Bland. Came in on Monday night, had a medical workup by Jimmy Morgenstern, and had surgery yesterday afternoon. Echo showed a reduced left ventricular ejection fraction, so we did her under an epidural. The catheter dislodged during the case, and Fred Green had to put her under a general anesthetic so I could complete the surgery. She went into bradycardia first. Fred tried unsuccessfully to reverse that with IV meds, then the cardiology team put in a pacemaker, but to no avail. She then went into asystole, but the code-blue team couldn't get her back."

"Green put her under all right. Permanently."

"I don't know what else he could have done."

"That's my job. To find out," he said, with a suspicious glint in his eye.

Mrs. Bland had been laid open, so to speak, by the traditional Y-shaped autopsy incision. I watched as Jeff deftly cut the trachea, esophagus, and carotid vessels at the neck. He then detached the lower intestines and rectum from the anus and lifted all the internal organs out of the chest and abdominal cavities as one large mass. The bowel, liver, kidneys, pancreas, heart, and lungs made a resounding "clump" as the autopsy technician threw them onto a large flat stainless-steel pan adjacent to the autopsy table. The tech then began separating the various organs so that Jeff could describe the tissues from the gross anatomical viewpoint.

He dictated his findings into a microphone suspended from the ceiling and controlled the recorder with a foot pedal.

"Lungs are congested, full of frothy edema fluid, with old black scars, suggesting chronic nicotine abuse."

He looked at me. "Got a cigarette?"

Laughing, he continued. "Heart atrophic, muscle diseased and damaged, with signs of recent myocardial infarction. The coronary arteries are partially, but diffusely, calcified."

He continued by describing the abdominal contents, although it sounded to me as though there were no problems with those organs other than those one sees with the lack of blood supply that occurs during a cardiac arrest.

"Looks like she had a bad heart, Brady. The general anesthetic pushed her over the edge, and she lacked the reserves to compensate. Of course, the trauma of a hip fracture probably initiated some additional coronary narrowing due to spasm, but she was already doomed. She just needed a little shove.

"Of course, I'll have to do the usual tissue sectioning, look at everything under the microscope, but I think you're in the clear on this one. Feel better?"

"Not really. What about the brain?"

"I don't routinely pry open the skull unless there's some valid reason. Did she have brain cancer or some malady that might cause death?"

"Not as far as I know. Alzheimer's is what Morgenstern told me."

"So? All she'll have is cortical atrophy. They all have it. No big deal, and not worth my time, unless . . ."

"Unless what?"

He stood back from the autopsy table, took off his gloves, washed his hands, and lit a cigarette. I joined him.

Jeff watched his technician cut and prepare tiny slices of tissue from the large and small intestines, kidneys, bladder, liver, gall bladder, pancreas, heart, and lungs.

"What am I going to find on the next patient? What's the name?"

"Beatrice Adams. She was another Alzheimer's patient, admitted for dehydration and electrolyte imbalance. On admission, she was found to have a swollen right knee. Morgenstern called me, I ordered some films and an MRI. She had a three-or-four-month-old femoral condyle fracture with secondary myositis ossificans. I had nothing to offer her but PT. Unfortunately, she arrested and died on the floor last night."

"What from?"

"No idea. I guess that's why you're doing an autopsy."

"What kind of arrest did she have?"

"What do you mean?"

"Bradycardia, with asystole? Ventricular fibrillation? Supraventricular tachycardia? What?"

"Jeff, I have no—"

"Read the fucking chart, Brady. What did the head of the code-blue team write in the progress notes?"

"I don't have the chart, Jeff."

He stubbed his cigarette out on the table amid the remains of Mildred Bland. "Next table over, in the chart rack. We always insist on having the chart when we do the autopsy. Helps us figure out what happened."

I stepped the few feet to the adjacent autopsy table. The corpse was covered with a plastic sheet. I leaned to the end of the table, removed the chart from the rack, and stepped back. Jeff removed the tarp, as he called it, and he and the technician began the same procedure they had just completed on Mildred Bland.

I found a quiet corner, pulled up a chair away from the noisy job of sawing through the sternum and ribs, and read through Beatrice Adams's chart.

By the time I had deciphered the writing and walked back to join Jeff, he was dictating his gross pathological findings. I waited until he finished before I spoke.

"So, you want to hear?"

"Sure, Brady."

"The patient's vital signs showed, about one hour before her cardiac arrest, a marked reduction of her heart rate. Looks like it went down into the fifties. Morgenstern was called, but he was in the emergency room, taking care of an acute MI, and couldn't come right away, or so the nurse's notes read. He asked that the nurses draw some stat blood work, digoxin levels, electrolytes, and the like."

"She was on dig?"

"Apparently. Chronic congestive heart failure and electrolyte imbalance were her admitting diagnoses, according to this record. Anyway, the nurses started checking her vitals every fifteen minutes, as instructed by Morgenstern. About the time he arrived on the scene, one of the aides came running out of her room, saying that the patient's heart rate was down to forty beats a minute. To make a long story short, Jimmy called cardiology to get a stat pacemaker inserted, and started giving her drugs to get her heart rate up. Looks like atropine and isoproterenol, but the writing is hard to read."

"The drugs sound right."

"Anyway, the heart rate continued to fall and she went into asystole before the pacemaker could be inserted. She died. Resuscitation was not successful."

Jeff again removed his gloves, washed his hands, and lit another cigarette.

"So, we got two Alzheimer's patients, both with fractures, who die the same day. One during surgery, one on the floor, minding her own business. Both developed a slowing of the heart rate, frank bradycardia, then asystole. Both failed all resuscitation measures."

"And don't forget, Jeff, both were in their fifties. A little young for AD, don't you think?"

"Maybe."

I watched him ponder and blow smoke rings into the frigid, odorous air.

"How much do you know about Alzheimer's, Brady?"

"Not much. One of the Med-8 head nurses on the night shift told me about the three stages, which essentially are bad, worse, and awful."

"I mean, how much do you know about the pathology?"

"Nothing."

"Let's get some coffee. I'll buy."

We walked to his office, where he plugged in an ancient percolator and spooned in a dark Cajun chicory blend. As it perked, he lit another cigarette, an unfiltered Picayune no less, and placed his worn, stained shoes on the county-issue metal desk. The tiny room had no window and was lit only by a fluorescent ceiling fixture. Clutter was scattered everywhere—charts, loose papers, organ specimens in jars with preservatives, ashtrays with pungent, half-smoked butts.

"In AD, you get these tangles. Neurofibrillary tangles, they are called. The tangles represent death of the neurons, those little nerve structures that transmit information from one section of the brain to another, and then on to the rest of the body. The process is quite complicated, especially when you consider that the transmission process is entirely chemical. I won't bore you with the details—after all, you're just a carpenter, and I really don't want to cast my pearls before swine—but I'll give you a thumbnail sketch.

"Acetylcholine (ACH) runs the show. There are a lot of other chemicals that participate, primarily serotonin and norepinephrine, but ACH is the main neurotransmitter than ensures that the entire chemical complex runs smoothly. It is very important to appreciate that if ACH levels dwindle, dementia sets in. Alzheimer's is just another form of dementia, but it's a popular term. It's a catchword, like AIDS, you know. With a cute little name, the fundraisers can get the big bucks for research from—well, guys like you. Guys who think they're making a difference in disease research by buying an expensive table at a charity gala, but who have no idea how the money is being spent. But that's another story to discuss someday.

"So, why does ACH dwindle? Well, two reasons. One is there isn't enough of a particular enzyme to catalyze a reaction to make it work. It has been proven, through electron microscopy and brain chemistry studies, that AD patients have decreased levels of that enzyme, called choline acetyltransferase. Well, when that enzyme decreases, it allows a corresponding increase of another enzyme, ace-tylcholinesterase. Any idea what that little jewel does, Brady?"

"Breaks down the acetylcholine and reduces the ACH levels in the brain?"

"Very good. There may be hope for you yet. So, in current brain research, what scientists are doing, since they can't seem to fabricate the enzyme that catalyzes the ACH reaction, is to insert acetylcholin-esterase inhibitor into the neurotransmission reaction. Get it?"

"I think so. If you infuse into the system the inhibitor of the enzyme that breaks the ACH down, then theoretically, it will allow more ACH to be produced, possibly slowing down, maybe reversing, the progression of the Alzheimer's?"

"Exactly."

Jeff is so much smarter than I am, and he's always made me feel like his pupil.

He stood, went to the percolator, poured me a cup of his brew into one of the many mugs sitting on the scarred wooden table next to the coffee pot.

"Straight up?"

"Yes, thanks." I couldn't help but notice the inscription on the side of the mug he handed me: PATHOLOGISTS SEE DEAD PEOPLE.

He returned to his chair, opened a desk drawer, poured some bourbon into his coffee mug, and sipped.

"I appreciate the lecture on brain chemistry, but I don't see what it has to do—"

"Brady, are you aware that acetylcholinesterase inhibitors are currently being used in everyday medical practice?"

"No."

"I thought not. They are commonly used in the treatment of cardiac arrhythmias, such as supraventricular tachycardia and atrial fibrillation. These drugs slow the heart down. In other words, they cause therapeutic bradycardia."

He sipped his coffee, I sipped mine.

"Point is this, Brady. I read both patients' charts before I started the autopsies. You do remember from med school that I have a photographic memory?"

I nodded.

"Neither of the two patients were on a drug that could induce bradycardia. Sure, both had heart trouble, with narrowed coronaries, left-sided heart failure, decreased cardiac muscle function, and therefore decreased cardiac output. Nothing a little digitalis, some diuretics, and potassium supplement wouldn't control, especially in a couple of older, inactive AD patients."

"And what does that mean?"

"I have no idea. Might be a coincidence, maybe a fluke, maybe an adverse reaction to medicine. Or," he chuckled, "maybe somebody has been putting a little something extra in those patients' mashed potatoes."

He picked up an intercom phone. "Frankie? Crack the skulls on those last two stiffs. I want to take a look around."

CHAPTER 10

RESCUE

Thursday, May 18, 2000

"**S**o why is she still on the ventilator?" I asked the recovery room nurse.

"Don't know, Dr. Brady. She will not wake up. Dr. Green's been in here several times. He used a nerve stimulator on her temples and cheeks with no response. He thinks she could have pseudocholines-terase deficiency. We drew the lab work, but with this storm, the lab is operating under emergency conditions and with limited personnel, just like us. The eleven-to-seven clinical pathology supervisor is still running the show as best she can. She told me a few minutes ago, when I sent the specimens upstairs marked stat, that there was no such thing today. Only one of her seven-to-three shift employees has shown up so far. Two of our day-shift nurses made it in, thank God, but the nursing supervisor won't let us go home. Cardiac is doing two emergency bypasses right now, so some of us from yesterday's night shift have to go over there and staff their recovery room as soon as we get some of these post-op patients up to the floor. It's a mess."

"How long before we know about the test results?"

"No idea," she said, as she stepped to the bedside of one of the four patients in the normally jam-packed recovery room.

I wondered why Fred Green had not ordered that particular lab test on Agnes Cutkelvin prior to surgery. Since she was a nursing-home patient, and essentially in a noncommunicative state and couldn't give a history, I thought it was hospital policy to determine in advance if a patient might have a genetic absence of the enzyme that allows the metabolism of certain anesthetic agents. Without pseudocholinesterase, paralyzing drugs used in surgery for muscle relaxation in order to allow intubation and prevent muscle spasm during the operation could not be broken down and excreted. Therefore, the patient couldn't breathe on their own, couldn't be extubated, and essentially had to be kept alive artificially until the drugs cleared the system.

A while back, I had an intimate experience with pseudocholinesterase deficiency when my senior partner and mentor, Dr. Ed Wilson, had been given a large bolus of succinylcholine, a commonly used paralyzing agent for surgical procedures. He was a known pseudocholinesterase-deficiency patient from previous operations, and he had died. Unfortunately, the drug was administered postoperatively via his IV once he was breathing on his own and had been moved to a hospital room. Normally undetectable after being broken down by body chemistry, the succinylcholine, still in his system, was discovered by none other than Jeff Clarke. It was, of course, discovered a little too late to help the man, but not too late to discover the sinister activities of the killer . . . but that's another story.

I could not remember the half-life of succinylcholine, a measure of its breakdown through natural deterioration over time. How much time it took was critical for Mrs. Cutkelvin's recovery from anesthesia. Jeff Clarke would know, but I wasn't quite ready for another session with him.

Mr. Jeffries was fortunately doing well. He was awake and breathing on his own, although still sedated. Very sedated. The recovery room nurses were not a pack of fools and didn't want to take a walk on the wild side with him any more than the ER nurses had.

I decided to go visit with Cynthia Dumond and headed upstairs to Med-8, the first leg of my hospital rounds. Although Jeffries and Cutkelvin were to be moved up there from the recovery room, my current census on the floor was zero due to the two Wednesday deaths, so I didn't really have to make an appearance. But I wanted to speak to Cynthia in person about the events surrounding Mrs. Adams's and Mrs. Bland's demise.

I found her in the nurse's lounge, feet up, sound asleep. I tried to back out quietly and let her rest, but my squeaking boots woke her up.

"Wha-? Oh, Dr. Brady. Excuse me. I'm exhausted from last night. We haven't been relieved yet, and I was walking in my sleep," she said, sitting up and rubbing dried matter from her eyes. Her normally coiffured hair was in disarray, her small black-and-white nursing cap tilted off to the side.

"I thought if I could sleep for just a few minutes—"

"Oh no, I didn't mean to disturb you, Cynthia. I just wanted to say how sorry I was over the passing of the two patients I was seeing up here. With Mrs. Bland dying in the operating room and then Mrs. Adams arresting here on the floor . . . Dr. Morgenstern called me last night, told me I was two for two."

"That wasn't very nice of him, Dr. Brady. He's a good doctor, but his sensitivity level leaves something to be desired."

"I guess that comes from treating too many incurable diseases and seeing too many medical tragedies over the years. In my business, I don't see much dying, and I hate it, as a matter of fact, which is why I went into orthopedics. I like to see patients with problems, fix them, and have them ease on down the road."

"Well, Doctor, I see quite a bit of death up here, but I never seem to get accustomed to it. Each one of these old folks that passes on gets me down. Really down. You'd think after all these years . . ." she said, her voice catching in her throat.

"Cynthia, I think you're a wonderful nurse, and a great human being. The way you fixed Mrs. Adams's hair and face yesterday, well . . . anyway, just wanted to tell you in person that I was sorry."

She stood, we hugged, and I moved on. This sniveling idiot had to stop in the stairwell to blow his nose on the tissue Nurse Dumond had given him. I needed to check my testosterone levels.

"Hey, sweetie," I said to Mary Louise. I had completed rounds, the patients were in good shape, and none were too interested in going home until the water had subsided. I hoped that Medicare and the private managed-care companies would make exceptions for bad weather and allow me to extend the pre-approved hospital stays without penalty, either for me or my patients.

"Jim Bob, I was starting to worry! It's after noon. Are you coming home?"

"Well, I've been delayed." I told her about the two autopsies, the conversation with Jeff Clarke, and the plight of my ankle-fracture patient who still had not awakened from anesthesia. I had called her from the recovery room and therefore had to plug one ear to hear the conversation over the din of monitors, respirators, ringing telephones, and nurses yelling at each other across the gurneys.

"What are you going to do? You know, it's been raining all morning. According to the news reports, the water hasn't begun to run off yet, even though the rain has slacked up compared to yesterday. I'm worried that you won't be able to get back here."

"Well, I have to stay here until this woman wakes up, or until I find out exactly when she's going to wake up. I'd like her to be somewhat stabilized before I leave. Plus, I want to see if Jeff found anything unusual when he sectioned those two brains."

"I think studying dead bodies is gross. Beyond gross. Reminds me of necrophilia."

"I don't think Jeff sleeps with the corpses, Mary Louise. I think he enjoys the study of medicine from a more scientific standpoint than those of us who deal directly with patients. I like the personal contact, he doesn't. But he's one of the smartest damn people I've ever known. He's a walking medical encyclopedia."

"Jim Bob, I want you home just as soon as you think it's safe to leave. And if you don't think your truck will make it, turn around, park it, and call me."

"If my truck can't get through the water, how do you think—?"

"Just call me. Okay?"

"Sure." I laughed to myself, thinking about how my darling wife could possibly rescue me from a little high water. Me, the owner of a four-wheel-drive Chevy Silverado pickup. Ridiculous.

"Morgue."

"Hey, Dr. Brady here. Dr. Clarke still around?"

I heard the receiver thump against whichever table housed the telephone, and in the background, the answerer, whom I assumed to be Frankie, the technician, yelled to his boss and asked him if he wanted to speak to me.

"Now what, Brady? I'm trying to get some work done."

"Sorry to bother you, Jeff, but I've got a little problem in the recovery room I want to ask you about."

"I can't solve your problems with the living," he said irritably. I wondered how many of those spiked coffees he had consumed.

"I think you can with this particular patient. Remember the Ed Wilson case?"

"How could I forget?"

"Well, I operated on a patient about eight this morning. She's another Alzheimer's from a nursing home, same one that the two you have downstairs came from, by the way. I repaired her broken ankle. Fred Green gave her a general anesthetic, which she hasn't awakened from yet. The recovery room nurses have drawn some lab work to test for pseudocholinesterase deficiency, but the lab's short-handed, so I don't have a result yet."

"Why didn't Green get it before the surgery? That's policy on the pre-op evaluation if the patient's incommunicado. He should know that!"

"Good question. Probably because I rushed her up to surgery. The ankle was partially dislocated, the circulation was impaired, and I considered it a stat case. Plus, Fred's been up all night with no relief in sight. Point is, what's the half-life of succinylcholine?"

"He gave an unknown patient, with an unknown history, the one drug that might not be metabolized properly. What a putz!"

"Jeff, just tell me what the natural half-life is, so I can quit worrying."

"Shit, Brady, doesn't Green even know that?"

"He might, but he's doing another case, so I didn't go ask him. You do know, don't you?"

"Of course I know, but I think it would be more fun to have you sit up there and stew about it."

"I'd like to go home, Jeff, but I can't leave until I know whether this woman is going to come out of it or not. Please?"

"Please? Please! God, I hate it when you get all humble! I like you as a sparring partner, not as some schmuck doctor, like all those clinical practitioner weenies you cavort with."

He was silent. I responded in like kind.

"She's another nursing-home resident, huh?" he finally said.

"Yep."

Silence again.

"Six to eight hours from the time of the last dose."

"Thanks. By the way, any comments about your findings on my two patients' brains?"

"They each had one," he said, and hung up.

I waited at my office for word from the recovery room on the status of consciousness and spontaneous respirations for Mrs. Cutkelvin. A few employees managed to make it into the office during the morning, but not enough for any of the doctors to have clinic hours. In fact, most of the docs never showed up. A moron, I believe Jimmy Morgenstern had called me.

I piddled around with the stacks of paperwork on my desk, then finally got motivated and signed, dictated, did whatever I had to do to move the amoebic mass from the desktop to the Out box. I longed for a Trash icon for my desk.

My private phone line rang a little after three p.m.

"Hello?"

"Brady?"

"That's me."

"Fred Green here. I just extubated your patient. Oxygen saturation is good, pulse is good, strong respirations. She's going to be fine."

"Thanks, Fred."

"I'm very sorry about the faux pas. I should have drawn that lab work pre-op. Guess in all the rush—"

"Don't worry about it. Did you get the lab values back yet?"

"Yes, and I'm embarrassed to tell you she has the lowest level of pseudocholinesterase I've ever seen. The value is almost nonexistent. Guess we lucked out on this one. I undermedicated her in spite of her weight. If I had given the full dose complement, based on her kilogram mass, she would be sleeping until tomorrow."

"Good thing, huh? How about Mr. Jeffries? Did you move him to the floor?"

"Sure did, but on a Valium drip, though. He's a wild man. Just make sure the nurses don't overdose him."

"That'll be up to Morgenstern. He's the real doctor. I'm just the mechanic."

"Right. I have to go."

With the situation under control, paperwork done, patients alive and well, and a doctor with a clear conscience, I made the trek down to Level B, started my chariot, and headed out of the parking garage onto University Boulevard. Water was still running in rivulets from north to south. It didn't appear any deeper than it had at six that morning, so I crossed Main Street and headed west.

I dodged two stalled cars and a compact truck. All I could see of the truck was the roof, topped by the familiar red, white, and blue sign announcing DOMINO'S PIZZA.

As I swung around the pizza delivery truck, I veered into what I thought was one of the driveway entrances into the Rice University campus. My truck suddenly lunged forward, then listed severely to the right, and dropped into a hole. It was apparently a very large hole, since I thought I heard the axle to the right front wheel snap. Then the engine died.

I waited to wake up from a bad dream. Finally, I picked up the phone.

"Mary Louise?" I said.

"Are you on your way home?"

"Yes and no. I'm calling from the cellular. Got a little problem here."

"What's wrong?"

I told her.

"Stay put. I'll call you right back. Don't leave the car yet, hear me?"

"Yes."

I watched the rain, no longer coming down in sheets, but steady nonetheless. Periodically, I turned on the windshield wipers so that I could see but left the engine off. I was afraid that attempting to restart the ignition would draw water into the air intake manifold, creating more of a problem for my new vehicle than it already had. I patted the dash and apologized.

I smoked a cigarette and tried to crack the window so that the smoke and fumes wouldn't suffocate me. Unfortunately, the rain was slanted just enough to blow directly into my face. So, I moved to the passenger side of the bench seat, cracked that window, and smoked in relative peace.

Two cigarettes later, the cellular rang.

"Hola, chica."

"How far are you from the office?"

"Maybe a couple of blocks. Why?"

"I want you to walk carefully back to University Tower, then call me from the security desk to await further instructions."

"Sounds like a line from *Mission Impossible*."

"Almost. 'Your mission, should you choose to accept it . . .' Can you make it back to the office building?"

"I guess."

"Call me when you get there. I love you."

"Ditto."

I considered removing my boots but remembered my tender feet, not to mention unknown slithering creatures enjoying freedom from ditches and damp ground under pier-and-beam houses. I had on a pair of old refurbished-yet comfortable sharkskin boots. I figured that sharks spent their life in water, so what was a block or two?

The passenger door was difficult to open due to the exterior water pressure. Unfortunately, once the gate was opened, the murky waters flooded the interior in a matter of seconds. I jumped out as quickly as I could and shut the door. But not before rising water covered the front seat.

I was drenched, soaked to the skin before I had walked twenty yards. I had no umbrella, of course. That particular device was not considered manly for a Texan driving a pickup truck. As I trudged through the edge of the neighborhood of Southampton, which had become lakefront property, I tried to keep my mind off the dangers of lightning and snakes by calling myself names, such as Dumb Shit, Stupid Shit, Fuckhead, and Ass Wipe, words I last used to describe myself to my pledgemaster on Hell Night in my college fraternity.

I made my way into my building's portico drive-through, devoid of cars by the way, and took the elevator to the second-floor cross-walk, home of security.

I called Mary Louise as instructed. She ordered me to the roof.

"What? There's nothing up there but—"

"Be there. Fifteen minutes," she said, and hung up.

The security guard on duty had been there for over sixteen hours, and he was nonplussed at my request to accompany me to the roof of University Towers. The exit to the roof was an alarmed door, requiring a special key card and alarm code for entry and exit. That safety device had been installed some years previously after a first-year medical student had plunged to his death from the top of the building after a failing grade on a microbiology exam.

Nevertheless, the security guard was too tired to argue. We took the elevator to the top floor, belonging to another medical group. He permitted himself entry with the customary two key cards and led me to the internal stairwell. We walked up the double flight of stairs and encountered a door marked EXIT: AUTHORIZED PERSONNEL ONLY.

He inserted yet another key card, punched in a five-digit code, and opened the door. We stepped out onto the roof and stood under a small eave.

"Smoke?" he offered.

"Sure. Mine are drenched."

I inhaled one of his unfiltered cigarettes and almost choked, but immediately felt the warmth of the pollutants in my chest. It was therapy for pneumonia. No bacterial organism could withstand what I had just breathed into my lungs.

"Lose your car, Doc?"

"Yep. New truck, too."

"Must be pretty bad out there."

"Bad as I've seen it, and I've been in this town thirty-two years."

We heard the rhythmic hum about the same time. The security guard looked at me. He had a serious nature about him. A man of secrets, maybe, or victim of a much rougher life than mine.

"Feels like Nam all over again. Pourin' down rain, can't see your nose in front of your fuckin' face, standin' in stinkin' water full of snakes, Hueys hoverin', pickin' up the dead and the dyin'. Bitch of a war. Doc, were you there?"

I shook my head. "Med school deferment. I was reclassified 1-A at the end of my internship year, but then the war ended."

"Lucky man," he said, lighting another cigarette off the burning ember of the last one. "Here's your ride, dude. Looks like you got some pull."

The blue-and-white helicopter touched gently down on the heliport atop University Tower. I read the Houston Police Department insignia on the fuselage, then saw the face of my friend Detective Lt. Susan Beeson, smiling through the partially fogged starboard window.

CHAPTER 11

MORGENSTERN

Thursday, May 18, 2000

After a long, steaming-hot shower, Mary Louise brought me a thick white cotton robe and a pair of wool hunting socks that I last used on a pheasant hunt in McCook, Nebraska. She led me into the sunroom and sat me down in my non-designer recliner. On the small TV table, the wooden one from Crate and Barrel, was a large bowl of chicken soup bordered by a few wheat crackers and a carafe of hot tea.

"Jewish penicillin?" I asked.

"Works for the Protestants, too. And drink every drop of the Earl Grey."

She wore black leggings, thick red socks pulled up to her mid-calves, and a loose bulky red V-necked sweater. Her blond hair was pulled into a ponytail, held loosely in place with a silver and turquoise clip.

"And what about you Catholics? Does it work for you, too?"

"Don't forget, I'm one-fourth Jewish. Remember, my Irish grandpa married a Jewish girl he met in Austria during World War I. She died when Mama was a child, so Grandpa raised her Catholic. She married within her faith, wiping out thousands of years of Jewish tradition in Grandma's family. You know, of course, how I was raised."

"Yes. Fish on Friday, Confession on Saturday, and Mass on Sunday."

"And then the confusion set in at SMU, hanging out with all those Methodists."

"And then, worst of all, you move to Houston and meet a non-church-going Protestant medical student who, by the way, is still struggling with the basic tenets of the faith."

"Best thing that ever happened to me," she said, leaning down and kissing my wet hair. "You should have dried your hair. I don't want you getting sick and dying on me. You're still shivering."

"A little. The soup will help. And so will the attentions of man's best friend," I said of Tip, who had barely left my side since my arrival on the Post Oak Tower rooftop heliport. He wedged his big sandy-colored head just inside my TV tray and made my lap his chin's temporary home. He stared at me with those dark baleful eyes and said he was glad that I was okay. I think.

Mary Louise had a sandwich, watched me eat my soup, and scanned the channels for updates on the Great Flood.

All four local network affiliates carried the same story: the worst flooding in Houston since Hurricane Alicia. The San Jacinto and Brazos Rivers had flooded their banks, closing major highways and thoroughfares in Harris, Chambers, Liberty, Montgomery, and Brazoria Counties. Thousands of residents had been evacuated from low-lying areas into shelters that were themselves also surrounded by high water. All available emergency personnel had been dispatched to various central locations throughout Houston. The governor had called out the National Guard to assist the local police and fire departments. President Clinton had been notified of the emergency and was considering declaring Houston a disaster area once he made a tour of the devastation.

"How did you manage, in the midst of all this trouble, to retrieve me via whirlybird?"

"I called Susan after your noon phone call. I was afraid you'd get stuck up there. She said that if worse came to worse, she'd come pick you up, in whatever she had available. Pretty nifty, huh?"

"That was my first ride in a helicopter. I didn't realize we are the beneficiaries of a heliport atop this apartment building. Were you aware of that?"

"Not until Susan asked. I called Raj, who fortunately was able to make it in this morning, who then obtained permission for its use from the powers that be."

"It was nice to see your and Raj's smiling faces when we touched down. I appreciate it. I can't wait to get the reimbursement bill from the City of Houston."

"We'll worry about that later. Nothing's too good for my baby."

"I guess a Real Doctor would have stayed at the hospital and helped out with . . . with whatever."

"Was anything else going on that you could have made better by staying? Something the orthopedic house staff couldn't handle?"

"Not that I know of."

"Then your place is with me. It's your job to take care of your family, especially in critical situations like this one."

"Looks to me like it's the other way around. You seem to be taking care of me."

"I know that's the way it looks, but after your soup, you should be revived enough to . . ."

"Ah. To take care of you."

She winked. I was feeling better.

Afterward, we lay in our king-sized bed under the covers, safe from outside influence. Mary Louise had let Tip back into the room. He made himself comfortable on our bed, positioning himself equidistant between my bride and myself. After all, he wouldn't want to show favoritism, in case something happened to me and the mistress of the house was solely responsible for him.

Although it was only a little after six, darkness had settled over the apartment. From the twenty-seventh-floor view, I could see clouds full of rain moving rapidly from the south, passing like a specter through Transco Tower and the Galleria complex. Wind sang through invisible cracks in the weatherstripping of the large master bedroom window. Large droplets of water continued to sling themselves silently against the double-paned glass.

My pager sounded. I quickly picked it up off the night table next to me and shut it off, hoping not to waken my sleeping bride. I activated the built-in light source and read a 790 exchange. University Hospital.

I sat up, punched in the numbers on the touch-tone portable phone, put on my robe, and walked into my study. I sat at my desk and watched the rain from a different perspective, with downtown Houston as the backdrop.

"Med-8."

"Dr. Brady here. Did you page me?"

"Yes, sir. Dr. Morgenstern needs to speak to you."

My stomach churned, and I felt a little nauseous.

"Jim Bob?"

"Hey, Jimmy. You still up there?"

"Hell, yes. I'm one of a handful of medical docs that made it in today, so we're trying to take care of the entire patient population of this hospital. A bitch, huh?"

"Sounds like it. I tried to page you earlier after the two cases I did this morning, but I couldn't get ahold of you."

"I've been pretty damn busy. I'm answering emergencies only."

"You're not calling with any more bad news, are you?"

He was silent for a little too long. I felt it coming.

"What is it, Jimmy?"

"Cutkelvin, the ankle fracture?"

"Yes?"

"She died."

My head ached and my stomach turned. There were no words.

"Jim Bob? Are you there?"

"Barely."

"What exactly happened in surgery? With the breathing problem?"

I related the events of the morning, which seemed like an eternity ago.

"Huh. Sounds like it was a typical pseudocholinesterase-deficiency response. The anesthetic, the succinylcholine, should have been out of her system by this evening, though, wouldn't you think?"

"I guess. You want to tell me what happened?"

"Don't know exactly. The nursing shortage here is of disaster proportions. Vital signs are being erratically checked. When the nurses last charted her signs and called me stat, her heart rate was down to forty beats per minute. By the time I got up here, it was down to thirty. I called a code blue and called for a cardiology resident or fellow to put in a pacemaker, but nobody came. NOBODY. One of the nurses and I did our best to give her CPR. I pushed the usual drugs to jack up her heart rate, but . . . zip. I'm sorry."

"I should have never left the hospital."

"Don't blame yourself. She was fine when you went home. Just one of those things, I guess. There's nothing you could have done."

"Jimmy, I've had three patients die in the last, what, twenty-four hours? And all died of an irreversible decreasing heart rate. Two were post-op. All three had Alzheimer's, and all three came from Pleasant View Nursing Home. Don't you think that's a little beyond the limits of probability?"

"I don't know what's going on. Could be just a bad coincidence. Your time in hell, so to speak. Happens to all of us. In fact, most of us much more than you. Most of your patients get well and then hurt themselves again. Don't get yourself too riled up over it. Especially since—hold on, my beeper's going off."

I waited.

"Need to go. I'll call you later," he said, and disconnected.

"Who was that?" asked a still-sleepy Mary Louise from my office doorway.

"Jimmy Morgenstern."

She looked at me with more than a little sympathy in her gorgeous blue eyes. "Not another . . ."

"Yes. Another. The ankle fracture I did, the one with all the breathing problems. Her heart rate dropped, and not enough staff was present to even try and save her. Not that they could."

She stepped behind my chair, put her arms around my neck, put her cheek against my cheek. I smelled her fresh scent, felt her blond mane with my hand. She kissed my stubbled beard.

"You think something's going on?"

"I don't know what to think."

"If anybody can figure it out, it's you. Want some more hot tea?"

"No. Wouldn't mind a little Glenlivet Scotch, though."

"Rocks, splash of Evian?"

"No, thanks. Just neat. I just need to think."

"I'll bring you the drink, then sort of steer clear, let you brood for a while. But only for a while."

I did just that, until the phone rang. I was afraid to pick it up. Could be another death, or another consult from Morgenstern that could turn into another death. Mary Louise answered it from her locale, and all was quiet again for a while.

"Want to talk to your son?" she asked, as she again stepped into the doorway of my study.

"Sure!" I turned on my extension's speaker phone. "Hey, boy! How's Bermuda?"

"Great, Dad. I've been trying to get through to you guys for hours. We've been seeing the news about Houston most of the day. Guess the phone lines have been jammed with calls, huh? You okay?"

"We're fine, J. J. Are you having a good time?"

"Better than you, Pop. Mom told me about the 'copter ride home. Cool move on her part, don't you think?"

"Very. It was my first time. You ever been up in one of those things?"

"Sure. Nice ride if you have the stomach for it. You okay on the . . . the, uh, patient problem?"

"Not really. I just hope it doesn't get any worse."

"Anything I can help you with when I get back?"

"Nothing that I can think of right now, but I'll let you know. How's the weather?"

"Blue skies with a nice easterly breeze. The temp gets into the 70s during the day, then back into the 60s at night. I could live here."

"How does Aimee like it?"

"She loves it. For her, it's like being back home in Florida without the summertime heat. We rented a catamaran today and had a nice sail in the Atlantic. Took some wine and cheese."

I laughed. "Did you do much sailing?"

"Enough to get out and back. We took a little respite on the boat, if you know what I mean."

"I think I do. Wasn't too bumpy, huh?"

"Oh, it was bumpy all right, but it added to the . . . excitement. I like Aimee. She's a cool chick. Could be long-term potential there, Pops."

Mary Louise was listening from the doorway, shaking her head. She mouthed the words, "He's your son."

"So, when are you coming home?"

"End of next week. We decided to stay a few extra days. I'm going to take some diving lessons. Aimee's a pretty accomplished diver, so I have to keep up with the Joneses, you know?"

"Sure. Just be sure the only shark's teeth you run into are on the beach and not attached to anything that's still swimming."

"Don't worry. You guys take care. Love you, Dad."

"You too."

Mary Louise remained in the doorway. "Still brooding?"

"Probably, but I'm tired of being alone."

"Come watch a *Seinfeld* rerun with me. Jerry bought a new couch, and Elaine's falling in love with the delivery man."

"Sounds exciting. What's Kramer up to?"

"He's buying a make-it-yourself pizza parlor."

"This I must see."

Partway through *ER*, the Michael Crichton-written medical show, I heard my beeper's pulsating, almost pleasant melodic buzz from my desk in the study. The number on the LED readout was that of my answering service, so I made the call.

"University Orthopedic Group."

"Yes, ma'am. Dr. Brady here. You rang?"

"Yes, Doctor. We have a call holding from Jacob Stern?"

"I don't know anyone named Stern. What's it about?"

"He says he's a rabbi and needs to speak to you about one of your patients."

"Put him through, then."

"Thank you, Doctor. Go ahead, please."

"Dr. Brady?"

"Yes?"

"Rabbi Jacob Stern. I'm sorry to bother you, but the wife of one of the members of my synagogue is desperately worried about her husband. I understand you operated on him this morning. Rufus Jeffries?"

"Yes, sir, I did. He had a broken wrist. I fixed it, and last I heard, he was doing fine. I didn't realize Mr. Jeffries had any family, or I would have tried to get in touch. Most of the nursing-home patients I see—at least the ones I've seen lately—don't have any family. I'm very sorry."

"No problem. Rufus has been in Pleasant View for a couple of years. It seems that when he fell, the nursing-home staff had him rushed to the emergency room at University Hospital and forgot to call Stella, his wife.

"She usually visits him every day, but because of the flooding problems, she couldn't make it in. When she called to check on him, she was told that he had fallen, and so on and so forth.

"She called me in a panic. I called the hospital, found out that a Dr. Morgenstern had admitted him. I then contacted the medical floor, and one of the nurses told me that you had operated on him. Stella wouldn't rest until I talked to you personally."

"Well, sir, when I left the hospital about three o'clock, he was doing all right. He was very restless, though, so they still had him on a Valium drip. In truth, he was very combative, especially in the ER this morning. I haven't heard anything from the nurses, so I would assume that all is still well."

"Good. I spoke to Dr. Morgenstern earlier in the evening. He gave me the same report you did. I didn't want to bother you, but as I said, Stella insisted."

"So, you're his rabbi?"

"Yes. Why? The name Rufus Jeffries doesn't sound Jewish enough?"

I laughed. "Well, what's in a name?"

"His father brought his family to Texas from Poland in the late 1930s during . . . well, during the trouble in Europe. There weren't many jobs in the construction business for a man named Reuben Jankovics, so he changed the family name to Jeffries."

"I see. Well, I'm glad times have changed."

He paused. "Maybe not as much as you might think, Doctor. But thank you again. And if you would be so kind as to take down my number and call me if any changes occur in Rufus's condition?"

"Yes, sir. I'll be happy to."

I hoped there would be no need to call.

The last phone call of the evening occurred after eleven, while we were in bed. Mary Louise was sleeping. I was still brooding, but from the reclining position.

"Brady? Jeff Clarke. You asleep?"

"I'm in bed, Jeff. Are you still at work?"

"Yep. I have no wife to go home to, so I'm partying in the lab with some of my very cold and very quiet friends."

"Are you drunk?"

"I hope so. But I don't need a lecture from you about the evils of alcohol. I can't hurt my patients any more than they have already been hurt. I called you for a reason. Want to hear?"

"Sure, Jeff."

"Those two brains I looked at today, Adams and Bland? Classic Alzheimer's on gross exam. Atrophy of the cerebral cortex and a twenty to thirty percent reduction in brain mass. Typical findings.

"It was late, and Frankie didn't want to cut the sections, but I made him anyway. I've been looking at them for a while. On Adams, I see the usual neurofibrillary tangles, the hallmark pathological finding in AD. In case you don't remember, these tangles are found in dying neurons. Her specimen also contains senile plaques, which are degenerated nerve bundles surrounding amyloid protein cores. Some of her slides even show a little aluminum accumulation in the plaques and the tangles."

"Aluminum? Is that normal?"

"Sure. In the early days, researchers thought that maybe exposure to pots and pans caused Alzheimer's, because of the aluminum particles found in the brains of autopsied patients. But now, that theory has been debunked."

"What about Bland? You didn't find any, what did you call them, neurofibrillary tangles?"

"Yes, tangles. And no, I did not see a single one. She had some degenerative plaques, a typical finding in any nonspecific dementia, but no tangles."

"What does that mean?"

"Probably means she had a non-Alzheimer's senile dementia. But that's not important, Brady. Do you want hear what's REALLY important, or do you want to bullshit with me about the ridiculous nit-picking some academic pathologists do over the various microscopic findings in dementia disorders?"

"I'd love to hear what's really important, Jeff."

"Then quit asking dumb questions. The reason I called," he said, "was to tell you that I've found something extraordinary in both specimens. Evidence of nerve regeneration."

I sat up, putting my feet on the floor.

"Jeff, nerves don't regenerate. That's why paralyzed patients and stroke patients and patients with degenerating neurological diseases don't recover. That's why there's a Lou Gehrig's disease, and facial nerve palsies after a stroke, and temporal lobe epilepsy after meningitis, and—"

"I damn well know that, Brady. But I'm telling you that, just as sure as I was the valedictorian of our med school class, there is fucking nerve regeneration in both these brains. Definite signs of the creation of new brain tissue. Brand new neurons!"

"That just can't be, Jeff."

"You're right, it can't be. But it is. I need more specimens. Did you bump anybody else off since yesterday?"

"You know, Jeff, you can be a real insensitive prick. Don't you think that I might feel bad about these patients dying on me? That maybe I might not appreciate your joking about it? Huh?"

He was silent, then said, "I'm waiting."

I reluctantly told him about Mrs. Cutkelvin, the ankle fracture from the morning and my latest fatality.

"Fan-fucking-tastic, Brady! What a pal you have turned out to be. You keep bumping off people from the old folks' home, and I'll be famous. I can see the headlines now:

"DR. JEFFREY CLARKE AWARDED MEDICINE'S
NOBEL PRIZE FOR DISCOVERING CURE
FOR ALZHEIMER'S DISEASE"

"Jeff, I don't see how—"

"Neither do I, Brady, you wonderful goy, you! But I will. Trust me, I will. So whatever you and Morgenstern are doing, keep it up. I need a series of these cases to figure out the details!"

CHAPTER 12

DEATH

Friday, May 19, 2000

I woke up sometime during the night to relieve myself of all that hot tea Mary Louise had forced down me. At the time, I hadn't cared about the stimulant and diuretic effects. At three or four in the morning, however, it became a significant factor in my sleep deprivation. The Glenlivet consumption had not been enough to counteract its effects.

We had pulled the blackout shades down in the bedroom, so it was, as usual, pitch black. So black, in fact, that I sat on Tip as I tried to get back into bed. He whimpered a little, but no serious harm was done. I lay in bed after patting him to let him know that I hadn't done it on purpose, and I tried to get back to sleep. I tossed and turned for a while, stared at the clock, and worried about getting adequate sleep for the next day.

I finally got out of bed, put on my robe, and went into the sunroom, not that there was any sun at that time of the morning. Nor had there been at any time of day for several days. I walked out onto the terrace and lit a cigarette, thinking a little nicotine would relax me. I had hoped it would counteract the stimulant effect of the Earl Grey. Some doctor I was.

I sat down in one of the mold-proof chairs and appreciated the absolutely clear night sky. The temperature was cool, with a healthy breeze. The clouds had dissipated, and the three-quarter moon shone brightly across the Houston sky.

I noticed the "moon maiden," hair askew, with closed eyelids and the typical pucker on her sensuous lips. For me, there had never been a man in the moon, only the maiden, always in a state of repose or physical pleasure.

I thought about the demise of the three female Alzheimer's patients from Pleasant Valley. Beatrice Adams, Mildred Bland, and Agnes Cutkelvin. All had died of a dramatic slowing of the heart rate, followed by cessation of the heartbeat. None had responded to the usual medications that stimulated and accelerated the heart rate. No one had responded to the insertion of a pacemaker, but I couldn't remember how many had received one. Cutkelvin did not get one due to the lack of available personnel, but the other two? I would have to check.

I rehashed all that chatter from Dr. Jeff Clarke about nerve regeneration in patients Bland and Adams, but it made no sense to me. I attributed his theory to the fact that he was probably very drunk. We doctors knew that nerves, once interrupted, did not regrow. If they did, even partially, then there would be fewer people with quadriplegia, paraplegia, and stroke disabilities. In fact, if nerves could regenerate themselves, then senile dementias such as Alzheimer's would either not exist or would be a significantly milder disease process. And all that hoopla about Mrs. Adams's specimens showing the hallmark tangles of Alzheimer's and Mrs. Bland's not? Jeff said it wasn't important.

Maybe it all was bunk, due to Jeff's mental state. He would probably sober up and call me in the afternoon. He would say that he had autopsied Agnes Cutkelvin, the latest tragedy, and that he had reviewed her specimens. His opinion would be that she had classic Alzheimer's. And, upon reviewing the other two patients' specimens, he realized he had made an error. That there was, in fact, no regeneration, simply a phase of degeneration that resembled potential new growth of nerve tissue. And that Mrs. Bland did in fact have the classic neurofibrillary tangles as well, documenting her Alzheimer's disease.

An error. It had to be. There is no neuronal regeneration. That is a scientific fact.

We both slept through the alarm and were awakened by the persistent whining of the Tipster, who desperately needed to relieve himself. My immediate response was panic, not for my dog, but for me. After all, rounds, patients, surgery—

"Mary Louise! Get up! We've overslept! It's after seven!" I said, running into the bathroom to quickly shower. "Please walk Tip! I don't have time!"

As I was hurriedly soaping down and washing my hair, the shower door opened and in stepped the gorgeous woman that I slept with at night. She was nude, in all her glory.

"Mary Louise, any other time, I would be thrilled to see you like this, but—"

"Jim Bob. It's Friday. What do you do on Friday?"

I stood there for a minute, water pummeling my face as it had the day before during my walk from my stalled truck, and looked at her.

"Isn't Friday your day off? Normally?"

I nodded, enjoying the warm, controllable, indoor shower, and started to calm down a little.

"And do you know which particular Friday this is?"

I thought as hard as I could but did not remember. I shook my head.

"The Friday before the Saturday that you are to give your lecture. Remember?"

It was starting to dawn on me.

"Oh. With the flood and the deaths, I guess I forgot. New York."

"That's right. My husband is to present a lecture on some erudite subject, of which I have no idea—being a retired retailer of women's fashion—at his alma mater tomorrow. We're leaving Intercontinental Airport at one thirty today and are scheduled to have dinner with some of your colleagues this evening at the St. Regis Hotel.

"So, since the weather's cleared, and the flights are probably running again, we're making that trip. And if you want to go in, make rounds, check on your patients, and maybe drop by your office and see if any of your associates managed to drag their lazy butts into work today, that's fine. But you don't have to hurry. No surgery. No patients. Just rounds, maybe, if you choose.

"Of course, you were there most of the day yesterday and you almost got killed trying to get home. So, I think you've put in your time. And if you want, you can call your resident—what's his name?"

"Tim Kelly."

"You can call Tim, have him see the patients—how many are there?"

"Four. Five, counting the broken wrist I operated on yesterday, and the only one from the nursing home that's still alive."

"Okay. Five people. So, you can go in and see those five people, four of whom have been there a while, right?"

"Right."

"And one who won't know YOU were personally there. Right?"

"Well, the circulation and neurological status of his hand has to be checked, and . . ."

"Or, you could relax a little and have Tim make rounds for you. Can Dr. Kelly competently perform that duty for you?"

I gave her my best thoughtful look, then nodded.

"Then what's your hurry, big boy?" she said, stepping the rest of the way into the shower. She put her arms around my neck and pulled my body next to hers. She opened her mouth, put it against mine, and kissed me deeply.

"Maybe you can take me to breakfast," she whispered, "or maybe you can have me for breakfast."

I put my hands on her hips, then her buttocks, and held her close.

"I'll call the office, see if Fran or Rae made it in, then call Kelly and see what he's up to."

She pulled away from me slightly and looked down. "Well, at least I know what you're up to."

I made it to work a little after nine, with plenty of time to see about my patients, check in at the office, retrieve my slides for Saturday's lecture, and sign out to my group's on-call doc for the weekend. It was each physician's responsibility to provide a typed or handwritten summary of their hospital inpatients to whichever surgeon was taking weekend call. The purpose was to make their miserable job easier. At least they would have some idea of what was wrong with each patient.

I stopped by my office first and played back messages on my private line from both Fran and Rae, saying that they were still homebound due to persistent high water in their respective outlying communities. I had noticed during the drive to the medical center that, just as the water had quickly risen on Wednesday and Thursday, it had just as quickly disappeared in the early morning hours on Friday. There was little or no standing water to be seen during my fifteen-minute drive into work.

The majority of local schools were still closed and would be so until Monday. Some banks and retail businesses would also remain closed for the convenience of their employees, or so the radio reports had said.

A memo on my desk from our administrator Peggy Peterson informed me that she had decided to allow all doctors to sign out as early as they wanted on Friday to the doctor on weekend call. Although the customary changeover time was five p.m., a number of our patients resided in the hinterlands, and therefore clinic visits were anticipated to be sparse due to persistent high water in the suburban areas. Still, I pitied the doctor with the duty. To cover for the thirty orthopedic surgeons in the group, to tend to God only knew how many hospital inpatients, and to try and counter patient panic over what had turned into a two-day clinic closure would be nigh on impossible. Call that weekend would later be categorized as Nightmare on Fannin Street.

I strolled leisurely over to the hospital and started rounds on Med-8 with Mr. Rufus Jeffries. Since the night shift had been relieved by then, an unfamiliar day-shift nurse accompanied me into his room.

"Morning, Mr. Jeffries," I said, carefully palpating his radial pulse beneath the surgical bandage and the external fixator. "Your pulse is fine. Can you feel me touching your fingers?"

There was no response. To say that he seemed much calmer than he did in the holding area outside the operating room the day before would be an understatement. His thin white hair was neatly combed, he had on a fresh gown, and he was lying on fresh sheets. Cynthia Dumond's presence on the night shift was duly noted by this observer.

"Can you move your hand for me, sir?"

Again, nothing.

"I don't think he's communicative, Doctor. We've had no response from him since I came on duty. And, according to the night shift's report, he—"

"Nurse," I said, peering at her name tag through the bottom half of my bifocal lenses, "how do you pronounce it? Lefkanovich?"

"Lef-kan-O-vic. I'm Ukrainian."

She looked to be in her twenties, was tall and thin, and wore little makeup. She wore her black hair short, with long bangs that almost covered her eyes. She had a serious look about her.

"Ah. Excellent. Mr. Jeffries is of Polish descent. His rabbi called me last night. The family changed their name back in the 30s from Jankovics, I believe he said."

"Yes?"

"I don't want anything to happen to this man. Please take a lesson or two from the eleven-to-seven supervisor, Cynthia Dumond. You're familiar with her, right?"

She nodded.

"I've seen her bring around these AD patients with attention and conversation. They can respond if they are stimulated to respond. You saw what she did with Mrs. Beatrice Adams. Remember her?"

"Yes, Doctor."

"Pretty amazing, wouldn't you say?"

She hung her head. "Yes, Doctor."

"Somewhere inside these people there is, I believe, the capacity to communicate. I don't know what triggers it, but as sure as hell it isn't silence. Talk to the man, no matter whether you think he's hearing you or not. It might surprise you. Okay?"

She nodded.

"And, if there is the slightest problem—and I mean, the least, little, seemingly nothing kind of abnormality, you get Dr. Morgenstern up here stat. Understand?"

"Yes, Doctor. Sorry. I didn't mean to appear . . . insensitive."

"We all get a little calloused sometimes. You have to try hard not to be. It's just that this guy here is special to me."

"Is he a relative or something? Friend of the family?"

"No. He's the only living Alzheimer's patient I have left in the hospital. The other three died this week. And I can't deal with another death."

She seemed very surprised by my comment, staring at me the way she did. "I'll watch him very closely, Doctor."

I patted her on the shoulder, still a socially acceptable gesture in the year 2000. "Thanks."

As I was writing a progress note on the hospital chart, Jimmy Morgenstern came slowly striding down the hall, dressed in an expensive suit with a double-breasted jacket, white shirt, and bright, patterned tie with matching handkerchief. In spite of his natty outfit, he looked tired. His eyes were puffy, the white streaked with hyperemic capillaries.

"Hey, Jim Bob. How are you feeling?" he said, shaking my hand.

"I'm feeling like I don't want Mr. Jeffries to be another statistic for the week. Mary Louise and I are leaving for New York this afternoon and won't be back until Monday. Please keep him alive."

"It's not like I'm bumping them off," he said, obviously insulted. "They're dying on my service, not yours. My mortality stats are off the chart. At this rate, the monthly Medicare audit is going to eat me alive with sanctions and financial penalties. I wish to God I'd never agreed to take Frazier's sickies."

"Sorry, Jimmy. I didn't mean to imply—"

"Forget it. Have a safe trip."

I stopped by the autopsy suite and went looking for Jeff Clarke. He was hovered over the enormous frame of Agnes Cutkelvin.

"What did you find, Jeff?"

"Fat, and lots of it. We haven't cut the brain yet. But don't worry, you'll be the second to know what's in there."

"Any retractions on the statements you made to me last night? About nerve regeneration in the other two patients?"

He continued sectioning organs and making verbal descriptions of their gross characteristics into the overhead microphone.

"Jeff?"

"What?"

"Did you hear me?"

"Look, Brady, I was little drunk. I looked at the slides again this morning after an entire pot of coffee. Let me make it simple for you. When you're looking at tissue, there is a remodeling process going on all the time. When death occurs, that process stops, like a freeze-frame on a video recorder. On both brain specimens, you could see macrophages at work. Remember those little cells whose job it is to clean up messes, so that new reactions and new messes can be made?"

"Yes."

"Okay, so I thought last night, when I saw the cleanup process going on, that there was a rebuilding process going on. But this morning, I'm not so sure. I'm going to get some EMs and take a closer look."

"EMs?"

"Jesus, man, did you go to medical school? Of course, you did. I witnessed it! Electron microscopy specimens. I want to look at the reactions down on the biochemical level. That will give me time to take some tissue from this one—Cutkelvin—combine it with the other two—Adams and Bland—look at them in series on the EM, and compare them to some other cerebral tissue slides I have of various dementias, maybe make some EMs of those as well."

"So, Jeff, the bottom line is . . ."

"Is that I don't know jack shit for sure! Now leave me the hell alone, Brady!"

"Aye, aye, captain."

"Oh, go fuck yourself and the horse you rode in on. And do not discuss this with anyone yet. Got it?"

I saluted him, artfully dodging a piece of liver he threw at me.

On the way home, my beeper exploded. The LED readout provided an all-too-familiar number.

"Med-8. May I help you?"

"Dr. Brady. Someone call me?"

"Hold, please."

"Dr. Brady? This is Nurse Lefkanovich." She was sobbing.

"Oh, God."

"I'm so sorry," she cried. "Right after you left, while Dr. Morgenstern was still here, Mr. Jeffries's monitor sounded. His heart rate was at forty-eight. We called a code blue, and Dr. Morgenstern did everything he could, but the patient just would not respond. I'm so very sorry. I wish . . ."

I hung up the phone and silently cried for a man I didn't really know. Maybe I was crying for myself.

CHAPTER 13

BONHOFFER

Friday, May 19, 2000

By the time Continental Flight 160 touched down at La Guardia Airport, I was somewhere between bulletproof and invincible. "Witty and charming" and all those cute phases of early inebriation were long past. We had seats in the first-class section, since the trip was deductible and I was to receive a small stipend for presenting a paper. When the hostess asked if she could get me anything prior to takeoff, I had requested a double scotch on the rocks. After the first two, I didn't remember much, which I guess was my intent.

The cab ride to the St. Regis Hotel was a blur. Mary Louise checked us in, then put me in a freezing cold shower and ordered a pot of coffee.

"We have to be downstairs at seven thirty, Jim Bob. Are you going to make it?"

"I don't know," I said, drying my hair with a large white cotton towel, with another wrapped around me. "Got any aspirin?"

"Sure. How many?"

"Six."

"Six? You can't—"

"Yes I can, with an antacid chaser."

Once I started to focus a little better, I appreciated our room. The entry led into a nice sitting area with antique furniture, an FM-stereo/CD player, and a console television. The bedroom was ample, with a king-sized bed and another stereo and TV. There was an honor bar in the oak cabinet that housed the TV in the sitting room, from which I pulled two diet colas, washed down the six aspirin, and added four antacid tablets, icing for the sludge cake in my stomach.

"Sorry about overdoing it on the plane. I just couldn't think about those four patients for one more second. Hope I didn't babble too much or embarrass you beyond repair."

"Don't worry, sweetie," she said. "I still love you, but I'm not sure about our temporary neighbors on the plane. You might have been a tad obnoxious," she said, patting my cheek. "Are you through in the bathroom?"

"God, how embarrassing. No, I need to shave, brush my teeth, comb my hair."

"Why don't you use the half-bath by the foyer?"

"We have two bathrooms?"

"It's a half-bath. This is New York. We're uptown now."

"I thought we were in Manhattan."

"Uptown, with a small *u*. We're at East Fifty-Fifth, between Madison and Fifth Avenue, which is still Manhattan, silly."

"I guess you know the city better than I do, huh?"

"I spent enough time here buying the latest fashions for the store, remember? I was in retail for twenty years. I'm going to get ready," she said, kissing my cheek and retiring to the bathroom, the full-sized one in the bedroom.

I finished my toiletries and donned a black double-breasted suit with a thin gray stripe, a light purple shirt, and a tie that Mary Louise said matched. My head continued to clear, thanks to the scotch antidote, so I experimented with the TV and stereo remotes in the sitting area and waited for my bride to finish dressing.

When the sliding door into the bedroom opened and she stepped out, I was taken aback. She wore a short black cocktail dress that came to just above her knees. Her blond hair was piled on her head, with strands dangling in front of her ears and over her forehead in strategic locations. I was familiar enough with her routine to know she had worked hard to make herself look like she just "threw" her hair together.

The dress she wore had a plunging neckline which exposed just enough of her chest to make one curious. Maybe more than curious.

"I hope no one we're meeting for dinner has a heart condition."

"Why?" she asked, smiling.

"Well, one look at you and there'll be a rush for nitroglycerine at the drug store. That is an unbelievable dress. Turn around."

She modeled it for me, swirling in expert fashion on a pair of black suede pumps with three-inch stilettos, marked by a row of vertical rhinestones along the back of the heel.

"Some outfit."

"Think I should wear this?" she said, wrapping a red-and-black silk scarf around her neck and shoulders, which partially covered her chest and neck.

"That totally changes the look. I really shouldn't comment because my head is still swimming. You look great, regardless of how you wear the dress."

"I think I'll wear the scarf down there and maybe take it off when we sit down to eat."

"I hope I sit next to you, not across from you."

"Why is that?"

"I wouldn't be able to eat for, you know, the view."

"You've seen them a million times."

"Maybe, but it's always like the first time to me."

She smiled and put her arm through mine. "Now you're trying to make points."

"Yes, I am."

From our suite on the twelfth floor, we descended in the mirrored elevator to the marbled lobby of the St. Regis. We were greeted by all who saw us: bellhops, doormen, registration employees, the concierge. It seemed a friendly place, which I appreciated, now that I was sober. The events of the week still weighed heavily on my mind, but I did my best to push the hospital deaths out of my conscious thoughts.

We walked the short corridor toward the four-star restaurant, Lespinasse, passing the "pipe" room and the piano bar, complete with a nodding and smiling keyboardist playing show tunes. I longingly stopped in front of the drinkers' bar, stared at the oak-paneled walls and the oriental rugs, and heard the sounds of ice clinking the sides of crystal glasses. Mary Louise tugged on my arm, and we moved along.

We were escorted into a private dining room, with numerous tables set with fine china, silver, and crystal goblets. A number of people were milling about, most of whom were strangers to me. In the corner, we spotted our old friends, Richard and Michael Carnes. They waved, came over to us, and we exchanged hugs.

"So, how was the trip?" asked Richard, host of the weekend's events, and an orthopedic surgeon whom I had met during my fellowship in New York at the Hospital for Special Surgery. After the completion of his medical training, Richard and Michael had returned to their native Long Island to live and work. We saw them twice a year, at this reunion dinner for past trainees at Special Surgery and at the national meeting of the American Academy of Orthopedic Surgeons.

"Great, from what I can remember," I said.

"Bad week?" he asked.

"The worst. I'll tell you about it later. It's been, what, six months since we've seen each other?"

"It was last fall, when we were in Orlando at the national convention. Want a drink?" Richard's nasal, distinctly Northeastern accent seemed shrill compared to the slow, Texas drawls I was used to.

"Sure. What are you having?"

"House wine, but I'd love to have a scotch with you in the real bar, and maybe sneak a smoke?"

"Mary Louise, Richard and I—" I said, interrupting the two women who were catching up on recent events in each other's lives.

"I know where you two are going. Just be back in time for dinner. Okay?"

"Sure. Michael, I see you haven't grown any," I said to Richard's wife, a petite, chocolate-haired girl just over five feet tall in heels.

"And I see you haven't learned any manners," she said, smiling.

"No, Michael. You can take the boy out of Texas, but you can't take the Texas out of the boy."

I kissed my wife's cheek as she and Michael continued their huddled, hushed conversation.

I followed my old friend into the bar. Richard was six foot three inches, the height I should have been had I not inherited short femurs from my mother's side of the family. He was thin with a runner's build and hair that was once red but was now mellowing to gray. We each ordered a single-malt scotch and lit a cigarette, still legal indoors. I immediately unloaded events of the past week on someone who would understand the pain and frustration of losing patients.

"Four deaths in one week? That would put me over the edge, too, Jim Bob."

"Tell me about it. I got so wasted on the plane, I was almost blinded."

"Can't say that I blame you. All Alzheimer's, huh?"

"Yep. Three post-ops, and one nonsurgical fracture. And all died of bradycardia that was unresponsive to drugs. Damnedest thing I've ever seen. You heard of anything like that?"

"Never, and I do the same kind of work you do, hip and knee reconstruction. I've done quite a few fractures in dementia patients, even had a few deaths, but nothing vaguely reminiscent of your experience. I don't have a clue. We'll ask around tomorrow at the meeting. Some of these guys here in New York have considerably more time in practice than you or I do, not to mention experience. Maybe someone can help you."

We toasted ourselves, then saw our wives at the door, motioning us to return to the dining room.

"I vould like to velcome you all to zis meeting, zee eighteenth annual reunion of zee Hospital for Special Surgery residents and fellows," Dr. Rheinhold Bonhoffer announced, as he stood at the podium in the front of the Lespinasse private dining room. The audience, numbering well over a hundred, politely clapped.

"He must be eighty years old, Richard," I whispered.

"Eighty-two, to be exact. And he's giving a paper tomorrow, so you'll get your fill."

"Still speaks with his Hamburg accent."

Richard peered at me over his reading bifocals. "What else?"

"Ve vill all enjoy zee meal zis evening. Zen, tomorrow, after zee hangovers have passed . . ." he said, and waited for the polite laughter to subside, "ve vill convene in zee morning at precisely nine, at our most illustrious institution, and bask in zee glow of zee new and important information that vill be passed on amongst us. Zank you all for coming, and a special velcome to all zee spouses zat have joined us as vell. Zere are no planned activities for zee spouses. However, I have no doubt zat you vill find plenty to do in our fine city. Doctors, remove your credit cards: EN GUARDE!"

Once Dr. Bonhoffer took his seat, tuxedoed waiters came to each patron and asked for one of three choices of appetizer, salad, and entree. I chose the sea-bass soup, a romaine salad, and venison served with cabbage and pearl onions. I tried to catch up on old times with the Carneses and also be reasonably polite to the attendees and their spouses seated at our table, but the food was too delicious for intense conversation.

I had hoped that the espresso and New York-style cream cheese-cake would revive me, but alas, jet lag and blended airplane scotch got the best of me. We bid adieu to the Carneses and turned in early for Eastern Standard Time, which was an hour later than my Texas Body and Mind Time.

I remember getting undressed, but my next clear, conscious thought was that of the doorbell ringing and the sight of Mary Louise in her luxuriously thick white robe, with its St. Regis insignia, coffee urn in her hand. We enjoyed fresh croissants, bagels with cream cheese, and smoked salmon, and washed them down with what tasted like Mocha Java blend.

We met the Carneses in the lobby around nine thirty and headed over to Fifth Avenue for a morning of shopping. Richard and I both had papers to present after lunch, which allowed us to play hooky and enjoy the clear spring weather with our better halves in the morning. After all the years that had transpired, it still thrilled me not to be present at Dr. Bonhoffer's "precise" nine o'clock gathering. Because we doctors spend so many years in school, I think that our emotional maturation process is delayed, maybe even stunted permanently. We never seem to grow up, but then I could be just speaking for myself.

We stopped at St. Patrick's Cathedral, a must-see on Fifth Avenue. Mary Louise and I lit candles for our deceased parents. Feeling dutifully sanctified, we hit Bergdorf-Goodman, Bulgari, Zegna, Saks Fifth Avenue, and FAO Schwarz. By the time we hit Bendel's, I was shopped out. I made the trek to the third floor with the rest of the crew, then decided to take a breather, found a comfortable chair out-side a small, exclusive hair salon, and rested my weary bones.

I lit a cigarette and sat facing the mirrors lining the walls oppo-site the cutting chairs, minding my own business, thinking my own thoughts. From inside the salon, a small black-and-white King Charles spaniel appeared, slowly walked to the open double doors of the salon, and peered at me. I assumed she was a female, what with those two pink bows in her hair. I leaned over in my chair, put my hand out, and watched her tentatively yet gracefully step over the threshold, walk the eight feet or so, and smell the tips of my fingers. She liked what she smelled, which probably had some reminiscent odor of Tip, combined with nicotine, because she rubbed against my black pants and smelled the tips of my black ostrich boots.

She was impeccably groomed. I stroked her soft, silky coat as she turned around, sat on her haunches, licked her lips, and wagged her tail energetically. I leaned back as she leaped into my lap and made herself comfortable.

Just as we were getting to know each other, I heard a loud shriek from inside the hair salon.

"Fifi! Fifi! Oh my God, someone's taken my Fifi!"

I really was trying to stand up, hold what was apparently Fifi, and walk inside to alleviate the worst fears of my new friend's owner, when the woman rushed through the doorway and ran right into me.

"What are you doing with my dog? Jacques!" she yelled. "Call security! We have a dog thief!"

The woman was quite tall and thin, with very wet jet-black hair. She had a towel wrapped around her shoulders over the salon cape that was meant to protect whatever likely-expensive top she was wearing underneath. I scanned her frame, noting the tight stretch pants, what we used to call pedal-pushers in the sixties. Below the span of bare ankles, she wore high-heeled backless white furry shoes, left over from a bedroom scene in a Jayne Mansfield or Marilyn Monroe movie.

"Ma'am, I was just petting your dog. She wandered outside, then jumped into my lap. I had no intention—"

"You're a despicable man," she said, snatching Fifi from my arms and holding her tight.

"Did the bad old man hurt my baby? Huh? Is my baby alright?" she asked, clutching the small dog as though it had been ransomed and rescued.

Security came, of course, as did Mary Louise, Richard, and Michael. It was quite a scene. When the dust settled, I was cleared of any wrongdoing and received an apology from the security staff and the store manager. When we left, the woman was still clutching Fifi, whispering sweet nothings in her ear. Fifi, it seems, might not have been quite so enamored, since, as I walked away, she jumped out of her owner's arms, came running to me, put her little front paws on my leg, and "ruffed" me a sweet goodbye. As we walked down the stairs, I could hear the wet-haired woman yelling something about Fifi getting her ass back where she belonged. I think Fifi and Tip would have made a great pair. So did Fifi, apparently.

The excitement brought hunger, so we four ambled over to Wolf's Deli at Fifty-Seventh and Sixth for pastrami sandwiches, stuffed cabbage, and potato pancakes. Richard and I left the girls after lunch—they were ready to do some "power shopping"—walked back to our hotel, picked up our slides, and caught a cab to Seventieth and York.

The Hospital for Special Surgery is an orthopedic hospital affiliated with the Cornell Medical School. It is an impressive eight-story structure, tucked in a side street adjacent to New York Hospital. From the facade, one would never suspect that many of the finest orthopedic surgeons in the world have trained at HSS.

We arrived at the amphitheater a little early, gave our slides to the projectionist, and sat in the back of the room. Dr. Rheinhold Bonhoffer stepped up to the podium just after we sat down.

"Oh, God, we're too early," Richard said.

"I didn't realize he was speaking just before my talk."

"I did. And I'm after you. I was hoping we'd miss the old—"

"Excuse me, doctors. I vould appreciate quiet during my presentation," he said. Everyone immediately was silent, just as though we were still in the training program.

"Zee material I vould like to present involves research I haf been doing for years. Most of you know about it. I haf been studying spinal cord injuries in mice and haf published a number of papers on zee subject of nerve regeneration. Zis paper I am going to discuss concerns zee use of NGF and its effects on zee spinal cord lesions induced in mice, simulating zee type of spinal cord injuries humans sustain.

"Zee first slide, please."

"I've listened to this shit for years, Jim Bob," Richard whispered. "Same old stuff."

"What's he been doing?"

"Trying to make nerves grow with NGF, neuron growth factor. Everybody thinks it's a bunch of crap, but what he's done is develop a vaccine, if you will. He injects mice, whose spinal cords he's severed, with NGF. He swears he's getting spinal afferent and efferent nerve regeneration. We all know that's not possible," Richard said. "You can't create neurons. Only God can do that."

I thought of Jeff Clarke and his excitement the previous Thursday night, then his sober reassessment Friday morning. He thought he had seen nerve regeneration in Mrs. Adams and Mrs. Bland, and then in Mrs. Cutkelvin, but he wasn't sure. He said he was going to do electron microscopy studies, and I wondered if he had, and what they revealed.

I tuned in to Professor Bonhoffer's lecture and listened with a fair amount of interest to what he had been trying to do. He had combined three of the major biochemicals responsible for allowing acetylcholine (ACH) to function to create NGF. He had used acetylcholinesterase inhibitor, serotonin, and norepinephrine. He had tried to synthesize choline acetyltransferase, the enzyme that prevents the breakdown of ACH by inhibiting the enzyme that destroys it, but, like other researchers, he had been unsuccessful. He had injected NGF intravenously, as well as intrathecally (directly into the sac that contains the spinal cord) into hundreds, maybe thousands of mice and rats.

He revealed, in microscopic specimens of his reactions, that local nerve endings had seemed to regenerate with NGF. He also showed spectacular electron microscopy photographs depicting the molecular reactions produced by NGF. He illustrated the regrowth of nerve bundles on the cellular level. I had to admit it was fascinating. I wondered if Jeff Clarke knew of this man's work.

I leaned over in Richard's direction. "This is pretty interesting stuff."

"Right. I'm going for a smoke before your talk. Want to join me?"

"No, I think I'll listen to the rest of his lecture. You know, Richard, if this NGF actually works, think of the potential in the human population."

"Potential is all it will be. That's where Bonhoffer blew it."

"What do you mean?"

"He injected some of that shit of his into some paraplegics at the Veterans' Hospital when he was on staff there and lost his faculty appointment. Overnight he became a professor emeritus."

"You're kidding."

"Nope. The ethics committee recommended it. You know the rules, Jim Bob. You have to have FDA approval for a human experimentation project. Bonhoffer had no approval, just went about it in his own little arrogant way and got caught."

CHAPTER 14

BELLADONNA

Saturday, May 20, 2000

Saturday night at the Plymouth Theatre, a few blocks from Times Square, I tried to pay close attention to Steven Sondheim's musical-drama *Passion*. It had received wonderful reviews and a Tony nomination.

My thoughts, however, were cluttered with ponderings on nerve regeneration research. I had wanted to speak with Dr. Bonhoffer after the lecture series had ended, but unfortunately, after my talk then Richard's talk and the subsequent panel discussion, he was nowhere to be found. There were too many questions from the audience participants, and the discussion period ran past its allotted time.

I found the professor's experiments on paraplegics at the Veterans Hospital fascinating, illicit though they may have been. That study might be a matter he would not want to address, but I had hoped to press him to divulge some of the nonpublished findings, not that I knew exactly what I was looking for. I reasoned that some information was better than no information.

After the play, we took a cab to Petrossian on West Fifty-Eighth for a late-night dinner of caviar, smoked salmon, and champagne.

"So, how did you guys like the play?" Michael asked.

"Loved it," Mary Louise answered. "Wonderful sets, wonderful music."

"Jim Bob?"

"I like everything, Michael. Even if a performance is bad, if it's live and I have good seats, it's my kind of gig. I could summarize my concept of the performance in these words: To die truly loved is to die truly happy. What did you think, Richard?"

He was silent for a moment, sipping his Veuve Clicquot from the thin crystal champagne flute. "Let me summarize as well: A sick, obsessive, strangling love is better than no love at all."

Funny how interpretations differed.

Richard and I attended meetings Sunday morning. I searched valiantly for Dr. Bonhoffer, but he was noticeably absent from the conference.

We met the ladies for lunch at the Russian Tea Room on Fifty-Seventh, famous for its caviar plates and what must have been thirty different varieties of vodka. We tried a few, of course. After all, when in Rome . . . To work off our lunch, we took a walk through Central Park and fed pilfered lunch bread to the Canada geese and a multitude of green-headed mallard ducks lolling in one of the murky ponds.

We then took a cab downtown and spent the afternoon wandering the art galleries and antiques stores of Soho, which I learned is an abbreviation for "South of Houston Street." I also discovered that Tribeca stands for "Triangle Below Canal Street." I always get a little smarter when I travel to New York. I wished, however, for more mystery and intrigue in the abbreviations of those two sections of Lower Manhattan. The monikers were too mundane for the Big Apple.

We passed a woman just outside an art gallery who was taking a smoke break. She was holding a cellular phone to her ear with her left hand, which contained a burning cigarette between her index and middle fingers. While she was talking, she reached into her jacket pocket with her right hand, shook out a cigarette, put it into her mouth, and lit it.

I stood and watched the irony of it all for a moment, until she took the phone away from her ear and said, not too politely, "What the hell are you looking at? Never seen anybody talking on the phone before?"

I just smiled, put the index and middle fingers of both hands together, and put all four to my lips, in a phantom smoking gesture. She looked at her hands, shook her head, and laughed, "Sorry. One of those days," she said.

We wandered over to Mulberry Street, toured Little Italy, and settled for dinner at a fabulous little restaurant called Il Cortile. The chef prepared some of the finest calamari, fettuccine, and cappelletti I had ever eaten, and followed it with their famous black sambuca and espresso. It was yet another Manhattan meal to die for.

Monday was our departure day. It was a good thing for me, because another day of eating in the city and none of the clothes I brought would have fit.

"Jim Bob, we have to leave in an hour. Do you plan on getting ready or just traveling with that St. Regis robe on?" Mary Louise asked, as I was lounging in the sitting room, drinking coffee, eating a bagel, and watching the *Today* show. I was still thinking of how to get hold of Dr. Bonhoffer.

"Sorry. Just mulling over the trip, trying to get in the right frame of mind to return to work tomorrow."

"You have today off. Can't you just relax and enjoy it? You're in the office all day tomorrow, so there's no surgery to prepare for."

"I know. I guess I'm a little afraid to return. Somebody else might die. And I'm especially afraid to take another consult from Frazier's nursing home!"

She walked over to the couch, still dressed in her robe as well. I couldn't help but notice how but she seemed to fill her robe out much better than I did mine. She sat down beside me and ran her fingers through my uncombed hair.

"I'm sorry about all the trouble you've had. It will be okay. Just give it, time."

"It's just that my patients aren't supposed to die. It seems too coincidental to have four patients from the same nursing home, with the same disease, all die of the same problem within a week's time. I just don't get it. Maybe—"

"Maybe you need to quit thinking about it. If you really think there is some problem with Ted Frazier's patients, other than the fact that they are old and sick—"

"But none of them were that old. From the late fifties to the early sixties."

"They had medical problems, didn't they?"

"Well, yes, but I don't see how those particular medical problems could have resulted in the same terminal event. Of course, I've been out of medical school for almost thirty years, and I'm sure I've forgotten far more than I remember about the pharmacology and biochemistry of disease."

"Why don't you talk to Ted when you get back? And Jimmy Morgenstern? I'm sure they can explain it to you, since they're both medical doctors."

"Mary Louise. I'm a medical doctor!"

"Yes, but you're an orthopedic doctor. You said yourself you don't remember all that much about internal medicine. So why don't you stop making yourself feel bad about those deaths, at least until you can talk to Ted and Jimmy? I'm sure there is a logical explanation for what happened in each case. Besides, you really can't quit taking consults from those two, can you?"

"Not really, not without repercussions."

"Like reduced referrals, that sort of thing?"

"Something like that. You have to take the good with the bad when it comes to referrals from an internal medicine doctor."

She kissed me like she always did when she was trying to start something. And it would be just like her to try and take my mind off my troubles with sex. What a despicable woman.

"What are you doing? I haven't even brushed my teeth. Besides, I'm not that easy, just because I'm a man. And you said yourself, we only have an hour to get dressed, pack, and check out."

"First of all, your breath doesn't bother me. Secondly, you're very easy. Thirdly, we have an hour, which, if I know you, is more than enough time."

She smiled that smile of hers.

"You think so, huh?"

"Yes, I do."

And she was right. I am easy, and it didn't take very long. It reminded me of what my dear old departed dad used to say: Men are dogs. That's why man's best friend is one.

After I was dressed and packed, I called HSS, identified myself to the receptionist, and requested a phone number for Dr. Rheinhold Bonhoffer. None of the dozen or so nationally prominent surgeons I had spoken to over the weekend had ever heard of any specific relationship between Alzheimer's disease and death by bradycardia syndrome, especially in patients with no prior history of heart block. I wanted to pick Dr. Bonhoffer's brain about that issue and a few others.

So, while Mary Louise had the bellhop take down the bags and assist her in the checkout process, I called the good professor's number at an address on Seventy-Sixth in the Upper East Side.

"Guten tag," the familiar voice answered.

"This is Dr. Jim Brady calling for Dr. Bonhoffer."

"Zis is he."

"Dr. Bonhoffer, I spoke to you Friday night at the Hospital for Special Surgery dinner at the St. Regis. I did a fellowship at HSS in the late seventies."

"Yes, Dr. Brady. I know who you are. Vat can I do for you?"

"Yes, sir. Well, I heard your fascinating lecture Saturday afternoon about the research you've been doing with mice, spinal cord injuries, and neuron growth factor. I'd like to ask you a few questions, if you please, sir."

He was silent for a moment. "Vell, go ahead. Get on vit it."

"Yes, sir. I have recently treated four patients with Alzheimer's disease, each whom had a fracture of one sort or another, three of whom underwent surgery. All died within twenty-four hours of admission to the hospital from terminal bradycardia. All four were autopsied. I don't have the results of the last patient's death, but I can give you a brief description of the first three. The first two showed signs of what the dissecting pathologist initially thought was nerve regeneration in the brain. The third patient's findings were equivocal. The pathologist, on second look at all three specimens, wasn't as certain of his findings as he had been the day before and decided to perform electron microscopy studies. Since I've been here all weekend, I do not know the results of those studies yet.

"My first question is this. Have you done any experimental work with any of the dementias, such as Alzheimer's, using your neuron growth factor? And can you explain the signs of possible nerve regeneration in these patients I've told you about? Lastly, can you help me at all with the bradycardia phenomenon?"

Silence.

"Zose are tough questions, Doctor."

"I know. I'm sorry. Would you like me to repeat them?"

"I may be old, Doctor, but I am not an imbecile."

"Yes, sir. I know. I'm sorry."

"Dr. Brady, you are sorry quite a lot."

"Yes, sir, I am. Sorry."

"Vat is all zis 'sorry' business? You Americans apologize for everyzing! Just be quiet for a moment, so I can collect my zoughts."

I watched the second phone line in the room repeatedly blink. I knew it would be Mary Louise, telling me to get my butt downstairs, that the cab was waiting. But I was afraid I would miss Dr. Bonhoffer's response, so I didn't answer it.

I waited some more.

"Are you avare, Dr. Brady, zat I did some experimentation in human subjects, using my neuron growth factor?"

"Yes, sir," I said, hesitantly.

"How much do you know about zat?"

"Not much, sir."

"I tried to help some young boys, Viet Nam veterans who had been paralyzed from zee vaist down by shrapnel vounds. Zey all had T10, T11, T12 vertebral fractures, vit a severance of zee spinal cord in each case. Perhaps not entirely ethical, you understand, but certainly my treatment could make zem no vorse. I mean, after all, paraplegia is not reversible, at least, not at zis point in time."

"Yes, sir."

"Vell, I unfortunately have no experience with the dementias. But, since zese diseases are characterized by neuron loss, as is paraplegia and quadriplegia, I vould tink zat zey might be similar, ya?"

"Yes, sir."

"So, vat I can tell you is zat by intravenous and intrazecal injections of NGF, zese boys regained some degree of sensory and motor nerve recovery. A few of zese patients died over zee course of treatment due to unrelated causes. Autopsy specimens did show some degree of new nerve growth in zee spinal cord afferent and efferent nerve rami. I vas quite pleased."

"Yes, sir, I'm sure you were. You saw neuronal regeneration at the cellular level? In other words, the creation of new nerve bundles?"

"Zat is correct, Doctor. Somevat like . . . an act of creation, don't you zink?"

"Yes, sir," I said. He was quiet, and I was sweating over what I was hearing. And over the thought of Mary Louise busting through the door any minute.

"A few of zee patients developed a slowing of zee heart rate, a side effect I considered related to zee dose of NGF. Neuron growth factor markedly increases zee concentration of acetylcholine, vich vould cause zee bradycardia. Understand?"

"No. How does an increased level of ACH cause a slowing of the heart rate?"

"Did you go to medical school?"

"Yes, sir, I did. Sorry."

"Zere you go, being sorry again," he said.

"Yes, sir. Sorry."

"My God, man, I zink you have a problem with zis 'sorry.'"

I was quiet, mostly so he could continue and finish before Mary Louise was finished with me.

"Zee biochemical reactions of acetylcholine and its enzymes and inhibitors are not vell understood, at least from a zerapeutic standpoint. Vat I surmised, in zose patients of mine zat developed bradycardia, vas zat zee portion of NGF zat is comprised of acetylcholinesterase inhibitor vas being absorbed via zee bloodstream and affected zee biochemical reactions in zee heart muscle. As you know—or in your case, probably don't know—zis particular family of drugs is used to treat zee tachycardiac arryzmias, especially zee supraventricular arryzmias. Zose are increased heart rate abnormalities, Doctor.

"So, by deduction, I assumed zat zee reduction of zee heart rate was simply zee equivalent of zee effect one vould obtain by giving one of zese drugs to a patient vit a normal sinus rhyzm."

"Interesting, Doctor Bonhoffer. Let me reiterate, if you don't mind. One of the components of NGF, the acetylcholinesterase inhibitor, contains a chemical compound that is used to treat cases of rapid and irregular heartbeat. So, you surmised that if you give this drug to a patient with a normal, regular heart rate, that it would, by its nature, slow the heart rate down?"

"Yes."

"I zee. I mean, I see." Idiot.

"Do zese comments help you at all?"

"I don't know, Doctor Bonhoffer, I'll have to think about it. My colleague, the pathologist in Houston, also proposed the theory you just surmised. May I call you again if I have more questions? I'm trying to catch a plane back to Texas, and my wife is probably tapping her foot on the sidewalk at this very moment."

"But, of course, Doctor. I enjoy discussing my pet project. It is too bad zat zee powers zat be stopped my research. It vas quite promising."

"Yes, sir, it sounds like it. Well, thank you again."

"One more item zat may interest you, Dr. Brady."

"Yes, sir?"

"I vas able to control zee descending heart rate vit a little atropine, injected IV at zee time of zee injection of NGF. Not completely, but partially."

"Really. Well, thank you again, Doctor. I sincerely appreciate the information."

I tried to hang up and get downstairs before Mary Louise came back upstairs to yell at me, but I felt as though he wanted to say one more thing.

"I also tried scopolamine, Doctor Brady, but it made zee patients, shall I say, somnolent."

"Sleepy?"

"Sleepy, lezargic, zat sort of zing."

"How did you administer scopolamine?"

"Have you ever had motion sickness, Doctor Brady?"

"No, sir."

"Ah. Zen you've never had zee pleasure of wearing a patch behind your ear. Simple, but effective. You change zee patch once, sometimes twice a day. It gives a nice blood level and picks zee heart rate up a little. And all zese patients of mine zat had a little slowing of zee heart rate due to NGF just needed a little boost. Of course, too much of zee atropine or zee scopolamine vould induce tachycardia, or sometimes an arryzmia."

"Yes, sir, I believe I get the picture. I appreciate your talking to me, but I—"

"One more point of interest, before you return to zee land of zee cowboys and zee horses and God only knows vat else you people have down zere."

"Yes, sir?" I said, looking at my watch, starting to get a little frantic. I didn't want to miss the flight any more than—

"I tried to control zee bradycardia vit atropine eye drops in a few patients."

"You mean, like when you go to the eye doctor, and they dilate your eyes? That kind of atropine?"

"Yes. You see, in ancient Rome, dilation of the pupils vas considered extremely attractive, desirable, and seductive. So, handmaidens vould pick leaves and flowers from zee belladonna plant, grind it up, and apply small amounts to zee eyes."

"I see," I said, and again looked at my watch, about to develop an arrhythmia myself, worrying about getting downstairs and to the airport on time. I could not shut the guy up.

"But zere was a problem in ancient Rome, Dr. Brady."

"Yes, sir?"

"Do you know vat it vas?"

"No, sir. I don't have a clue. Too much hedonism, promiscuity, and moral turpitude?"

"No, Dr. Brady. A problem vit zee belladonna plant. It's toxic. Poison. Too much, and zee patient dies."

"Yes, sir. So why would a woman having her eyes dilated die?

"Doctor, I'm surprised at you. Your medical knowledge is unfortunately quite limited. Zrough absorption, obviously. Zee mucous membranes around zee eyes are quite vascular. Zee atropine content of zee belladonna plant varies, from plant to plant, and from flower to flower. Zat is vy zee ancients stopped its use. Zee effects ver too unpredictable. A lady goes to see zee ancient cosmetologist, or zee ancient medicine man, asks for a little belladonna to dilate zee eyes for an important engagement zat evening. And she never shows up for zee date. Vy? She's dead, overdosed on belladonna, depending on zee strength and concentration of zee atropine in zee plant, and zee sensitivity and vascularity of zee eyeball."

I was mulling all that over when the door to the hotel room opened. Mary Louise slammed it against the adjacent wall, stood there, arms folded, with one of those looks.

"Doctor Brady, I have a question for you. Doctor Brady?"

"I really need to go, Doctor Bonhoffer. Maybe I can call you when I return—"

"Vy are zee patients of yours who have died showing zee pathological changes of neuronal regeneration I have seen in my own paraplegic study?"

"Excuse me?"

"Your patients, on autopsy, possibly have zee same findings zat my patients had. How is zis possible? Ver zey under some sort of . . . specialized treatment?"

CHAPTER 15

HOME

Monday, May 22, 2000

"**W**hat were you doing on the telephone all that time?"

"Does this mean you're speaking to me now?"

Mary Louise turned to look at me from her bulkhead seat adjacent to the window. She had on a pair of black slacks, a black silk blouse, and a black-and-white checked Escada jacket, one of my favorites. Her legs were crossed, and she was swinging her high-heeled shoe to and fro. Her long blond hair was combed out straight and hung past her shoulders. She pulled her sunglasses down toward the end of her nose, tilted her head down slightly, and looked at me with her piercing blues.

"If you remember, my darling, the cab driver had to maintain warp speed to get us to La Guardia in time for our flight. I didn't talk to you then, because I was hanging on for dear life. By the time we arrived at the airport and were able to check our bags, we had to run in order to avoid the airlines giving away our seats to standby passengers. We sat down, and the hostess offered us a drink, which I gladly took. The pilot has just turned off the seat belt sign, and now we have an opportunity to talk. I was never, at any time, not speaking to you. I was simply too rushed and too stressed out to engage in meaningful conversation."

"Really?"

"Really.

"And besides that, I made mad, passionate love to you right before we were to leave the hotel, thinking that would settle you down, improve your mood, and allow you to relax a little. But I don't think it worked, since you just had to make a phone call, which lasted for what, twenty minutes? Thirty?"

"Sorry about that. I was talking to Dr. Bonhoffer."

"Who?"

"Professor Rheinhold Bonhoffer, the German doctor that gave the introductory speech at the dinner Friday night at the St. Regis."

"What could you possibly have to discuss with a man you hardly know that was so important that we almost missed the flight?"

I explained the scenario to her.

"Jim Bob, I'm no doctor, that I grant you. But it baffles me as to why you think the research that man was doing has anything to do with the four deaths you had last week."

"I don't know if it does. I called him to see if he had done any experimental work with Alzheimer's and his NGF. He said he hadn't done any neural research on the dementias."

"But even if he had, how would that relate to your patients with Alzheimer's? They weren't being treated with his drug, were they? I mean, it's experimental, isn't it?"

"Yes. Bonhoffer's done most of his work with mice. Richard told me that Bonhoffer tried a human experiment without approval from his academic institution or the FDA. He got into trouble and lost his position at HSS and was relegated to emeritus status. However, the good professor told me on the phone this morning that it was working."

"What was working?"

"The NGF. Some of the paralyzed patients had partial return of feeling and some gains in movement."

"That's wonderful, but I still don't understand how that relates to you and your patients."

"Neither do I, except that Bonhoffer asked me a penetrating question. He asked me if my patients were under a special treatment."

"What kind of special treatment?"

"I don't know. Something that would cause them to have microscopic brain alterations similar to those he'd found in his experimentally-treated paraplegics."

"How could that be?"

I shook my head.

She patted my knee. "You need some new jeans."

"These are my favorite blue jeans, with the perfect amount of fade."

"Wouldn't you like some 'blue' blue jeans?"

"Those are for city slickers."

"And you're not a city slicker?"

"Nope."

"We live in the city."

"Yeah, but my heart's in the country, where I grew up."

"You grew up outside of Waco."

"In a small town in Texas."

"But you grew up just outside the city limits of Waco."

"Maybe, but my heart was in the country."

"Ah. Just like now. Your heart's in the country, but you live in the city. Just to be clear, you're not now, nor have you ever been, a city slicker. Not that anybody would ever suspect otherwise, what with that white western shirt with pearl buttons, faded jeans, and . . . what kind of boots are those?"

"Texas horned lizard."

"Texas horned lizard. They're pretty small, huh?"

"Yeah."

"Probably wiped out an entire family to make those boots."

"And a few distant cousins, twice removed. But then, I don't wear loafers or wing tips like my colleagues. And most of my boots are made of some kind of animal skin. I think I have a representative pair of most all the skins. Except foreskin, of course."

She laughed. "And you've always worn boots."

"Always. No loafers for this boy."

"Because your heart's in the country, and always has been. And only city slickers wear shoes. A Texas cowboy wears boots, even if he's only a Texas cowboy in his heart and mind."

"I'm glad you finally got that straight, Mary Louise."

"Gosh. And it only took me twenty-nine years of marriage to figure that out."

"Better late than never, darlin'. Some people never figure out that just bein' a Texan is a state of mind."

"Really?"

"Yep."

"Well, I guess you should know."

"Yes ma'am."

We fell asleep after lunch and a glass of wine or two, so the flight home seemed rather brief. The plane landed on time for a change. We collected our bags and headed home to the Post Oak Tower.

I dropped Mary Louise off and had the valet haul our luggage upstairs. I drove to the veterinary clinic just before closing time and picked up my boy Tip. As usual, he acted as though I'd been gone on sabbatical for a year.

Since it was after seven, and most doctors and employees were gone, and because I hated to leave him after just picking him up, I took Tip along to the office. I wanted to check my mail and enlighten myself as to any problems that had arisen while I was out of town.

A handful of my remaining partners looked askance when I arrived at the office with Tip, but there were no comments.

My desk was cluttered with debris: charts, patients' questions, insurance forms. To top it off, Fran had placed the mail from the previous two days in a large cardboard box. Mostly advertisements, thank the Lord, with no certified attorney letters. I breathed a sigh of relief.

There was a large stack of messages and calls to return. Among them, Dr. Jimmy Morgenstern, Dr. Ted Frazier, Sergeant Kenneth Adams, and Rabbi Jacob Stern. Memories of the prior week came flooding back into the forefront of my mind, not that they had actually departed during my four-day sojourn to New York.

I sat at my desk long enough to decide it was too late to call anybody. I gathered up my box of mail, gave the old Tipster a good rub on the head—which he appreciated greatly—and headed for the ranch, the one in my mind.

Once safely home, far removed from the medical-world's ills, I poured myself a short Macallan scotch, propped my boots on the pine desk in my office, and pondered. Tip's eyes were closed, but I saw his feet moving as though he were running. Doggie dreams. I amused myself by trying to imagine what dogs dream about. Chasing cats? Running with a pack of dogs, marauding neighborhood garbage cans? Being let loose inside a McDonald's with no one around to say BAD DOG? Playing frisbee on the beach? Finding a mountain of cat poop to rub their impossible-to-clean manes into?

My reverie was disturbed by the persistent ringing of the phone.

"Mary Louise? You want to get that?"

No answer.

"Mary Louise?"

I heard the answering machine pick up and Jimmy Morgenstern's basso profundo voice.

"Hey, Jim Bob. Thought you'd be back by now. Guess you know that we lost Mr. Jeffries the morning you left. Sorry about that. I'm contacting you because this guy named Stern keeps calling me. Rabbi Jacob Stern. He told me the wife is all upset about losing her husband, which I can of course understand, and she's got Stern all worked up about it. He wants to talk to you. Neither Ted Frazier nor I have been able to calm him down. Please, and I'm begging you now, call him as soon as you get in."

He left the number.

"Oh, and by the way, Ted sent two more patients over yesterday. One has a broken hip that needs to be nailed. The other one is strictly a medical problem, lucky for you. Anyway, none of your partners would take the hip fracture case, so it's yours. You can do him on Wednesday. His name is Pullig, Charles Pullig. He's on Med-8, but you probably already figured that out. One good thing is that you won't have to carry on a conversation with him. He has . . . yep, you guessed it, Alzheimer's. I'm starting to think that's all Frazier's got over there at his nursing home."

He paused. "You're there, aren't you? And you just don't want to pick up the phone?"

He paused again.

"Guess not. Anyway, call Stern, and see Pullig in the morning. Hope you had a good trip."

I could have picked it up at any time, but sometimes I just can't deal with conversations. On occasion, I need to listen to the message, let my mind sort through the problem, and deal with the issue later.

I walked into the master bedroom. Mary Louise had the reading light on, her reading glasses on, and the covers pulled up to her neck. Her current read, Dick Francis's *Wild Horses*, was lying faceup on the covers with its reader fast asleep.

I closed the novel and put it on the nightstand. I carefully took off her reading glasses, trying not to wake her, and turned out the light. I gently patted her head. Her body moved from side to side, acknowledging the pat, but other than that, she did not stir.

I stood by the bed and watched her sleep for a moment and thought about how lucky I was to have found her.

"Rabbi Stern, I hope it's not too late to call you. I just got back from New York, and—"

"Doctor, I appreciate your calling. Obviously, Stella Jeffries is beyond consolation due to the sudden and unexpected demise of her husband, Rufus. Can you tell me what happened?"

"Well, sir, I operated on his broken wrist Thursday morning. I performed the procedure under a Bier block—that's a numbing procedure for the hand and wrist—with a little sedation. I think I told you how hyperactive he was."

"Yes, you did."

"He did fine during the procedure. He also had no problems that evening and was fine when I made rounds Friday morning. I went over to my office to take care of some last-minute items before I left town, and shortly thereafter, the nurse called me and said he had passed away. Dr. Morgenstern was on the floor making rounds, so he was there on the scene immediately and did everything possible to bring Mr. Jeffries back. Unfortunately, he didn't respond.

"I can't say that I'm just as upset as you, but he was the fourth patient from Pleasant View Nursing Home who died while under my care last week, and I'm not feeling too special as far as my doctoring abilities are concerned."

He was silent for a moment.

"Rabbi Stern?"

"Sorry, Dr. Brady. I was just thinking about what you said regarding those four deaths. Of course, I'm concerned primarily with the Jeffries family at the moment, but I can't believe there have been that many deaths from Dr. Frazier's facility. In just one week? That is perhaps unusual, Doctor?"

"Well, I would think so. I've been in the practice of orthopedic surgery for twenty-two years, and I've taken care of a lot of older and sicker patients than Mr. Jeffries, and this situation has never arisen before. I must say, it has distressed me greatly."

"Doctor, I'd like you to do me a favor. Would you consider it?"

"What's that?"

"I'd like you to come up here to Conroe and speak to Stella personally. It would mean a great deal to her, and to me for that matter. If you'll agree to that, I'll take you to lunch. I also might have some information that you may be interested in. When would be good for you, Doctor?"

"I don't know, Rabbi. I—"

"Please, call me Jake. And if I may, I will call you James."

"That's fine, sir. It's just that my schedule is pretty full, except for Friday. We usually go to the beach—"

"Friday is perfect. We can meet with Stella in the morning then I'll take you to lunch. There is a wonderful diner that prepares the most fabulous chicken fried steak you've ever tasted. Shall we say, ten o'clock?"

I wondered how I got myself in these situations. From being too damn nice, probably.

"All right, Rab—Jake. I'll be there unless an emergency comes in that requires surgery Friday morning, but I would know that by Thursday, I think."

"So, unless I hear from you, I'll meet you at the Agudath Jacob Synagogue on West Davis, Friday morning, ten a.m. Thank you, Doctor."

Mary Louise was sleeping. Tip was sleeping. J. J. was probably sleeping, although I wasn't sure if he was still in Bermuda or in his apartment on the eighteenth floor. I was probably the only member of my family awake at midnight.

I had unsuccessfully counted sheep, had a second scotch, and watched Leno and Letterman. Finally, I wandered out onto the terrace and lit a cigarette. Since I had to be in Conroe anyway, I thought I'd drop in to see Dr. Ted Frazier and that Pleasant View Nursing Home of his on Friday. And maybe I would go see Kenneth Adams, Beatrice's brother. I could personally see the people and places that had affected my life so significantly in the past week.

Maybe I would take Mary Louise along, and we'd spend the night in one of the resorts on Lake Conroe, then go down to our Galveston beach house on Saturday. It might be fun, and informative.

I reasoned that Mary Louise might be a nice addition to the meeting with Jake Stern and Stella Jeffries. After all, she's one-fourth Jewish, and that certainly couldn't hurt my chances of establishing some kind of camaraderie with the wife of the deceased. Not that I was worried about her filing a lawsuit against me. Certainly not. I mean, isn't it routine for a doctor to bump off four patients per week, of which her husband was one?

I was thankful that my old nemesis, Donovan Shaw, the Houston malpractice attorney who had made my life hell a while back, was out of business. He had been disbarred and had a nervous breakdown to boot. I don't, as a rule, wish ill upon anyone, but sometimes I feel myself straying off that path . . .

As penance, I started counting my blessings, and I finally fell fast asleep.

CHAPTER 16

REGENERATION

Tuesday, May 23, 2000

T uesday's office was, in a word, horrible. In addition to the regularly scheduled patients, most of the folks who had appointments
for the previous Thursday and couldn't make it in due to the flood
showed up as well. And the majority of patients decided not to call,
and thought they would just . . . drop by. After all, I had always run
an open-door kind of shop. The policy was, if you think you need to
be seen, we'll see you. Of course, I hadn't intended for it to apply to
an entire day of patients. There was no time to return neither Jeff
Clarke's call—Jeff had called no less than three times during office
hours—nor Kenneth Adam's call.

It was seven thirty p.m. before I found myself over on Med-8
at the hospital, seeing my newest consult, Charles Pullig. He was in
the same bed that Mildred Bland had occupied. Talk about déjà vu.
According to the chart, he was sixty-eight years old. He was held fairly stationary with cloth-and-Velcro restraints at the wrists and ankles.
Skin traction was applied to his left lower extremity. He appeared
dazed and confused and was generally unresponsive to my questions.
He groaned when I palpated his left thigh, the site of his fracture. The
pedal pulses were intact on the affected side. His eyelids appeared to
be a little swollen, with only half of his irises and pupils visible. The

eyeballs moved synchronously, in a rapid fashion, side to side. One of the other Alzheimer's patients I had treated in the past two weeks exhibited a similar finding, but it was the head that moved and not the eyes.

I wrote a note on the chart and left orders for him to be NPO after midnight and for a pre-op evaluation to be performed by the anesthesiologist on call.

As I was leaving the floor to go home, I ran into Jimmy Morgenstern, who was also making late rounds.

"Hey, Jimmy, I saw Mr. Pullig. Another jewel."

"That's right, J. B. Nothing but the best for my friends. You fixing him tomorrow?"

"Yeah. I've got four other cases, so it'll be later in the afternoon before I get to him."

"That's all right, he's not going anywhere. Listen, I called in a cardiologist to see him. He has a history of heart block and had an internal pacemaker implanted a while back. If we have any problems with his heart rate or an arrythmia, at least the pacemaker is already in place."

"Seeing as how the last four patients you've sent me all died of bradycardia, maybe that pacemaker will give us an edge for a change."

"It certainly can't hurt."

"Good. Well, see you later."

My beeper exploded its variably irritating siren as I made my way across the crosswalk over Fannin Street toward the parking garage. Sometimes the beeper seemed alive, changing its sounds to reflect my mood. The digital readout said DR. CLARKE. STAT CALL. EXT. 224.

I stopped at one of the in-house phones along the way, worried that he might have injured himself and needed my services. No such luck.

"Where the hell have you been, Brady? And why haven't you returned my calls?"

"Jeff. I was in New York until last night, and I've been working my ass off all day trying to catch up. I was just on my way home."

"Forget that. Come down to my office. I've got something to show you."

"Jeff, I'm really tired, and—" I heard the click, then silence.

We sat in a small amphitheater in the basement, just down the corridor from his office. It was a lecture hall, with rows of chairs in a large semicircle and two vertical aisles dividing the auditorium into thirds. The rows were tiered, with steps, like a football stadium or a basketball arena. We entered at the top, the back row, and walked down an incline, step by step, to the front row.

"Sit," he said.

I did as instructed, glad to be off my feet. He walked over to the lectern, hit a button, and a gigantic screen descended. He hit another button, and the lights dimmed. He picked up two small slide carousel remote control devices, one in each hand, and started the two slide projectors in the rear of the room. Remarkably detailed and incredibly enlarged photographs appeared on the screen, side by side.

"These are the slides of the cerebral cortex on Mildred Bland, your second Alzheimer's death last week. See the swirls and neurofibrillary patterns? Those are called tangles. And see that pink goo? That's amyloid. They're classic in AD patients, but nonspecific in related disease processes. That's one of the ways we distinguish Alzheimer's from some of the other dementias. With me so far?"

"Yes, Jeff," I sighed.

"Okay. Good. These next slides are from Agnes Cutkelvin, your third Alzheimer's death last week. See the tangles? Very similar to the specimen on Bland, wouldn't you say?"

"I'm no expert, but they look about the same to me."

"Good. Now check this out. This is the specimen on Beatrice Adams, your first—"

"Could we not keep score, please?"

"Sure. You're too damn sensitive, though. That ruins your investigative skills. Anyway, look at the slide, and tell me what you see."

"Jeff, I'm pretty tired. You wouldn't happen to have any coffee, would you?"

"Sure. Be right back."

I studied the dual slides of Mrs. Adams, sections of brain tissue magnified I didn't know how many times, searching for similarities between those and the previous two patients. I picked up the two clickers, flipped back and forth and compared the findings.

Jeff returned shortly with a steaming mug of black brew. I sipped and looked at the label on the mug, which read PATHOLOGISTS DO IT WITH THE DEAD.

"Well?" he asked.

"I don't see any tangles. Am I missing something?"

"No, you're not. Now look at these next few. These are from Jeffries," he said, moving the slide carousel backward and forward, so that I could assimilate the differences.

"What do you see, Brady?"

I diligently searched Mr. Jeffries's slides, and even got up and went over to the screen for a closer look.

"No tangles."

"Correct. What do you make of that, Brady?"

"No tangles, no Alzheimer's?"

"Precisely. At least, within a reasonable probability. What does that imply?"

"That Bland and Cutkelvin were true Alzheimer's, and Adams and Jeffries were misdiagnosed and had another form of dementia."

"I agree."

"So?"

"So, I went back over the medical records in detail, including the data that Frazier sent with the patients when he had them transferred here onto Morgenstern's service. I found something interesting. Both Adams and Jeffries had thyroidectomies done years before and both had Synthroid listed on the nursing-home medication sheet. I went back and looked at my autopsy notes, and sure enough, I had noted it."

"Wait a minute. If I remember correctly from medical school, thyroid-deficient patients, over a period of time, develop myxedema, which can cause some kind of mental problem."

"Exactly. Chronic thyroid deficiency dementia, or myxedema dementia, is its own syndrome, characterized by a puffy face and eyes, yellow skin, enlarged tongue, apathy, lethargy, depression, hallucinations, and ataxia. It's difficult to differentiate myxedema dementia from a psychiatric condition, or Parkinson's disease, or . . ."

"Alzheimer's disease. Shit!"

"Shit is right. So, maybe we're dealing with two typical AD's, and two separate but similar thyroid deficiencies."

"But wait a minute. If Frazier had those two patients on thyroid supplementation, they wouldn't have myxedema symptoms, which would mean they shouldn't have dementia. So, maybe they still had Alzheimer's, but without the tangles. Right?"

"I thought about that, and reviewed the lab work again. If the patients had been on replacement Synthroid, then their blood levels of thyroxine should be normal, or even high normal. Right?"

"Right."

"Wrong. Thyroid hormone levels were absent. Zero."

"What? Didn't Morgenstern prescribe their thyroid meds when they were admitted?"

"I called him about that today. He did in fact prescribe Synthroid for both patients. But remember, Jeffries was only here for twenty-four hours, maybe less. One dose does little or nothing for the blood level of thyroxine, especially if a patient is extremely thyroid deficient. Adams was, however, here for a few days."

"So, what did Jimmy have to say about that?"

"With regard to Jeffries, he said he didn't pay any attention to it. Jeffries died the morning after he was admitted, the day after your operation. Plus, that was the worst day of the flood, and he was swamped trying to keep too many other patients alive to worry about one thyroid level.

"As far as Adams was concerned, he said he thought that the test result was a fluke and had ordered another. Since he had placed her on thyroid medication, he figured he had her covered and was waiting for the results of the repeated studies. She died before he saw the repeat values. It takes a couple of days to do thyroid assays, you know."

"Huh. You think neither one of those folks were getting their thyroid meds in the nursing home, and that's why they had dementia misdiagnosed as Alzheimer's?"

"Yes."

"Well, the logical question would be, Jeff, that if they had been deprived of thyroid medication long enough to exhibit the signs of myxedema dementia or Alzheimer's and to therefore require nursing-home care, then whatever doctor was taking care of them before their admission to Frazier's nursing home is guilty of serious . . . neglect and malfeasance."

"That's correct, since you'd have to deprive a patient of thyroid medication for at least a year or so to induce a dementia-like state."

"Bottom line, though, that doesn't really tell us why they died."

"True. Just an interesting footnote," he said, with a smirk on his face that I recognized all too well.

"Jeff, when you get that look, it usually means there's more."

"Uh-huh."

"Do you want me to guess?"

He turned to the screen, clicked to the next two slides.

"Know what these are?"

"No."

"Electron microscopy specimens with reagent staining techniques. It gives color to certain biochemicals. These are EMs of the first two—of Bland and Cutkelvin, left and right respectively."

"I see a lot of red and green."

"I tagged the acetylcholine in red, the serotonin in green. For effect. Remember my lecture to you last week?"

"Sure. Acetylcholine makes the brain world go 'round. Serotonin and norepinephrine does too, but to a lesser extent. And, both substances are deficient, or absent in—wait a minute! There's a lot of red and green on those slides."

"Exactly. More than normal."

"What do you mean, more than normal? More than the normal brain?"

"Yes."

"But that's not possible, Jeff. If they had AD, then the content should be far less than normal. That's what you told me."

"Yes, I did. That's the way it should be. But it isn't. Now look at this," he said, clicking to the next two slides. "These are EMs from Adams and Jeffries. Same area of the brain, same staining techniques. What do you see?"

"A lot of red and green."

"Correct. Remember, that while the mental symptoms of myxedema are similar to Alzheimer's, there should be no tangles on the pathology slides. And we saw that, didn't we?"

I nodded.

"But, my old friend, the chemical pathology should be the same for both AD and myxedema dementia, and that is marked reduction of acetylcholine and serotonin in the microscopic cells of the brain. And, as you can see, that's not the case here."

"Jeff, I guess I'm confused. How could these four patients have had dementia of one type or another with all those good chemicals in there?"

"I don't know."

"Jeff, I think we've just confused ourselves more than we've clar-ified the situation, don't you?"

There was that grin again.

"What is this? *Let's Make a Deal?* There's more?"

He turned to the screen again, clicked on the next two slides. There were two graphs on each slide, one on top of the other. The vertical column of each read: MICROMILLILITERS. The horizontal column read: ACETYLCHOLINESTERASE INHIBITOR.

"Want to guess what this is?"

"You've charted the concentration of a biochemical that pre-vents the breakdown of acetylcholine, probably the brain tissue con-tent in each of the four patients."

"Yup. I took samples from ten different sections of cerebral tis-sue, from the cerebellum all the way up to just behind the pituitary gland. I plotted normal values versus the values found in each patient. Then I drew lines and connected the dots. The black line is the norm, the blue line is the patient value."

"From here, the patient values look high."

"High? Off the chart, I'd say! You know, some researchers the-orize that the reason these dementias occur is because there isn't enough of this inhibitor in the brain and the enzyme that breaks down acetylcholine—acetylcholinesterase—goes hog wild, dissolving every bit of ACH everywhere in sight. These four people had, com-pared to normal brain values, tons of inhibitor of the chemical that breaks down ACH."

"Meaning these patients shouldn't have dementia, right?"

"Right."

"Jeff, I have a question."

"I was hoping you would."

"When you did electron microscopy on those four brains, did you see any microscopic evidence of a process that could be remotely described as potential nerve regeneration? You said you were going to look into that, before I left. Because when I was in New York, I attended a lecture by this German professor who's been doing research on paraplegic mice with something called—"

"Neuron growth factor. Bonhoffer."

"How did you—"

"I had my computer do a literature search on acetylcholine-related subjects yesterday. Bonhoffer has published several articles on the subject in one of the obscure medical journals. Apparently, he's thought of as a renegade. A heretic."

I looked at Jeff. "Well?"

"Well what?"

"Did you find any evidence of nerve regeneration in any of the four patients?"

He clicked the next slides onto the screen. Using an electronic pointer with a small red arrow, he illustrated several microscopic areas on four successive sets of slides, one set for each of the four patients in question. He was silent as he pointed out the sections on the slides he was interested in.

When he finished showing me each set, he plopped heavily into the chair adjacent to mine.

"Those areas you just showed me. I guess they mean something to you?"

"Yes. Spontaneous combustion. Evidence of a nerve manufacturing process. Neuronal regeneration, the heretofore impossible. Creation of the uncreatable. It's pretty damned amazing, if you ask me."

"In all four patients, regardless of Alzheimer's or myxedema dementia?"

"Yessiree, Jim Bobby. They all are the same. Question is, why?"

I smiled. "Guess somebody's going to have to figure it out. Wonder who?"

Jeff's eyebrows arched upwards. "You don't see anybody else sitting here, do you?"

CHAPTER 17

THYROID

Wednesday, May 24, 2000

I arrived on Med-8 at six thirty Wednesday morning to check on Charles Pullig, my newest patient, prior to beginning surgery.

"Well, good morning, stranger," said Cynthia Dumond, from her position at the nursing station. "Been avoiding me?"

"Not at all, Cynthia," I replied, with a smile. "I was out of town for a few days at an orthopedic meeting in New York. I saw Mr. Pullig early yesterday evening, so I missed you. How have you been?"

"Oh, pretty good. Too much death and dying for me. I'm thinking about changing careers."

"That would be a shame. You're the kind of nurse that stands out as an example to your co-workers. It would be our loss—the doctors' and the patients'—if you left."

"Thank you, Dr. Brady. I appreciate your kind words. I just don't know if I can deal with all this anymore. I'm thinking of going to work for one of the major payers—they used to be called insurance companies—evaluating charts, determining benefits, organizing pre-approvals for treatment, that sort of thing."

"I see. It's called sleeping with the enemy. You would become one of those people that would, when my staff calls to get approval for someone's hip replacement, give them the third degree. Like how long has the patient had the problem, how have I treated it, have I gotten a second opinion? Pointless questions like that."

"I would hope not, Dr. Brady."

"You need to remember, Cynthia, that once you go to work for an insurance company—or provider, as they like to be called—your job is to save them money, whenever and however you can. We would be on opposite sides of the fence. Think you can handle denying patients treatment that they need and have already paid for?"

"Dr. Brady, you make it sound worse than it is. Patients will still get treatment in the 'new medicine.' It's just that routine screening procedures have to be carried out prior to authorization for a provider, to protect the patient from unnecessary surgery."

"That's how it all started, Cynthia. But now, the large providers question every doctor and often refuse to authorize needed procedures, sometimes even critical procedures. That's not just true in orthopedics either. Aren't you aware of that?"

She hung her head.

"I'm sorry, Cynthia. I was on my soapbox again."

"I'm hearing what you say. It's just that I can't take this floor anymore," she said, dabbing her eyes with a tissue. "I think what got to me was attending Beatrice Adams's funeral."

"Really? I'm surprised. I didn't realize you knew her all that well."

"This wasn't her first admission to the floor, Dr. Brady. She'd been here two or three times before."

"And she never had any trouble during prior admissions with her heart rate slowing down?"

"No, sir."

"Listen, I'm sorry," I said, frowning at my own outburst, then giving her my best encouraging smile. "Let's go see Mr. Pullig."

I felt like an insensitive fool for dumping my tirade onto Cynthia. And in fact, I didn't blame her for wanting to leave. I couldn't work on a floor that resembled a modern-day purgatory, where you couldn't be assured that the patients' outcomes were likely to be positive.

Charles Pullig was in the same condition as the day before. I leaned down close, pulled his sparse gray-white neck- and chest-hairs apart, and saw the faded remnants of a transverse scar, in the shape of a smile, over his lower neck.

"What are you looking for, Dr. Brady?"

"I wanted to see if this man's thyroid has been removed."

"I could have told you that. It has, and Dr. Morgenstern has him on thyroid supplements."

"Huh," I said, raising up, stretching my back muscles. "Turns out that Mrs. Adams and Mr. Jeffries had thyroidectomies, too, Cynthia."

"Yes, sir. Quite a few of Pleasant View transfers are on thyroid medication. Do you find that unusual, Dr. Brady?"

"I don't know enough to say. What do you think?"

"I certainly don't think it's unusual for this population of patients."

The staff opened a second room for me in surgery, so I ran a little ahead of schedule. I did two knee-joint replacements and two hip-joint replacements, one of which was a revision. By four o'clock, I had only one case remaining, Charles Pullig's fractured hip.

The day shift, except for orthopedic head nurse Loretta Birdwell, had gone home. An unfamiliar night crew staffed the case.

"Doc, don't be surprised by these night crawlers. They're different from my day crew," Loretta said, as I scrubbed at the sink just outside the OR.

"What do you mean by 'night crawlers?'"

"Different breed of cat on the three-to-eleven shift. Tend not to be family people. Loners. Rovers. Night people. Also different from the eleven-to-seven shift, who generally don't like people at all. They work while most of us sleep, and most of them, they're a real trip."

"I really don't care who I work with, long as you're around to keep it all together."

"Yeah, I know. Can't live without me, huh?"

"Nope. Wouldn't even want to try."

The case started smoothly despite the fact that the circulating nurse had put the Rolling Stones album *Voodoo Lounge* on the compact disc player. When I complained about the volume of Mick Jagger's raspy, sensual voice, Loretta mentioned that I must be getting old. And, come to think of it, I didn't remember ever complaining about the music volume in surgery before. Great. Next would come hemorrhoids, colitis, arthritis, and impotence. And in time I would be standing at cocktail parties discussing my bowel habits with total strangers.

"Turn up the music," I said.

"What? I thought you said—"

"Pump up the volume, and forget what I said before," I yelled.

The young nursing tech thought he was out of earshot when he muttered something about a fucking surgeon who couldn't make up his mind.

I was about to give him a piece of what was left of my mind when the anesthesiologist spoke up.

"Heart rate's dropping, Brady."

"What is it?"

"Sixty-two."

"He has a pacemaker, I thought."

"That he does, but it's not firing properly for some reason. All his other vitals are okay, except his oxygen saturation is dropping."

"Loretta, look at the chart. See which cardiologist saw him pre-op."

As she did, I worked faster, putting the hip fragments together as best as possible, and reducing them under the titanium plate. An added problem was that Pullig had undergone previous surgery for a fracture lower in the femur. I had to remove an old broken steel plate before I could apply the new one for the break higher in his leg.

"Dr. Richard Peterson. Know him?"

"I know his wife. She's a radiologist here. Get him on the phone, please."

I continued working as fast as I could.

"He's in bradycardia now, Jim. Down to fifty-four."

"Just hang in there," I said, sweating from hammering the old hardware out and struggling with insertion of the new. My nerves were probably shot, but I was determined not to lose another patient.

The OR phone rang and Loretta answered. It was Peterson.

"Tell him to get over here. Mr. Pullig's pacemaker is not working, and his heart rate's down to fifty-four."

She gave him the message.

"Says he's in the middle of his office, seeing private patients. Said you'd have to wait at least an hour or find someone else."

I stood up from my operating chair, told Tim Kelly, the orthopedic resident, to start putting the screws in the side plate for me, and went to the phone, bloody gloves and all.

"Peterson," I said, grabbing the phone away from Loretta, "if you don't get your money-grubbing ass over here right this minute, since you're the one who said this pacemaker was working fine, I'm going to storm over to your office and beat the shit out of you with this old steel bone plate I have in my hand, the one I just removed from my patient who's dying because you won't come see him!"

I handed the phone back to Loretta. She held it against her ear for a moment, then hung up.

"Doc?"

"Yeah?"

"He said he'll be right here."

I had to admit, Peterson was good. He arrived in the operating room in what seemed like nothing flat and had exchanged the old pacemaker for a new one by the time I had my skin incision closed.

I stepped outside, removed my surgical hood and mask, and washed my face and hands in the scrub sink.

"Sorry about the misunderstanding. I didn't realize it was an emergency," he said to me, as he exited the OR.

"You're lucky no harm was done," I said, still belligerent. "Heart's okay?"

"Ticking along at seventy-two beats per minute. Camille mentioned your name to me last week, said she had studied some x-rays for you?" he asked, changing the subject and trying to be Mr. Nice and Polite.

"Yes, on one of my Alzheimer's patients with a fracture. She has since died, as have three other patients who I was asked to consult on. Guess I'm a little edgy, worried about losing another one."

"I can understand that. Sorry about the . . . the confusion," he said. Richard Peterson was shorter than I, with coal-black hair, dark skin, rimless glasses, and a trim, athletic body, a healthy cardiologist's well-worked-out body. I presumed that was from regular exercise, limited alcohol consumption, nicotine abstinence, and a low-fat diet. Since he was in the business of keeping heart patients healthy, it looked to me like he was living his own advice.

"Thanks for coming so quickly. I probably wouldn't have fulfilled my promise about beating the shit out of you."

He smiled. "I didn't want to take any chances. You don't look like someone I'd want to piss off."

He extended his hand. "See you this evening, then?"

"Excuse me?"

"Camille said your wife invited us to dinner, at your home tonight. You didn't know?"

"Well, I haven't spoken to Mary Louise all day."

"I see. See you at seven, then."

Another Brady special: open mouth, insert foot.

All in all, it was a pleasant evening. There were six of us. J. J., our son, was back from his excursion to Bermuda and brought along Aimee Mason his traveling companion and latest love interest. I did observe during the course of dinner that J. J. appeared to be smitten, an unusual occurrence for a young man who had said many times that he wouldn't consider marriage until he was over thirty. He had three years to go. He and Aimee made small talk to themselves, like the rest of us weren't there. And I could tell they held hands under the dining table when two hands weren't required for eating.

Aimee was gorgeous, with short blond hair, bright blue eyes, a beautiful smile, and . . . well, she was a full-figured kind of girl, not unlike a younger version of J. J.'s mother. I remembered when I had fallen in love with Mary Louise, whom I had met while trying to select a gift for my mother, back when I was in medical school. She was working in retail at the time. I knew she was the one for me, although it took a great deal of convincing for her to realize the same.

The night was pleasant, and not too windy, so we took our coffee and dessert out on the terrace.

"Wonderful dinner, Mary Louise," said Camille Peterson, dressed casually in slacks and a light sweater. Even with heels, she was still tiny.

"Yes, I agree," said Richard. "That's some of the best lamb I've ever had. Where did you find that mint jelly?"

"Cooke's, a little specialty shop on Kirby. They carry some of the best meat and spices in town, I think. I bought the vegetables there as well," responded Mary Louise, obviously pleased that her guests had enjoyed her delicacies.

Through the glass doors, I saw J. J. and Aimee standing in the sunroom, holding each other close, talking intimately. J. J. was probably wondering how to leave gracefully and get down to the business they were most interested in.

I smiled to myself and lit a cigarette. In the past, when J. J. had taken a female on a trip, even a weekend excursion, he couldn't wait to be alone again. This relationship was obviously different.

"Oh, I'm so glad to see you light up," said Richard as he pulled a large cigar from the breast pocket of his suede jacket. He deftly removed the tip with a cigar clipper and lit the aromatic stogie with a gold flameless lighter.

"I can't believe a cardiologist smokes."

"Just about my only vice, Jim. I don't inhale, of course," he said, then burst out laughing.

We four enjoyed a light conversation, our coffee, Mary Louise's bread pudding, and the springtime Houston evening from the twenty-seventh floor.

"I checked into that neuropathy business for you, Jim, regarding the patient from the nursing home. I came up empty with respect to a correlation with Alzheimer's disease."

"That's okay, Camille. The patient died."

"I'm sorry to hear that. I believe Richard mentioned something about that on our way over here. Said you'd had several deaths this past week?"

"That's correct."

"That's why I went into radiology."

"That's why I went into orthopedics."

She nodded. "I did find out something interesting when I reviewed the radiologic literature on neuropathic joints like the one—what was her name?"

"Beatrice Adams."

"Like the knee joint on the Adams woman. I reviewed, out of interest, the various radiologic manifestations of the dementias, since Alzheimer's disease, of course, is a type of dementia. There is one particular type of dementia that classically is associated with the development of lower extremity neuropathy. Know what it is?"

"Camille, I haven't a clue."

"Myxedema dementia, from chronic thyroid deficiency."

CHAPTER 18

JEFF CLARKE

Thursday, May 25, 2000

Thursday came and went, a busy office day but with no major problems. The folks from Wednesday's surgeries were all alive and well, including Charles Pullig, whose new pacemaker was keeping his heart ticking along at a smooth seventy-two beats per minute.

The everyday routine of orthopedic practice got me through a full clinic load even though my subconscious gnawed at me constantly. I suspected Camille Peterson's revelation of Beatrice Adams's joint abnormality, consistent with Jeff Clarke's findings on myxedema dementia and chronic hypothyroidism, to be a significant piece in the jigsaw puzzle of my patients' deaths. I could not dismiss that the brain autopsies showed consistently high levels of the chemical neurotransmitter ACH, which should have precluded the existence of any mental problems in the first place.

I thought about those patients and Ted Frazier and Pleasant View Nursing Home and brain chemistry all day long.

Jeff Clarke called about five o'clock as I sat in my office and stared out the window at traffic.

"Afternoon, Jeff."

"So, what time are you picking me up tomorrow?"

"Say what?"

"Tomorrow. What time are we leaving? To go to Conroe?"

"How do you know about that? And why would you be going with me?"

"Jake Stern's my cousin, son of my mother's sister."

I sat up. "What?"

"You heard me."

"So, you've been talking to him, too?"

"Sure. You don't think I've been doing all this extra work out of the goodness of my heart, do you?"

"Well, quite frankly, I wondered about that. You seem to be involved in this situation more intensely that I would expect for . . . for a guy like you."

"What do you mean, a guy like me? I like solving puzzles as much as the next guy. That's what I do for a living, Brady! I solve the messes you clinicians create!"

"Jeff, I just meant that you've been more pleasant than I would have expected about all the extra time you've spent helping me out, especially for a hospital pathologist."

"Yeah, well I'm not doing it just for you. I'm doing it for Jake."

"So, why didn't you tell me before?"

"There was nothing to tell, Brady, until Jake called me this week and asked me to check on Rufus Jeffries's demise. One thing led to another. He said you were going up there tomorrow, and Jake thought I should tag along. I figured you'd go see Frazier while you're up there. Am I right?"

I shook my head.

"Well? Am I right? Are you going to Pleasant View, and might you snoop around?"

"Yes. I called Ted this morning, said I wanted to talk to him about the four patients that had died, and asked to see his facility, since I was going to be in the neighborhood."

"And what did he say?"

"He said he'd love to have me visit, and that his nursing home is a state-of-the-art facility."

"Of course. You knew he would say that. So, what time do we leave?"

"Jeff, I had planned on taking my wife along, and thought we'd spend the night at April Sound, that resort on Lake Conroe."

"But she can't go."

"What?"

"She can't go. I called her. I didn't want to intrude on you two, in case you were going to make a weekend of it. I called her at home this morning. She said she couldn't go and told you that last night. Did you forget?"

I hadn't forgotten. I wanted to forget the conversation I was having with Jeff, though.

"Eight-thirty, Jeff. My office. Be on time."

"Great! And Brady?"

"What, Jeff?"

"Let's stop by the Montgomery County Sheriff's Office. Your first death, Beatrice Adams, she's from Conroe, nearest relative Kenneth. He's her brother, and turns out—"

"I know all about it, Jeff. I've already called his office to make an appointment."

"Then it looks like we're both on the same track. Just wanted to make sure you didn't leave me out of anything . . . fun."

Fun was not the word that came to mind when I considered spending an entire day with Jeff Clarke.

Over a quiet dinner at home, twixt barbs between George and Jerry on a repeat episode of *Seinfeld*, I gave Mary Louise a rundown on Friday's itinerary.

"I'm to meet Rabbi Jake Stern—who, as it turns out, is a first cousin of Jeff Clarke—at ten. I'm supposed to discuss the death of Rufus Jeffries with Stella, the deceased's wife, who will be at the synagogue with Jake. Then we go to lunch at a diner that is supposed to have the best chicken fried steak. I've got an appointment with Ted Frazier at the nursing home at two, and then I'm supposed to talk with a deputy sheriff by the name of Kenneth Adams, whose sister—"

"I know all about it, thanks to Jeff. He told me the whole story when he called me this morning."

"Yes, he told me. Sorry about that."

"It's not your fault. He talked to me like I was his best friend. You know, Jim Bob, except for seeing him once or twice a year at University Hospital functions, I haven't really talked to Jeff since you two were in medical school. He hasn't changed much—still his witty, charming, caustic self. He had me in hysterics."

"Are we talking about the same guy? Jeff Clarke? Charming?"

"I've always thought he had a way about him. He has a great command of the English language and is sharp as a tack. Wasn't he married at one time?"

"I think so. Why?"

"Well, he's not the most attractive man in the world, but a girl can overlook a lot of physical flaws if a man has a sense of humor. He's still heavy, I guess?"

"Yes. An overweight Gene Wilder would be my best description."

"Gene Wilder's hilarious. I'm glad he's back in the business. It took him a while to get past Gilda Radner's death, or so all the magazines said."

"Why did you ask if Jeff was married?"

"Oh, I have a few prospects in mind for him."

"Why the sudden interest in his social life?"

"He asked me if I knew any women that might like to go out with him."

"You've got to be kidding."

"No," she said, taking a bite of her fajita.

"Too bad you couldn't make the trip tomorrow. I'd much rather be traveling with you than Mr. Witty and Charming."

"You'll have fun. Besides, sounds like most of it will be business. I have to attend a March of Dimes board meeting and a luncheon at the Women's Center. By the way, I saw Stephanie Frazier, Ted's wife, today at lunch at the Grotto."

"Yes?"

"She was sporting a new sapphire ring—eight carats, I believe she said."

"My God!"

"That's what I said. It just about put my eyes out. Must have cost Ted a fortune."

"I didn't realize that the nursing-home business was so lucrative."

"Neither did I. And by the way, we walked out of the restaurant together. Guess what she was driving?"

"No idea."

"Rolls Royce Silver Cloud."

We ate in silence for a minute.

"Boy, I love these fajitas," I said. "The meat tastes a little different."

"Turkey again."

"What?"

"Turkey fajitas. Aren't they delightful? These are even better than the ones I served you a week or so ago. Since your cholesterol's too high, and since you've expanded into a size 40 waist, I thought I should help you with your diet."

"Thirty-eight waist, if you please."

"Sorry, Charlie. Remember, I buy your clothes for you and take them to the cleaners."

"You're kidding. I thought there for a while that you had a new dry-cleaning outfit you were using. My clothes have been feeling so tight, I assumed you were taking our laundry to one of those places that shrink everything. Some of my friends at the hospital mention it frequently. Then, my boxers and jeans started to feel comfortable again, so I figured you had changed vendors."

"No. I just bought new clothes for you. In a larger size."

She stood. "Want anything?"

"I was going to have another beer, but I think I'll switch to diet cola."

"Good idea, big boy," she said, laughing.

I made rounds Friday morning, and to my delight, everyone was just fine, including Charles Pullig, whose pacemaker-induced pulse was steady. I still didn't understand what the reduced thyroid level had to do with the deaths of Mrs. Adams and Mr. Jeffries, but I sure as hell didn't want to discover the connection through another autopsy.

I was pulling for Pullig. Sounded like a campaign slogan.

I completed the paperwork on my desk, got a cup of coffee, and waited for Jeff. I was amazed at his promptness.

"Dr. Brady," Fran, my secretary asked, "are you expecting a Dr. Clarke?"

"Yes. Show him in, please."

You could have knocked me over with a feather. He was clean-shaven, his red curly hair was trimmed, and he was dressed in a suit, white shirt, and tie.

"Well, what do you think, Brady?"

"Jeff, I can't believe it's you. When did this . . . this transformation occur?"

"Yesterday, after I talked to your wife. It's time to get back into circulation. I realized, after talking to Mary Louise, how much I've missed having an erudite conversation with an intelligent woman."

"I must say, I'm impressed. You look like a different person."

"I'd better. This is a Zegna outfit. Double-breasted suit, shirt, and matching tie. Cost me fifteen hundred dollars."

"I think it was money well spent. You look great."

"Are you ready?"

"Yes."

"Are you going dressed like that?"

"What's wrong with the way I'm dressed?"

"Let me see. Black slacks and a black leather western jacket with fringe. And what's that underneath? A white western shirt with pearl buttons?"

"Since when did you care about how I dress, much less yourself?"

"Since yesterday when Mary Louise told me she was going to fix me up with a couple of her friends, maybe double-date with you guys. Good news, huh?"

I could hardly contain myself.

CHAPTER 19

STELLA

Friday, May 26, 2000

"**S**o, Brady, this is a nice car, although I would have figured you for a truck man. I mean, a Lincoln Town Car's a pretty good ride, but for you? How come you're not driving a pickup?"

We were on Interstate 45, headed north toward Conroe. Jeff hadn't stopped yapping since we had left the office parking garage.

"I have a truck, Jeff. It's in the shop. I had a little problem last Thursday. The flood, remember?"

"You should have a four-wheel-drive vehicle. You see, that is the problem with people. A four-wheeler's a little uncomfortable. The ride's a little rougher. But when the going gets tough, everybody wants one. Needs one, even. But for most days, and most weather? The softies of the world want a smooth ride. Then, when they get into trouble, they want someone like me to bail their ass out. But no, not this boy. Let me tell you something, Brady . . ."

And on it went for the next hour. I distracted myself from Jeff's one-way conversation by counting mammoth pine trees that lined the interstate and watched for the red dirt, or red clay, that characterizes East Texas. It starts a little north of Conroe, becomes strong up at Huntsville, Livingston, and Woodville, then continues north and east all the way to Texarkana and into Louisiana. Pine trees and their thousands of cones scattered over the red clay were just about everywhere you looked.

The smell of pine sap is mostly what I remember about the Brady summer family reunions in Sam Houston National Park. We used to gather in the town of Cold Spring, named for . . . the obvious. We would camp out for two or three nights, sing old gospel songs by campfire light, and eat fried chicken, potato salad, and coleslaw. I've forgotten the names of many of my distant relatives, but I remember the red dirt and the pine trees. And the wood ticks, who loved to burrow themselves into the most remote of bodily locations.

I finally exited off the freeway onto Highway 105, which runs through Conroe, and found West Davis Street. I observed the thirty-miles-per-hour speed limit in the tourist town of 25,000 and put myself on alert for local law-enforcement officials, still called Smokeys in the local vernacular.

Temple Agudath Jacob was surprisingly modern, considering its surroundings. It was nestled in a grove of pine trees and fronted by large oaks and elms lining a long circular driveway. The structure was a combination of dark wood and brownish-red brick, with a central spire. It could have been any modern church or meeting hall, except for the iron-sculptured Star of David positioned on the lush green lawn.

I parked under the portico in front of the main entrance, and Jeff and I entered the synagogue's vestibule, which led to a spacious auditorium that resembled all the other houses of worship that I had visited.

"Gentlemen!"

"Hey, Jake," Jeff said, embracing his cousin Rabbi Jacob Stern, who had scampered down the central aisle from the front of the synagogue. "This Dr. Jim Bob Brady."

"Doctor," the rabbi said, extending his hand. He was short, bald, and stocky, with a strong grip. He had bushy eyebrows and a graying black beard. I saw a resemblance between Jeff and his cousin in spite of the absence of hair on his head.

"My pleasure, Rabbi," I said, returning his strong handshake, but losing the age-old subconscious grip-strength contest between men.

"It's Jake, please. And I shall call you James, after one of Jesus's brothers. James kept the faith alive, you know. He was a very loyal and faithful Jewish brother. He headed up a synagogue in Jerusalem, or so the story goes. But then, I'm sure you're aware of our history."

I smiled. "I'm not much of a historian, Jake."

"Ah. The quintessential scientist, then?"

"Just enough to get through a chemistry major in college, then medical school. In my spare time, I like to play music and read, mostly the *New York Times* bestseller list."

"A musician. What instrument?"

"Piano, but any kind of keyboard will do."

"Excellent. Perhaps you will play for me sometime. A sonata, perhaps, or one of the great Beethoven concertos. You do play the classics, James?"

"Oh, yes sir. Elmore James, T-Bone Walker, Howling Wolf, Robert Johnson, and Sippie Wallace, with a little Hank Williams, Merle Haggard, and Jerry Lee Lewis thrown in."

"I see. A Delta blues man, with Nashville seasoning."

"Exactly."

"I hate to interrupt this impressive stream of bullshit, Jake, but we have business to attend to here. We have a schedule to—"

"Jeffrey, Jeffrey, Jeffrey. Always the impatient one. Never had time to savor the joys of life. Working with dead bodies has caused you to be detached from your brethren and your relatives. You should be ashamed of yourself."

"Jake, I didn't come up here to be chastised for my way of life. I hear that from my mother. We're here to get information, and I'm sure Brady here doesn't want to involve himself with the family's squabbles. So, can we get on with it?"

The good rabbi turned to me. "See how he talks to a teacher? To a man of the cloth, as you Christians say? You are a Christian, are you not, James?"

"I grew up a Methodist, married a Catholic girl whose grandmother was an Austrian Jew, and haven't darkened a church door for years until today. Oh, I did go into St. Patrick's Cathedral while in New York last week and lit a candle for my deceased father. I don't know if that counts or not, since I'm still wrestling with the idea of life after death."

"Very good, James. God loves those of us who continually ask questions. All the great prophets questioned their faith—Abraham, Moses, Elijah, Jesus. And they ultimately had their faith tested to the fullest extent. They questioned, but eventually had their faith restored, and so will you."

We followed Jake Stern through a side door in the sanctuary, down a hallway, and into his private office. It was large, with a bay window overlooking the grounds. He had several clay pots in the office, some with flowering cacti, some with geraniums.

A large leather sofa flanked one wall, opposite his massive oak desk. A handsome coffee table, made from a lacquered oak tree stump, was centered in front of the sofa. Adjacent to the sofa and table sat two overstuffed leather chairs, one of which contained a diminutive woman.

"Stella?" Jake said. "This is Dr. James Brady, the orthopedic surgeon from Houston who took care of Rufus's broken wrist before he passed away. And this is his friend, and my cousin, Dr. Jeffrey Clarke, a pathologist from the same hospital."

She stood and greeted us both. She had immaculately coiffured silver hair and just enough makeup to disguise her aging face. She was dressed well, in a black suit with a scarf, and wore low black heels. She was a woman in mourning.

"Doctors," she said, shaking my hand first, then Jeff's. "Thank you for coming."

"So, sit please. Jeff, you and I will take the couch. James, take the other chair next to Stella," the rabbi said.

We sat and stared at each other for a moment or two, then Jake spoke.

"Stella wanted to hear from you, James, about the demise of her husband. If you please, simply tell her what happened."

"Sure. It was Thursday, a week ago, when I saw your husband for the first time, Mrs. Jeffries. He was transferred to University Hospital by Dr. Ted Frazier, who runs the—"

"I know very well who he is," she interrupted.

"Yes, ma'am. Well, Dr. Frazier called Dr. James Morgenstern, an internal medicine colleague of mine, who accepted your husband in transfer. He then consulted me. Your husband had a broken wrist that needed pinning to hold the bone fragments in place.

"When I first saw him in the emergency room, he was very wild. Dr. Morgenstern sedated him and kept him sedated while he was in the hospital. I took him to surgery later that morning—I had another case to do that was more of an emergency—and applied what is called an external fixator to his forearm.

"He seemed to do fine on Thursday. I stayed around the hospital most of the day in case I was needed, since most of my colleagues were unable to get to work due to high water. That was the worst day of the flood, you know. And as I said, when I went home that afternoon, he was fine.

"I made rounds the next morning—that was last Friday—and he was still doing fine. However, by the time I finished some paperwork in my office in preparation for a trip to New York to give a lecture, he died. It couldn't have been more than a couple of hours after I saw him."

"That's all?" she asked.

"Yes, ma'am."

She stared at me for a while, then at Jeff. "And you?"

"Excuse me?" Jeff asked.

"What do you have to add?"

Jeff looked at Jake, who nodded.

"Well, Mrs. Jeffries, I'm a pathologist. I did the autopsy on your husband. I must say, other than the broken wrist, and a normal amount of plaque buildup in the blood vessels for a man his age, I didn't find anything to explain his death. According to his chart, which I reviewed thoroughly, he died of terminal bradycardia, also called asystole. That simply means his heart rate slowed down so low that blood could not be pumped to the vital organs, resulting in a cardiac arrest. The code-blue team made every effort to save him, as did Dr. Morgenstern, but they were unable to get his heart started."

It was Jeff's turn to receive her icy stare.

"And that's all?"

Jeff pondered that for a moment and again looked at his cousin. Jake Stern nodded.

"Well, Mrs. Jeffries, I don't want to be offensive to the memory of your dead husband, but we did find some irregularities during the autopsy. Dr. Brady has reviewed this data with me, and we are both a little puzzled by what we found. That is one of the reasons we agreed to come up here to see you."

"What do you mean, irregularities?"

"Okay, let me explain. Your husband carried a diagnosis of Alzheimer's disease. This disease is a form of dementia, which scientists think is due to the loss of certain chemicals in the brain. Those chemicals allow the transmission of neural impulses, which allow us to think, speak, remember, socialize, know the difference between appropriate and inappropriate behavior, and a myriad of other important functions.

"Normally, at the time of autopsy, there is a dramatic lack of these chemicals, primarily acetylcholine, but also serotonin and norepinephrine in smaller amounts, in the brain tissue. Well, in your husband's case, there were massive concentrations of these chemicals, which is distinctly contrary to normal findings in the Alzheimer's patient."

He paused and waited for questions. There were no questions, but Stella Jeffries's intense stare did not diminish.

"Another unusual finding, Mrs. Jeffries, was an abnormally high concentration of a particular enzyme called acetylcholinesterase inhibitor, which prevents breakdown of acetylcholine. Realize that the inhibitor levels are normally markedly reduced in Alzheimer's patients, which allows the destruction of ACH, which in turn leads to the mental effects of Alzheimer's disease. The problem is, we can't explain its high concentration."

"So, what you are saying is that, based on your findings in Rufus's brain, he should not have had the mental problems he had?"

"Yes, ma'am, that's correct."

"So, what does all this mean?"

"Quite frankly, I don't know yet. As I told Jake the other day, Dr. Brady here has had four patients from Pleasant View Nursing Home who have died in the last couple of weeks. Three died the day of or the day after he performed surgery for fractures, and one, who did not have surgery, died after having been in the hospital for several days. One of the reasons I started looking into these matters was because of Dr. Brady's concerns about the patient deaths. As he said, his patients do not usually die. And, as the chief of pathology at University Hospital, I can attest to that.

"In the course of my in-depth study of these four patients, I have discovered that the other three had the same chemical findings in the brain as your husband. But Mr. Jeffries and one other patient, by the name of Beatrice Adams, did not have the classic pathological findings in the brain that you should see with Alzheimer's. There were no tangles."

"What is this word, tangles?" she asked.

"It describes a certain kind of nerve degeneration pattern in the brain. It was described by Dr. Alzheimer, after whom the disease is named."

"What are you saying, Jeffrey?" interjected Jake Stern. "He acted like he had Alzheimer's, but didn't?"

"I'm saying that from the pathological standpoint, he did not have classic Alzheimer's. He may have had some other form of dementia, but technically not Alzheimer's."

"Then what did my Rufus have, Doctor?" Stella asked.

Jeff shook his head. "We're not sure. But I did note that Mr. Jeffries had his thyroid gland removed some time in the past, correct?"

"Yes," Stella said, "but that was years ago. He's been taking his thyroid pills every day for as long as I can remember."

"Yes, ma'am. I noted that thyroxine was on the nursing-home medication sheet that Dr. Frazier sent over with your husband when he was transferred to University. The problem is that your husband's blood levels of thyroid hormone were nonexistent."

She sat forward in her chair. "Meaning?"

"Meaning he wasn't taking his medicine."

"Or he wasn't receiving his medicine?" she responded.

"Either way, Mrs. Jeffries, my point is this. Your husband would have had to have been without his thyroid medication for a year or more to get dementia bad enough to look as though he had Alzheimer's disease. And that process would have had to occur before he even went to Pleasant View. Do you see?"

"Yes, I see, but I'm telling you, he took those pills every day!"

"Did he see his doctor regularly?"

"Yes, he had a checkup every six months."

"Do you have any of his pills? His thyroid pills?"

She looked at Jeff for a moment, then reached down into her purse and brought out a brown pill bottle.

"Rabbi Jake told me that you said to bring these with me if I could find them. They are old. Rufus was in the nursing home for over two years, and all his medication has just been sitting in the medicine cabinet. I never touched a thing. I was waiting for him to . . . come home," she said, dabbing at her eyes.

Jeff took the pill bottle and read the prescription.

"Jeff?" I asked. "The prescribing doctor?"

"Theodore Frazier."

CHAPTER 20

PLEASANT VIEW

Friday, May 26, 2000

"Let me get this straight," Jake Stern said, as he drove Jeff Clarke and me to lunch at Lulu's. "Ted Frazier took care of a large number of patients in this city for a very long time, one of which was Rufus Jeffries."

"For over twenty years, I think he told me at a fundraiser last week," I interjected.

"Then, six years ago, he retires from his office practice and takes over the administrative position at Pleasant View. But apparently, at least according to Stella Jeffries, he maintained a small clinic at the nursing home and continued to care for some of his long-term patients, Rufus among them. Is that a correct interpretation?"

"Sounds like it, Jake," Jeff said. "He continued to prescribe medication for those selected patients and treat their ills."

"Stella said Rufus had been at the nursing home for about two years. She also said, and I agree with her, that he had progressive symptoms of Alzheimer's for about two years before it got to the point where she could no longer handle him," Jake continued. "I remember an event she didn't tell you two about, and that was when he set fire to their house."

"What?!"

"That's right, James. She had slowly and gradually put everything she thought was dangerous out of harm's way. She went outside one morning to do some extra watering of the yard. It was summer, and you know how hot these Texas summers can be. She was standing in the front yard, speaking with a neighbor, looking back toward the house, when she saw smoke billowing from the back of the house. Rufus had turned on one of the grills on the top of the stove and had lit the morning paper with it, which had caught the curtains over the sink on fire. Apparently, the heat blew out the glass in the window just above the sink. If they hadn't seen the smoke coming out of the broken window, I believe the whole house would have burned down, with Rufus in it. That's when she decided to put him in a nursing home."

"Which would imply the following," I said. "Frazier's been at Pleasant View for six years, and Rufus had been there for two. But he had symptoms of a gradually worsening dementia for two years before he entered the nursing home. So, if this thyroid deficiency business has anything to do with his demise, it means that sometime between four and six years ago, he began to be thyroid deprived."

"But why, Jim Bob?" asked Jeff. "Most of what we've discovered is just theory. Circumstantial evidence, the lawyers would call it. And maybe it's all bullshit. I mean, it sounds like the plot of a B movie. Why would a doctor deprive his patients of thyroid medication in the first place? To cause dementia? And what for? To get more patients for his nursing home? I would think there are plenty of older people who need care of one sort or another, enough to fill up all the available nursing-home beds around the entire state of Texas. I mean, from what I've read, there is a shortage of nursing-home beds as it is."

"I don't know what to make of it, Jeff. Do you, Jake?"

"There are three nursing home facilities in the community. As I understand it, they're all full with waiting lists."

"See what I mean? What possible motivation would the man have . . ."

I waited for Jeff to finish his sentence, but it didn't happen.

"I'll be interested to see how the analysis of those thyroxine pills turns out, Jeff. When do you think the lab will get that done? Jeff? Are you still with us?"

"Huh? Oh, the pills. Tomorrow. I'll do it myself if I have to. I was just thinking."

"About what?"

"About all this crap we're into, Brady. And more than likely, it's all a colossal waste of my time. Unless . . ."

"Unless what?"

He was quiet again.

"Well, here we are, boys. Lulu's," Jake Stern said.

It wasn't exactly a shack, but the clapboard restaurant with the gravel parking lot could have used a coat of paint and a new roof.

We entered through a screen door and took a seat at a Formica-topped table for four. The aluminum chairs had plastic seat covers. The utensils were wrapped in paper napkins, and menus were already in place behind an aluminum napkin holder.

"Don't even look at the menu. We're all having chicken fried steak with home fries," Jake said, and told the waitress such when she arrived to take our order. He also ordered three iced teas, which came in enormous clear plastic glasses.

"Gentlemen, you're in for a treat. The best chicken fried steak in the world," Rabbi Jake Stern announced.

It was.

I think Jake would have loved to accompany us to Pleasant View Nursing Home. Unfortunately, as he told us when he dropped us at my rental car at the synagogue, he had rabbinical duties to attend to. He explained that the Jewish Sabbath began at dusk on Friday, with Saturday services for children and adults, and that there was God's work to be done. He made Jeff promise to call him after we had toured the nursing home and after we had spoken to Sergeant Kenneth Adams at the sheriff's department. Jeff, against my better judgment, had told his cousin about the last leg of our Conroe trip, which was to visit with Beatrice Adams's brother. Beatrice Adams had also been thyroid deficient, and Jeff wanted to ask Sergeant Adams if he knew of any thyroid treatment she might have had prior to her admission to Pleasant View.

Pleasant View wasn't difficult to find, since it was on the west side of town, right off Highway 105 and on the way to Lake Conroe. The grounds were beautiful. A line of blooming magnolia trees had been planted on each side of the entry drive. The parking lot was freshly asphalted and the divider lines for automobiles freshly painted yellow. Impeccably maintained flower beds with red, yellow, and orange hibiscus mixed with red geraniums were scattered about the property including the various parking areas.

There was an ample portico over the circular drive that led to the entrance, designed for easy pick up and delivery and to protect families from inclement weather. Jeff and I entered the building through massive oak doors with decorative leaded glass in the center.

The interior of the building exhibited a two-story atrium foyer, complete with central fountain and a myriad of foliage. Two young women in green uniforms were watering plants and replacing the wood chips that lined planter boxes adjacent to the fountain. I noticed a sitting area in the background with Oriental rugs and antique furniture, complete with a polished ebony grand piano. It was an impressive facility from the entry vantage point, resembling the lobby of a fine hotel rather than my perception of the decor at a chronic care center. I had not been to a nursing home since I was a kid on required visits to debilitated sisters and brothers of my parents, but they couldn't have been as nice as Pleasant View.

"May I help you?" an attractive young woman asked, as Jeff and I were gaping at the opulence of the lobby. He seemed as surprised as I was.

"Yes, you probably can. I'm Dr. Brady and this is Dr. Clarke. We have an appointment to see Dr. Frazier at two o'clock."

She produced a clipboard from behind her back, found our names, and invited us to follow her. We stepped through the opposite side of the lobby and into a corridor to the left. I saw Jeff feel the fabric of a chair on the way. I noted the piano was a Steinway, a concert grand.

The corridor was glassed-in on both sides, with views of the front and rear grounds. The grounds in back were similarly landscaped to the front, but with the addition of several covered arbors containing white wrought-iron patio furniture. Two of the seating areas were occupied by younger men and women visiting with white-haired ladies and gents seated in wheelchairs and bundled in various colored blankets in spite of the warm spring day. Friday afternoon was probably a popular visiting time.

The receptionist, or administrative assistant—she didn't identify herself—led us into a spacious seating area labeled "Consultation Room" by a bronze plaque outside the door. She told us to have a seat, which we did. The conference table was of dark mahogany and was surrounded by ten leather swivel chairs. At one end of the room was a beverage cart, and at the other, a media center complete with a large-screen television and a myriad of electronic equipment.

"Think this is where the board meets and decides how much to charge the family to take care of Grandma and Grandpa?"

"No idea, Jeff. Pretty snazzy place, huh?"

"I wouldn't mind hanging out here, Brady. Of course, by the time I'm ready to come to a place like this, I won't know where I am or who I am. Kind of a waste, don't you think?"

"It's for the families, not the patients, Jeff. A place like this gives the illusion of quality nursing-home care. And in his defense, Frazier could be rendering fantastic care. Who knows? This place reminds me of those fancy funeral homes and burial plots with the ornate statuary. I've asked Mary Louise to please not waste her money in case I go first. I have told her repeatedly to go on a cruise to some fabulous place—the Greek Isles, for instance—open a bottle of champagne, and scatter my ashes into the sea. That would be money well spent, rather than some damn mausoleum that's—"

"Hello!" said Dr. Ted Frazier, entering during my tirade to Jeff about wasted burial costs. He was immaculately attired in a suit similar to Jeff's and wore tasseled Italian loafers. I noticed his shiny manicured nails, his styled razor-cut hair, and his incredibly white straight teeth. Doctor Wall Street came to mind.

"Hello, Ted," I said, extending my hand. "Nice to see you again. This is Jeff Clarke, a friend of mine."

"My pleasure," he said, shaking Jeff's hand. "I didn't know you were bringing anyone."

"It was a last-minute idea. Jeff has relatives in the area, so he came along for the ride."

"I thought you might bring that gorgeous wife of yours. What business are you in, Jeff?"

"I'm the chief of pathology at University Hospital."

"I see. I know most of the folks here in Conroe. What are your relatives' names? I don't believe I know any Clarkes."

"My cousin is Jake Stern. He's the—"

"The rabbi at Agudath Jacob. Yes, I know him. I believe some of my patients are members of that synagogue. In fact, if I remember correctly, Rufus Jeffries was one of his congregation."

"That's correct."

"Hm-m-m. Is it possible that you were the pathologist who rendered the autopsy on Rufus?"

"Yes, I was."

"And perhaps you came along with Jim here to discuss the unfortunate demise of Rufus with Stella?"

"Yes, sir."

"Good. That's commendable. I'm sure Stella appreciated that. And did you also visit with her, Jim?"

"Yes, sir. She was quite distraught over her husband's death, and Jake Stern asked if I would come up here and explain what happened to him in person."

"That's excellent, and very thoughtful of you two. Seems you've had a run of bad luck with my patients of late, Jim."

"That's an understatement, Ted. Four deaths in two weeks. It's pretty disturbing for someone like me, who's not used to that sort of thing."

"Well, Jim, it's just part of the business. Sick old people die. All of my patients die, you know."

"Yes, sir. You told me that when we talked on the phone last week."

"Yes, I did. The four patients that died under your care were also my patients here at Pleasant View, so I understand your emotions about the subject."

I smiled and nodded.

"Well, let's have that tour, shall we? I'm on a tight schedule today. I have a board meeting at three. This is, in case you two are wondering, a private nursing home. While I am the administrator, there is a board composed of the facility's owners, of which I am one. We have a few community leaders on the board as well, those whose good names provided invaluable support in the development and success of Pleasant View. I'm sure you can understand that this is a business, like any corporation."

We could.

On the lower level of the west wing, there was the conference room, Frazier's private office, and offices for administrative staff and other support personnel. On the other side of the atrium entry was an east wing, with an identical glassed-in corridor that led to a medical clinic and a physical therapy unit, complete with sauna and swimming pool.

"I perform minor procedures as needed here in the clinic. I also still see a few private patients here two days a week. This is a modern, thoroughly equipped clinic, complete with x-ray, EKG, a small hematology lab, even a crash cart. We do have unexpected emergencies arise here, you know, and you cannot be too well-prepared," he said. "I'm especially proud of the therapy unit. The pool is wonderful way for older individuals to try and stay fit. Swimming keeps the muscles toned and is excellent for the cardiovascular system."

I noted several decrepit patients having their muscles gently exercised, both in and out of the water, by youthful therapists who appeared to be in excellent physical condition. The irony of it all became quite obvious to me, like a sudden revelation. It was something I had seen so many times but had never really "seen" before.

We returned to the central lobby and took an elevator to the second floor. Dr. Frazier explained the setup.

"We have two wings—one for men, and one for women. There are fifty private rooms in each wing, and I can assure you, there is a waiting list. We have the most modern equipment and a caring and loving staff who is quite attentive to the needs of our patients. I do not believe there is a finer extended-nursing-care facility anywhere. I'm quite proud of it."

We walked to the male side first. The rooms were numbered one through fifty, set up along three walls with a central nursing station. The central lounge, in front of the nursing station, had a number of chairs, two sofas, accent tables, a television centered on a brightly papered wall, a soft-drink machine, and a commercial coffee maker.

"Families can meet here with their relatives in residence, or in the privacy of the patient's room if they choose. They can also visit outside in one of the arbors, as you probably saw when you arrived. We try to make this facility as pleasant as possible, both for the patient and the family. I have tried to create as much of a home-like atmosphere as possible, and for some patients, perhaps even that of a fine resort."

"Could I see one of the rooms?" Jeff asked.

"Well, that would be somewhat irregular. We don't want to disturb an individual's privacy."

"Maybe you could pick one of the Alzheimer's patient's rooms. You seem to have quite a few of them. They wouldn't know we were there, or at least they wouldn't remember. Besides, my aunt may require custodial care in the future."

"Ah. A potential client. Let me see what I can do," Ted said, leaving our company to speak with the woman in white who seemed to be in charge, called charge nurses in hospital lingo.

"What's wrong with your aunt?"

"Not a damn thing. I want to see one of those rooms."

I smiled. "What for?"

"Because—"

"Right this way, gentlemen. We can take a peek into Room 28," announced Ted.

We walked the left hallway, past Rooms 1 through 18, turned right, and entered Room 28. I noticed an immaculately clean, white-tiled floor with freshly painted walls of blue and white. It looked to me I could eat off the floor, not that I would want to.

"This room is painted in one of the pastels, at the request of the man's son. He hoped it would remind his father of his beach home that he loved dearly," Ted said.

The room was large enough to accommodate a hospital bed, a nightstand, a small couch, and two chairs. There was a private bath, with supporting rails in the bathtub and on each side of the sink and the commode. A TV was mounted on brackets opposite the bed. The man in Room 28 was sleeping, with the sheet and white blanket tucked in military-style around him. He had on a large white bonnet.

Once back in the hallway, Jeff asked about the bonnet.

"Kwell day."

"Excuse me?"

"Kwell, Dr. Clarke. While every effort is made to keep these patients extremely clean, it is sometimes not possible to prevent certain dermatological infections in patients who are unable to care for themselves. Sometimes these patients can be uncooperative as far as personal hygiene is concerned. Kwell is a topical treatment for head lice."

"I remember that Mr. Jeffries had scabies when he was admitted to University," I said. "Same kind of thing?"

"Mr. Jeffries had this little habit of . . . shall I say, relieving himself in his bed. Then he used to play in it. Rub it into his skin, like he thought he was playing in the mud. We go to great lengths to prevent that sort of thing, but we can't watch them every minute, can we? We do as much preventative treatment as possible, and Friday is Kwell day. We cover the patients' heads, so they can't rub it off."

We returned to the elevator and took it down to the ground floor.

"What's on the third floor, Ted?" Jeff asked.

"Medical records and storage. There is quite a bit of unfinished space in case we decide to expand."

Once on the ground floor, Dr. Frazier escorted Jeff and I back to the entrance.

"Gentlemen, I hope you've enjoyed the tour. I've got to be running along."

"Before you go, Ted, I'd like to apologize for the deaths of your four patients. I don't know what else could have been done. It seemed they all developed bradycardia, which progressed into asystole."

"Jim, I've explained the situation to you several times. These things happen. I'm sure you did all you could. Now, if you'll excuse me."

"Thank God Charles Pullig has a pacemaker," I said. "A new pacemaker. He's doing fine."

Dr. Ted Frazier lost all expression for a moment. "What do you mean?"

"His old pacemaker malfunctioned. I had a new one installed when I repaired his hip fracture. I believe he's going to be all right."

"Good. Very good. Good day, gentlemen."

Back in the car, on the way to the Montgomery County Sheriff's Office, Jeff said that Ted Frazier seemed a little less than overjoyed about the prospects of Mr. Pullig's survival.

"You think so? I got that impression for just a minute, but he seemed to recover that award-winning, toothpaste-commercial smile of his."

"You know what, Brady? I really wanted to pull the bonnet off that man's head."

"What for?"

"To see what was under there."

"He said Kwell."

"Brady, Kwell's a shampoo. You don't leave it on. You have to wash it off a few minutes after application, otherwise it burns the scalp. And I'm sure, with all the money these patients and their families are spending to make their waning lives more comfortable, Frazier has no intention of burning up their heads and killing the golden geese. Nope. He was feeding us a line of bullshit."

CHAPTER 21

CRIME SCENE

Friday, May 26, 2000

We traveled east on Highway 105, took Interstate 45 south to FM 1488, and headed back west. The Montgomery County Sheriff's Office was located off the farm-to-market road, centrally located in a woodsy area of Montgomery County. I pulled into a paved parking lot in front of a series of one-story brown brick buildings. Several Ford Broncos with the sheriff's department logos were parked on either side of the entry.

"Afternoon," I said to a female officer whose nameplate said WOOD. She was dressed in a khaki uniform with an MCSD emblem and sergeant stripes on each upper shirt sleeve.

"I'm Dr. Brady. This is Dr. Clarke. We have an appointment with Sergeant Adams at four."

She looked up from her desk and her paperwork—seems that everyone who worked had that albatross—and inspected her watch. "It's three thirty."

"Yes, ma'am, I know. I wonder if he's here?"

"No, sir, not yet. He had to go out on call. Would you like to wait?"

"How long before he's back, do you think?"

"Can't say. He's in the north part of the county," she said. "Chop shop."

"Excuse me?"

"We've been staking out a chop shop. That's where thieves cut up stolen vehicles in order to sell the parts. We got lucky today. Ken's got the crew cornered, along with the used car dealer who was in charge of the ring. He's making a bunch of arrests and supervising the dismantling of the shop. It's a real good collar."

"I'm happy for him," Jeff interjected, "but we have to get back to Houston. I have to analyze this specimen," he said, pulling Rufus Jeffries's pill bottle from his pocket. He held it gingerly, with the label toward him. From Officer Woods's vantage point, the brown opaque bottle probably looked ominous.

"Could be deadly bacteria in this bottle; you just never know," Jeff continued.

She abruptly leaned back, away from the drug-store cowboy and the Zegna suit holding a potentially toxic substance. She backed up her chair, stood, and went to a filing cabinet behind her desk. She picked up the microphone and called out a number over what appeared to be a CB radio.

The speaker squawked. "Yeah?"

"Ken, can you talk?"

"Yeah, Chris. What do you want?"

"There are two gentlemen from Houston here to see you. Two doctors?"

"Shit! I was supposed to see them at four. I won't be there for a while, at least a couple more hours."

She looked at Jeff and I and shrugged her shoulders.

"Well, we'll just come back another—" I started, but Jeff interrupted me.

"Can we meet him? Where is he?"

She shook her head.

"Just ask him," Jeff said.

"Jeff, I'm supposed to meet Mary Louise at home, or at the beach, depending on what time I get back. I don't want to be up here all night!"

He ignored me.

"They want to meet you out there. Can do?" the woman named Chris Wood asked Ken Adams via the radio.

"I guess, as long as they don't touch anything. You know where I am, right?"

"Ten-four," she said, and put the mike back in its cradle.

"Do you know where Porter is?" she asked, clinging to the file cabinet.

We shook our heads.

"Okay. Go back down 1488 and turn north on I-45. Get off at the Porter exit, which is about ten miles, and head east. Go about a mile, maybe two, until you see a sign that reads LAKE HOUSTON ESTATES. Go right, which will be south. Now just before you get to the Estates, there will be a farm-to-market road. I forget the number, but it's called Jackrabbit Road. Go east about three miles till you see an old red farmhouse, with a gravel road . . ."

"Did you get all that, Jeff?"

"Hell, no. I think I can get you to the farmhouse, but after that, I'm not sure."

"Why didn't you just leave well enough alone? We could have headed back to Houston. You could have started analyzing that—that deadly bacteria. I can't believe you said that. You scared the poor woman to death," I said, and laughed.

"That was the point."

"Anyway, I could have possibly met Mary Louise at the apartment, or at least had a head start on Friday afternoon traffic to

Galveston. As it is, we're not going to get out of here until six o'clock, and I won't get to the beach before nine. Thanks a lot, Jeff."

"Sure, Brady. Anytime."

We wandered the back roads of Montgomery County for an hour and a half before finding the chop-shop crime scene. Four tan sheriff's-department vehicles blocked the driveway to a large warehouse.

"Police business. Move along," said an enormous white man as he leaned down to the driver's window. He had on a similar khaki uniform to Officer Woods and wore a large tan Stetson cowboy hat and black hunting boots. He carried what looked like an old-fashioned Colt .45 pistol, a six-shooter, in a large black holster, mixed with other law-enforcement devices. I noticed a can of mace, handcuffs, a nightstick, a portable radio, and a large Bowie hunting knife. It wasn't rocket science to determine that we were in the country.

"Yes, sir, I understand," I said, as politely as possible. I wanted no part of any of the tools of his trade, all of which seemed to enlarge through my open window as he straightened up and backed away from the car. "Sergeant Kenneth Adams instructed us to meet him here. I hate to be a bother, but would you mind seeing if he's available?"

The officer glared at me behind his mirrored sunglasses, stepped over to my car, and leaned his six-and-a-half-foot frame back down to my window level.

"Step out of the car, please."

Those words will strike fear in the heart of any Texan, especially when out of the city limits. Any city limits.

Jeff and I meekly slithered out of the Lincoln, Jeff promptly joining me on the driver's side.

The officer, who didn't have a name tag—probably so we wouldn't know whom to complain about—inspected us, looking up and down.

"Hey, Bill," he called to another officer at the entrance, "got us a couple of city boys looking for Ken."

"Yeah, I see. Nice suit, City," said the man named Bill. "Cost him a pretty penny I bet, Wally."

The only Wally I knew was the older Cleaver brother on *Leave it to Beaver*. This Wally was definitely not part of that TV family.

Wally stepped toward us, looking at Jeff's suit and my boots.

"Kind of boots are those?"

"Ostrich shank," I said.

"No bumps?"

"Not on the shank. The bumps come from plucking the feathers. The shank is smooth."

"Good lookin'. I've got a pair of regular ostrich boots in black. Have to wear these ropers on the job, though."

He nodded, seemingly to himself, then said to Bill, "Go get Ken."

As Bill walked away, the man named Wally asked what we were doing up there.

"Well, we're doctors from Houston. We're trying to get some information from Sergeant Adams about his sister. She died recently at University Hospital, and—"

"And you were her doctor? 'Cause Ken's been mighty upset about losin' his only relative," he said, again glaring at me.

"Not exactly. I was only a consulting doctor. I'm an orthopedic surgeon, and I was evaluating his sister's broken leg. She died before she left the hospital. I talked to him on the phone the night she died. I tried to explain the situation as best I could, but there are a few unanswered questions.

"Dr. Clarke here is a pathologist at the hospital. He performed Mrs. Adams's autopsy. Together we're trying to figure out something suspicious about her blood work. We're hoping your colleague can shed some light on the situation."

That seemed to satisfy the giant of a man, who could probably crush me with one arm. I couldn't help thinking about the movie *Porky's*, with Alex Karras as the local sheriff. The image of Ned Beatty on all fours, squealing like a pig in *Deliverance*, also crossed my mind. I quickly pushed both remembrances aside with a hopefully undetectable shudder.

"Dr. Brady? Ken Adams," he said, walking from behind where we were standing having our conversation with Wally. He came around the truck and shook hands with Jeff and me. "Sorry you had to make the trip out here. Not much I could do about it, though. Wally been giving you a hard time?"

Ken was a couple of inches taller than me, with a similar uniform to Wally, but with a different insignia. I assumed that meant he was higher up the ladder of authority. He had on a huge Stetson hat, with some of the same weaponry on his belt as his cohort. And he wore the requisite ropers.

"Oh, no," I said. "We were having a good talk about things of mutual interest. He's been very kind."

Not exactly true, but you never know when you're going to need a friend like Wally. There was no reason to disparage him, I reasoned.

"Good. Why don't you two walk this way with me, so I can still keep my eye on the goings-on here. Great break for us, finding this chop shop. We've had these dirtbags under surveillance for months, and finally got lucky. So, what's on your mind, Doc?"

"This is rather sensitive information, Sergeant Adams, and I—"

"Call me Ken."

"Okay, Ken. There are some . . . irregularities in the autopsy findings of your sister Beatrice. Jeff Clarke here," I said, introducing the two, "is the pathologist who's been working with me on this matter, and I'll let him explain it to you."

After shaking hands with Sergeant Ken, Jeff explained about the four Alzheimer's deaths, the pathology findings in the four patients, and the unexplained thyroid deficiency in Rufus Jeffries and Beatrice Adams, the sergeant's deceased sister.

"I guess we could have told you this on the phone, but since we were going to be up here anyway, we thought you might want to discuss it in person," Jeff concluded.

"No, this is better. I like talking to people face to face. What can I do to help you solve this problem?"

"We'd like to know," I said, "since we've discovered that your sister was on thyroid medication just like Mr. Jeffries, who was prescribing the pills for her."

"Well hell, gents, that's easy. She went to the same doctor for thirty years, same as me. Doc Frazier."

"Okay, Jeff, it's after six. If we can find our way back to the highway and make good time, I can drop you off at the hospital and get to Galveston by nine."

Jeff was quiet for a while. He didn't speak until we were on I-45, headed south toward Houston.

"I'm hungry, Brady."

"What? Well, so am I, but I'm not going to—"

"I'll buy you a Dairy Queen hamburger."

"Jeff, I could eat something, too. But I'm kind of in a hurry."

"Brady, you've got to take life a little easier, maybe stop and smell the roses once in a while and quit hurrying so much."

"You're one to talk, Jeff. You're the one who got the lecture from your cousin Jake, not me. Besides, I don't consider stopping at a Dairy Queen a smelling-the-roses kind of experience."

"It was just an example. Look, you're hungry and tired, and you have a long drive ahead of you. Let's get a burger and some coffee. You'll be refreshed and awake, and I won't have to worry about you falling asleep on the road and killing us both."

I looked at Jeff in the darkening twilight. He had removed his jacket and tie and was slouched in the seat. "You're not getting altruistic on me, are you?"

"No, just protecting my ass. I want you rested and awake while you drive me home. And I would feel really bad if you bought the bullet on the way to Galveston. Look! There's a Dairy Queen, right off that exit. C'mon, Brady. It's the right thing to do."

We pulled into the parking lot and stopped, since I couldn't talk him into going the drive-thru route. He said he might spill something on his suit.

I ordered a Hunger Buster, he a Belt Buster—names with caloric implications, I was sure—along with two fries and two coffees.

While he washed up, I phoned home. The answering machine picked up, and I left a message for Mary Louise that we had been delayed and not to expect me at the beach house until nine or ten. I then called the Galveston house, but no answer. We didn't have an answering machine there, and I couldn't remember her car-phone number. The message at the apartment would have to do. I knew she'd pick up messages sooner or later, so at least she would know I was on the way.

I washed my face and hands in cold water in the men's room, then joined Jeff at a plastic table by the window with a panoramic view of the intersection of Highway 105 and I-45.

"The bonnet is the key."

"What?" I asked between mouthfuls of an absolutely incredible burger.

"The guy? In Room 28? With the bonnet? I believe the key to unlocking the mystery is under it."

I waited for what I knew was coming.

"I want to go back and take a look."

"No way, Jeff. The receptionist would recognize us. Frazier may still be there at his board meeting. We'll have 'suspicious' written all over our faces. There has to be another way. And besides, I'm already late for the trip to Galveston."

"It won't take but a minute. There must be a back entrance. We can bypass the reception desk and find a stairwell. It's only one floor up, and we can take a look at bonnet man. I don't think any of the nursing staff saw us, and if they did, they probably wouldn't recognize us anyway. We can say the guy is one of our relatives, and we just wanted to check on him. Visiting hours are from ten to eight, so we would be well within our rights to be there, but we arrive just after visiting hours."

"How do you know about the visiting hours?"

"Read the sign on the second floor, during our tour of the men's section. What do you say? We'll be out of there in five or ten minutes, and we'll be on our way."

"I don't know, Jeff. It's too risky. We don't want to tip off Frazier that we're checking into his—"

"Brady, you're supposed to be one hell of an amateur detective. You don't want to spoil your reputation and go all crybaby on me now, do you? Well, do you?"

I shook my head and felt that rumble of deep-seated trouble in my gut. It could have been the burger, but probably not.

"Then c'mon, Sherlock. Time's a wastin'."

CHAPTER 22

PROWLERS

Friday, May 26, 2000

We parked in the most remote section of Pleasant View Nursing Home's parking lot to try and avoid detection. It was starting to get dark, but fortunately, the designer of the ultra-modern facility had graciously spaced a myriad of lights along the walkways and amongst the landscaped areas between the curbs. Otherwise, we would have been stumbling around like a couple of fools, not that Jeff and I didn't qualify for that label for simply sneaking around at night at the nursing home.

We walked around the east side of the building, along a path lit by the glow of lights interspersed in the pine trees. No one was out and about. The arbors were empty. We stepped across the grass, stood at the corner of the rear of the first floor, and peered into the atrium lobby. The young woman who had greeted us that afternoon was still at the reception desk.

We could see the two-car elevator bank and watched while visitors disembarked after having paid their dutiful visits to infirm relatives. We waited. And waited.

Finally, around eight thirty, the lobby looked quiet. The receptionist stood from her desk, picked up her purse, and walked briskly to the elevator bank. She stood there, checked her watch, and waited.

Shortly, Dr. Ted Frazier exited from one of the two elevators, smiled at the young woman, and together, they walked out the front door. Old eagle-eyed Jeff watched her lock the front door. I thought that was odd, but perhaps it was a routine procedure.

We continued across the grass, looking for a rear door into the main lobby. We found one, but it was locked. We walked back around to the east side of the building, the medical clinic and physical therapy side, and found that door to be an emergency-exit door. A sign on a bronze plaque warned DO NOT ATTEMPT TO OPEN THIS DOOR. ALARM WILL SOUND.

We then walked all the way around to the west side of the nursing home, where Frazier's office and other administrative personnel offices were located. We found the same kind of door with the same warning sign.

"Now what?" I asked.

"I don't know. Let me think."

"I don't need to think, Jeff. It's time to go home. It will be very embarrassing if two Houston doctors are caught sneaking around this place at night. That would not be good for our respective reputations. It's just not worth the risk."

"We've come this far, Brady. We can figure out something. Now think, dammit!"

I thought about Mary Louise, at the beach house, sitting on the deck in a sundress with a cocktail, enjoying the ocean breeze. I knew where I should have been, and it was not in Conroe with Jeff Clarke.

"The way I see it, Brady, we've got two choices. We can each position ourselves at one of the emergency-exit doors and wait for an employee to exit, one who might be taking a shortcut to either the east or west end of the parking lot. One of us can then slip in as the employee is walking away, and then go and let our fellow conspirator in."

"That's a great idea, Jeff, except the door will more than likely shut before we can get in. And, if an employee sees one of us rushing for the door, they're going to think they're getting mugged and start screaming. Also, nursing shifts usually run seven to three, three to eleven, and eleven to seven. Considering the time is just now after eight, it's unlikely an employee would be leaving at this hour. What's our other choice?"

"Go in the front door."

I stared at him, unable to speak for a moment. "Didn't you see the receptionist lock the door?"

"Yep."

"So how do you propose . . .?"

"There has to be a night bell for emergencies, supply delivery, late entries, that sort of thing."

"So?"

"So, we go around to the front door, check to see if there's a bell, and if there is, we ring it and wing it. Couldn't hurt, Brady."

"Ring it and wing it? You mean, with no plan, just say whatever comes into our minds at the time?"

"Something like that. C'mon, let's do it."

Jeff started walking toward the front entry. I followed him, not knowing what else to do, except get in the car and drive to Galveston alone, and leave my obviously insane friend to his own devices.

There was, in fact, a night bell, just to the right of the leaded-glass front door. Jeff rang it. Shortly, an intercom adjacent to the buzzer sounded, neither of which we had noticed on our previous trip to the facility.

"May I help you?" a woman's voice asked.

"Yes, this is Jeffrey Moore, Mr. Reginald Moore's son. Did I miss visiting hours?"

"Yes, sir, you did. Ten to eight. I'm sorry, but you'll have to come back tomorrow."

Jeff started to cry honest-to-God tears. I shook my head.

"Sir? Sir? What's the matter?"

"I'm leaving on assignment to the Middle East, on a midnight flight. I won't be back for a month or more, and I've got to see Dad before I go."

"Sir, I am very sorry, but we have a strict visitation policy, as I'm sure you know. We don't want to upset the patients by disturbing their routine. It's very important to establish a routine with the patients, and—sir? Sir?"

Jeff continued to cry. Wail would be a better description.

"Sir, I'll be right down."

Jeff took out a handkerchief, blew his nose, and dabbed at his eyes.

"What in the hell do you think you're doing?"

"Getting us in."

"And what is this Reginald Moore business? Who's he?"

"The guy in 28."

"And how do you know that?"

"I read it on the outside of his door when Frazier took us in there this afternoon."

I shook my head. "I can't believe I let you talk me into this escapade. I must have lost my mind."

Shortly, a pleasant, plump, middle-aged woman in a white starched nursing uniform and white nursing shoes appeared at the door. Jeff had resumed his sobbing. We apparently did not frighten the woman, as she opened the door and invited us into the lobby.

"This visit is highly irregular, Mr. Moore, and I could get into serious trouble for allowing it. But when I heard how upset you were, I just couldn't stand it. You never know about our patients. At their age, and with their problems, they could be here today and gone tomorrow."

Jeff continued to sob, even leaned in the direction of this extremely kind and sensitive woman, whose name tag read VIRGINIA GUYTON. She put her arms around him and hugged him. I could not believe my eyes.

"Come along now, Mr. Moore. Let's go see your father. And who's your friend?"

"Him? Nobody. Just a company driver. He gave me a ride over here and is taking me to the airport. He can wait in the lobby if that's all right with you."

"Of course, my dear. Why don't you have a seat over there," she said to me, the company driver. Where did Jeff get that? "We shouldn't be long," she said, smiling, turning, and taking Jeff's arm as she guided him toward the elevator bank.

I stood there like a fool, not having the foggiest idea what I was supposed to do next. As I watched Jeff and Nurse Guyton board the elevator, I sat on the foot-wide rim of the fountain which had been turned off, lit a cigarette, and thought about a plan. Did Jeff simply want to take a look under the man's bonnet, in which case he would be back in the lobby in minutes, and we could get the hell out of there? Or did he want to explore further? And what did I want to do now that I was inside? I considered that I should get up to the third floor and take a look at the medical records that Frazier said were there.

Or should I just stay put, wait for Jeff's return, and then head south to Galveston? The lure of a pleasant ocean breeze, a comfortable deck chair, a single-malt scotch, and the arms of the woman I love was powerful and sounded like just what the doctor ordered. That's what a smart man would have done.

I put my cigarette out in the still waters of the fountain, dropped the butt in a small trash can next to the reception desk, and walked over to the elevator bank. I punched the "Up" button, the opposite of what a smart man would have done.

After I pressed the third-floor button, the elevator rose slowly. The door opened to a small lobby, dimly lit with a fluorescent ceiling fixture. I stepped into a corridor that branched into right and left walkways, similar to the arrangement on the patient floor below. Frazier was right about the space being unfinished. The area that corresponded to the lounge on what I thought was the women's side on the second floor had a cement floor with no carpet or tile. Wires hung from the unfinished ceiling, and water pipes and air conditioning vents were visible.

I walked around to the other side of the elevator bank and found the same conditions on what would have been the men's-side lounge on the floor below. However, as opposed to the women's side, which was dark, I saw a light at the far end of the hall. I could hardly see, so I used my trusty Zippo to guide my way.

Once I had crossed the unfinished "lounge" area, I saw where, at one time, a nursing station had been started. I knew from having been on the floor below that the remainder of the men's wing should have had beds lining the three walls. As I wandered to the right, I saw partially constructed patient rooms, aligned in the same fashion as the floor below. There were no doors on any of the potential patient rooms. I wandered through all the open spaces and saw nothing of interest. I noticed the light I had seen at the far end of the hallway was an EXIT light over a stairwell door.

I walked back to the elevator bank, then explored the women's wing. Again, nothing of interest. No storage rooms, no medical records, just space that could be built out if needed.

I went back to the far end of the opposite hall on the men's side and approached the stairwell door. I opened it, jiggled the stairwell-side door handle to make sure that it wasn't locked from that side, and walked down the completed stairwell to the second floor. There was a door in the same location. I carefully opened it and looked in both directions.

Luck was with me. The door opened between Room 25 and Room 26 of the men's ward. After again checking to make sure the stairwell door didn't automatically lock, I stepped into the hallway and walked over to Room 28. I listened at the door but heard nothing. I figured Jeff would have found out some way to have a little privacy with his "father," so I quickly stepped inside.

The door to Mr. Moore's room shut quietly.

I noticed a pinpoint light above his bed, shining on his bare head. I walked the few steps to the bed, leaned down, and observed his sleeping face. He had pale skin, thick lips, and a swollen face.

From the darkness behind me, I sensed movement. I whirled around and saw a shadow standing against the wall next to the door.

"What took you so long?"

CHAPTER 23

PATCHES

Friday, May 26, 2000

"**J**eez Louise, Jeff, you just about scared the shit out of me."

"Sorry. I didn't want to say anything if it was Nurse Guyton. I wanted to keep my options open, you see."

I shook my head and looked down again at the sleeping face of Mr. Moore. His bonnet was off, and on closer inspection, I noticed he had only a few wisps of silvery-gray hair atop his head. His sideburns were shaved clean, as was his face, and the hair over his ears was close-cropped.

"I don't see much, Jeff, except a sleeping old bald man. Not enough hair to warrant Kwell, wouldn't you say?"

"Precisely. I told you it was a ruse."

"But it proves nothing, Jeff. This was an exercise in futility. Let's get out of here. I'll go back down the stairs to the lobby and wait for you there. Nurse Guyton will never know I was up here."

"You came from upstairs, didn't you?"

"Yes."

"And what were you looking for?"

"Nothing in particular. I was curious, looking for a hiding place for some sort of incriminating evidence, I guess. I didn't see anything out of the ordinary, just an incomplete space similar to this floor."

"Did you comb the entire third floor?"

"I think so. There's nothing to see but unfinished space, like Frazier said."

"What about the medical records he said were stored there?"

"I didn't see any. The layout is exactly like this floor. There is a lounge on either side of the elevator bank, adjacent to two separate, incomplete nurse's stations for a men's and a women's ward, with empty, unfinished potential patient rooms."

"Did you look into the unfinished rooms?"

"Yes. Well, certainly not every room, but most of them. I followed a light at the end of the hallway, walked to it, noticed the stairwell, and followed it downstairs to what I hoped was the men's ward on this floor. Lucky for me, it opened just a couple of doors from here. Now let's go home."

"Whoa there, fella. You're moving too fast. Take a closer look at Mr. Moore."

"Jeff, I—"

"Look closer. Remember what you told me when you came back from New York and look . . . very . . . carefully."

I leaned down again, nervous about being caught and having to explain our presence to Nurse Guyton and ultimately, to Ted Frazier. We were trespassing, so we might even have to answer to the police.

I gently turned the patient's face from side to side, looking as closely as I knew how to look. And then I saw them.

"Shit. There's a white cloth button behind each ear, Jeff. It looks like—"

"Scopolamine patches. For motion sickness."

"But why?"

"You're the one who put that idea in my head," he whispered. "Remember when old professor Bonhoffer from New York told you about his experiences with neuron growth factor and how he had some unexpected complications with bradycardia in his experimental patient study at the VA hospital? And that he had tried to control the slowing of the heart rate with atropine eye drops? And scopolamine patches?"

"Yes?"

"I think that's what Frazier's been doing. I think he's been giving these patients some kind of drug to regenerate neurons in the brain to try and improve their Alzheimer's condition. I'll bet he's trying to slow down the deterioration, maybe even reverse the neuronal changes. And I think the large doses of whatever he's giving them causes massive accumulations of acetylcholine in their system and the development of bradycardia. I think he's been trying to control the heart rate with scopolamine patches, maybe atropine, but who knows."

"But Jeff, the patients I've taken care of had a relatively normal sinus rhythm when they arrived. They developed bradycardia later."

"Like the next day, after anesthesia, in two of the deaths. The last patient, Pullig, developed bradycardia as well, except that you knew he had a pacemaker, had it switched out for a new one, and he's all right," Jeff pointed out.

"But Mrs. Adams died after being hospitalized for a few days. It doesn't fit in her case."

"I know. She didn't have surgery. I can't explain it all to you. It's a working theory, and we have to try to prove—"

The loud knocking on the door caused us both to almost jump out of our skins.

"Mr. Moore? Are you about done? I really must ask you to leave. I'm breaking all the regulations by letting you in after visiting hours. Surely you've had enough time . . ."

"Oh, yes, ma'am," Jeff whimpered, his voice breaking. Having a friend who can cry at will is a valuable asset, I thought. "Just another minute. I'll meet you at the nursing station."

"Fine," we heard her say through the door. We didn't hear footsteps. Her nursing shoes must have had Vibram soles.

"Okay, Brady, you go back upstairs, wait fifteen minutes by the clock, then go back down the elevator to the lobby. Check it out best you can and make sure no one sees you. Then let me in the side door on the west side, the one by Frazier's office, and we'll go upstairs and explore the third floor together, see if we can find anything."

"Jeff, as I told you, I've already checked it out. There is nothing up there. Besides, I really think we should get out of here. You never know, a security guard might make rounds, or Frazier—"

"Wimp."

"What? I'm not a wimp. I'm just being cautious."

"Wimp. Schmuck. Coward. You're a big talker but afraid to take action," he said, glaring at me, arms folded across his chest.

Some adult male primates, the kind that live in trees, will stare a biped primate down. If you continue looking at them—I've had experience with this in primate research centers—directly into their face, they become enraged. They will tear your eyes out if they can get close enough. That's the kind of look I gave Jeff, but he just stared back.

I finally gave up and hung my head. "Fifteen minutes, not a second longer."

"Attaboy."

I hoped that the smoke detection system in what was probably a non-smoking facility was inactive on the third floor. I stood at the small landing next to the elevator bank and smoked and fumed. I heard the elevator activate and figured that was Nurse Guyton escorting Jeff back downstairs to the exit at the front of the building. He said he'd tell her I must have gone to wait in the car. I then heard the activation of what I thought was the ascent of the elevator, carrying the nurse back to her station on the second floor.

I waited. And I waited. Whoever said that a watched clock runs very slowly knew exactly what they were talking about.

I had sneaked out of Room 28 and returned to the empty third floor via the stairs. After precisely fifteen minutes, I punched the down button of the third-floor elevator and heard the wheels and pulleys turn. I half expected someone to be in the car when it arrived, but I was pleasantly surprised, relieved even, to see it empty.

I pressed the button for the first floor and descended slowly.

I carefully searched the lobby as best I could from the small landing where the elevator deposited me, its nervous passenger. No one was stirring.

I walked the west corridor toward the administrative offices and looked for the emergency-exit door that Jeff and I had observed when we were outside snooping earlier. I found it, just to the side of a closed door with the nameplate, DR. THEODORE FRAZIER. Unfortunately, the inside of the exit door had the same insignia as the outside of the door, with one of those red aluminum handle-attachments that said EMERGENCY EXIT ONLY.

Obviously, I didn't want to alert the nursing-home staff of my presence in the building. Jeff could always run away if the alarm sounded, but I was on the inside, making it harder for me to escape. We should have simply gone through the front door, dammit. It probably had a bolt lock on the inside and might not have even needed a key. Of course, if the front door required a key to exit, I was out of luck anyway. I wished I could quit second-guessing the decisions Jeff and I had already made, because there was no turning back.

I tapped on the door. It tapped back.

I slowly pushed the handle down and opened the door just enough to see Jeff standing there. He opened it the rest of the way and stepped inside.

That's when the alarm sounded.

Jeff shut the door behind him and ran like hell. What else could I do? I ran after him. He abruptly turned a corner and ran toward a dark corner under an EXIT sign. He opened that door, and we raced up the stairwell to the third floor.

"How'd you know where the stairs were?" I gasped, out of breath and regretting the day I tasted my first cigarette.

"Guessed."

"Lucky guess, Jeff."

"Better to be lucky than good, Brady."

We slipped out of the stairwell and onto the third floor. We ducked into an unfinished patient room. It had no door so we couldn't hide. We stood off to the side of the entrance in the dark, leaned as close to the wall as we could, waited, and recovered our breathing.

We waited thirty minutes by the clock. Nothing happened, so we ventured out into the hallway. Maybe the alarm wasn't activated. Maybe the charge nurse sent someone to check the first floor who saw nothing out of order. Maybe an angel happened by. We were still safe and undetected.

It was by then just past nine. I was supposed to be at the beach, which was two hours away at least. I was going to be late. Very late. I wondered what Mary Louise was wondering.

Systematically, we went through all the unfinished patient rooms on that end of the floor and found nothing. We then passed through the nursing-station-to-be, and the lounge area, and past the quiet elevator—believe me, we stopped and listened.

We looked around the next nursing station, then started into the rooms. We split up, Jeff taking the left hall, Rooms 1 to 18, and I, the right, Rooms 33 to 50. We met at the far end, at Room 25, adjacent to the stairwell. Again, nothing.

"Didn't he say he kept medical records up here?" Jeff asked.

"Yes."

"Well, there's not shit up here, Brady."

"I told you that. Let's go. It's very late, I'm exhausted, and all for nothing, thanks to you."

"I just can't believe it. I thought sure we would find something. Anything."

"C'mon, Jeff. It just isn't meant to be. Let's go, huh?" I said, putting my hand on his shoulder.

"I guess," he said, disconsolately. "Let's go down this stairwell. It's closer."

"We came up the west side, by Frazier's office. Don't you think . . ."

"We'll come out on the clinic side, Brady. We can slip out the exit door there and run like hell if the alarm is activated like it was on the other side. We've probably pushed our luck far enough."

With that, he opened the stairwell door, and we trotted down the stairs. When we reached the ground floor, we opened the door into a small hallway which led to the emergency-exit door, same as the opposite side of the building. We noted an extra door, however, next to the Medical Clinic sign, in that small hallway, made obvious by a bright light shining from underneath the entry.

"I wonder what's in there?" Jeff asked.

"Ignore it, forget it, leave it alone," I said. "We're out of here, Jeff."

He ignored my comment and opened the door. It opened directly into a treatment room. The room was composed of white tile on the floor and walls and had a strong medicinal smell.

I wouldn't have minded making a U-turn and finding my way to the outside. There was a small problem, though. There was a man, completely naked, lying face down on an examination table. And there was a nurse, standing next to the patient, hunched over his head and neck.

She whipped her body around at the sound of the opening door, made herself erect, and stared. Jeff and I were too stunned to move.

"Dr. Brady?" she asked.

The three of us stood there for what seemed an eternity, her eyes darting back and forth between Jeff, me, and the patient. In contrast to the dim lighting of the stairwell, the bright, incandescent examination-room lights were almost blinding, but the face of Cynthia Dumond was clearly recognizable.

CHAPTER 24

CYNTHIA

Friday, May 26, 2000

"**C**ynthia, what in the world . . . ?"

"Brady? What in the hell is going on here?" Jeff asked.

"Dr. Jeff Clarke, meet Cynthia Dumond. She is the eleven-to-seven head nurse on Med-8, the floor where all my recent Alzheimer's-related deaths resided—until their untimely demises, that is. I might ask you, Cynthia, what you're doing here?"

"I might ask you the same, Dr. Brady."

She had a good point.

"Well, Dr. Clarke and I were . . ."

"We were visiting my . . . a relative of mine," Jeff responded. "I got here a little late, and one of the nurses—Guyton is her name, I believe—let us in. We decided to take the stairs down and, well, we got lost."

Don't give anything away until we know what Cynthia's role is here. Good move, Jeff. We still had a chance to get out of this situation safely, I hoped.

"And you?" he asked.

She hung her head and looked at the ancient-appearing man lying prostrate on the table for all the world to see. She gazed back at the two of us paralyzed at the entrance to the treatment room, stepped away from the patient, walked to the white-tiled wall adjacent to us, folded her arms, and stared at the floor.

We waited.

"Dr. Brady, I know this looks suspicious, but let me tell you why I'm here. Could you listen for just a moment?"

"I'm all ears, Cynthia."

"When we first met, during your morning rounds a few weeks ago, I told you that it seemed that all the patients that were admitted to my floor from this nursing home died. Do you remember that?"

"Very clearly, Cynthia."

"Well, some time before that—it's been several months—I became concerned. Very concerned. I mentioned it to my supervisors and to Dr. Morgenstern. Everyone made light of the situation. The patients are old and sick, they said, and old, sick people die. 'It's a way of life,' Dr. Morgenstern said, more times than I care to count. But it seemed to me that some of the patients were too young to have Alzheimer's disease and that they died of, in my opinion, rather mysterious causes. There weren't that many at first, but then the frequency seemed to escalate. From what I read in the charts of the affected patients, most died of a sudden, inexplicable slowing of the heart rate. Some died after surgery in the operating room, but some died in their rooms, with no apparent warning. The heart rate would slow down, then they would develop a heart block, an asystole, if you will. And this had been happening long before I met you.

"These events have concerned me deeply, and since I could get no satisfaction from the nursing administration at University or from Dr. Morgenstern, I decided to take matters into my own hands. I took a part-time job here on the three-to-eleven shift, Fridays and Saturdays. That's not a very desirable shift, so there's always a shortage. People want to go out to dinner, go to a movie, see their families, you know?"

"Yes?"

"It's been very hard on me, working the eleven to seven at University Sunday through Thursday, then the three to eleven here Friday and Saturday. But there's only Mother and me, and I have a lady that comes in while I'm gone, prepares her meals and provides for her needs in my absence. I really have no life other than my work. So—"

"Brady, I think this woman is wasting our time. If she's here, at this institution, at this time of night, doing God-knows-what to the stiff there, then she's got to be in league with Frazier and involved in whatever he's doing to his patients. I'm not buying any of her story."

"For your information, Doctor, this is not a stiff. He has a name, and he's just resting. This man had a fecal impaction, and I brought him down here to clean him out. I was cleaning him up when you startled me. I do not appreciate your insinuations that I'm doing anything improper."

"Yeah, and I'm Albert fucking Schweitzer. Unless this man's anatomy is reversed, you should have been working on the other end, not the head and neck area. Let's move out of here, Brady. This woman is lying. She's part of Frazier's conspiracy."

"Wait, Jeff. I want to hear her out. Go ahead, Cynthia, tell me what you're doing here. And I don't mean right here, since, for purposes of discussion, I'll buy your impaction story for now. I want to know what you've been doing here, at Pleasant View, to solve your unanswered questions."

"Well, I've been working with the patients to try and discover why these people have been dying. And I've been able to work around Dr. Frazier's schedule, as he has to escort his young wife to a number of charity events in the city. And I've learned quite a bit. Come and look at this."

We moved closer to see what she was indicating.

"See?" she said, pointing to a small two-inch-by-two-inch bandage over the patient's lower back, at the juncture of the pelvis and the lumbar spine.

I peeled the bandage off with one hand, holding the patient steady with the other. There was a small blood-encrusted spot in the midline of the patient's spine. I palpated the area and found that the scabbed-over puncture wound lay between two spinous processes, L-4 and L-5.

"Spinal tap?" I asked.

"Indeed. He's been getting a spinal tap twice a week. So have all the others," Cynthia said.

"Spinal taps? Why in the hell would the AD patients need a—" Jeff asked. He stopped mid-sentence and seemed to silently answer his own question.

"What, Jeff? What?" I asked.

"There's no medical reason to withdraw spinal fluid from a patient unless you suspect an infection in the brain or spinal cord— like meningitis or encephalitis—for diagnostic reasons. There are indications for intrathecal injections, though, like for anesthesia— spinal blocks, epidurals—or for treatment of certain diseases, like multiple sclerosis, where the neurologists inject steroids to reduce the inflammation in the spinal cord. I doubt Frazier's into diagnostic procedures, so he's got to be injecting the patients intrathecally with some kind of medication."

We looked at Cynthia for an answer.

"I don't know," she said. "All I can tell you is that almost every patient in this facility comes down here twice a week and gets a spinal tap. The nursing personnel have been told that the procedure involves a research project. The rumor is that Dr. Frazier is trying to find the cause of Alzheimer's disease, and that he has some kind of grant to study the patients. It's very hush-hush, and although we're not allowed to discuss it, most of the employees do anyway. Some of the nurses feel that he's treating the patients experimentally, and others think that the spinal taps represent what they are purported to be, which is for diagnostic purposes. Having worked here for a few months now, it's my opinion that Dr. Frazier is treating his patients with medication to help their brains recover from Alzheimer's, because . . ." She paused.

"Because what?"

"Because, Dr. Brady . . . some of the patients have been discharged."

"So?" asked Jeff. "That's not unusual. Patients don't always stay in nursing homes forever. Some have temporary disabilities, get better, and go home. Or they run out of money and go live with relatives."

She looked at the floor. "Alzheimer's patients, Dr. Clarke?"

"Cynthia, why would an Alzheimer's patient be discharged, other than to a hospital for an acute problem, or to the morgue in case of death?" I asked.

She continued to stare at the floor. "Because they get better."

Jeff and I looked at each other.

"What do you mean, they get better?" I asked.

"Remember Mrs. Adams, Dr. Brady? Remember that day you came in, and she was lucid? And I had her all fixed up for you?"

I nodded.

"A number of these patients stay that way and go home."

"I don't believe it," Jeff said.

"That's the same thing Bonhoffer told me, Jeff," I said. "His VA patients had improvement in their paralysis with the drugs he was experimenting with. Why not Frazier's patients? Of course, I can't imagine how he could get away with it. I mean, think about it. A family brings a demented relative to Pleasant View, thinking it's the last weigh station. Then they get a call one day from Frazier, who says it's time to pick up Grandma, because she's playing bridge again."

"The families sign a release," Cynthia interjected. "The admitting family member agrees to whatever treatment Dr. Frazier deems appropriate for the patient's condition. The release implies there may be improvement in the medical condition and that the patient may be able to reach a more functional level and return home. Families are told that Dr. Frazier's project is government funded and experimental, and no one is allowed to discuss it.

"Of course," she continued, "most of the Alzheimer's nursing-home admissions would not be expected to improve. Usually, their demise occurs in a nursing facility like this one. Families expect that. But to have a patient improve and return to a more functional level? That would be quite an accomplishment, wouldn't you doctors think? And I would expect most family members to be grateful and to honor the code of silence, since they signed an agreement to that effect. Families pay a fortune to have their loved ones here in hopes they will get better. And some do."

Jeff and I were stunned. Speechless. At least I was.

"What happens after the spinal taps?" Jeff asked.

"Excuse me?"

"What are Frazier's post-tap instructions?"

"Dr. Frazier gives strict instructions to the nurses to elevate the feet and lower the head after the treatments."

"He puts them in the Trendelenburg position?" Jeff asked. "For how long?"

"Eight hours."

"Eight hours?!"

"Yes, Dr. Clarke."

"To increase cerebral concentration, Brady. It's got to be!"

I nodded, still stunned.

We all stared at the patient, who still hadn't stirred. It occurred to me that the room didn't smell like feces, though it should after an impaction had been evacuated. Since older, demented patients are fairly inactive, it is not unusual for them to develop bowel problems, which is why the use of stool softeners and laxatives are common, not only in nursing homes but also in hospitals. Even otherwise healthy but immobile patients can develop lower intestinal sluggishness due to pain medication, which aggravates the condition as well. But every impacted patient I had ever seen who had an evacuation procedure, well . . . the odor permeated the walls. And the room we were stand-ing in smelled perfectly normal. I thought it strange. Something still was not right.

We three stood uncomfortably together, looking at the ceiling, looking at the walls, looking at the floor.

Finally, Jeff asked her a question. "What about the bonnets?"

"Excuse me?"

"When Brady and I took a tour here this afternoon, we were personally escorted by Frazier. He tried to avoid taking us into any of the patient rooms, but I wanted to see one, any room, I didn't care. He reluctantly took me into a Mr. Moore's room, Room 28. That's who Brady and I were here 'visiting' this evening. You probably have guessed that he's not a relative."

"Mr. Moore has no relatives any longer, Doctor Clarke. But I can understand your desire to justify your presence here tonight. I've been doing the same thing to you and Dr. Brady, so we're essentially in the same position."

"That may be true, but I'm still skeptical, Cynthia," he said. "If you want to gain the trust of Dr. Brady and me, you can answer a question."

"I will if I can, Doctor."

"This afternoon, the patient in Room 28 had on a bonnet. Frazier said it was for lice treatment. 'Friday is Kwell day,' he said. But I know that's bullshit. When we were up there a few minutes ago, he had scopolamine patches behind both ears. Can you explain that?"

"No, Dr. Clarke, except to say that Dr. Frazier's additional stand-ing order is to apply the patches for forty-eight hours after the spinal taps are done. He says the withdrawal of spinal fluid, even very small amounts, causes dizziness, as does the eight hours of Trendelenburg positioning. And, by the way, he says that putting the feet up helps avoid leaking of spinal fluid. The patches, he says, help prevent motion sickness after the patients have had their heads down for that long. It seems logical to me, and few seem to question Dr. Frazier's judgment.

As I just told you, some of the patients do seem to improve. Their improvement often waxes and wanes, but some develop a preponderance of good days. Beatrice Adams is a good example," she said. "Such a shame. She was so bright that day I made her face up for you. And then . . . she was gone."

She walked over to a floor-to-ceiling cabinet, opened it, and took out some fresh linens and a hospital gown. "I need to get my patient dressed, if you don't mind."

She went about the business of gently redressing the man in a fresh gown and covering him with two sheets and a clean white blanket.

"I need to get this patient back upstairs, or my co-workers will start to worry. If you doctors have nothing else to ask me, I'll be going."

She unlocked the wheels of the portable gurney, went to the head of the bed, and started to push the cart out of the room, toward a set of double doors on the opposite side of the room from where Jeff and I stood.

"Cynthia?"

"Yes, Dr. Brady?" she said, stopping, still facing the double doors, her back to me.

"We need more information, such as medical records, documentation of treatment, and a summary of the medications the patients are getting. Jeff and I also need to find out what drugs may be in the spinal injections, and also information about the scopolamine patches. If Frazier's doing research here that's on the up-and-up and he does, in fact, have FDA approval for this patient experimentation, then so be it. That would mean that Dr. Clarke and I are way out of line. But he and I have come this far, and we need to get a few more answers. Based on the autopsies of the patients of mine that died, I'm still concerned that Dr. Frazier's activities may be negligent. He could be killing people in the name of science, all for the greater good. Understand?"

She nodded.

"So, do you know where he keeps the records?"

She waited at the door, not moving. I still wasn't entirely comfortable with her role at the nursing home, but if she led us to the records, she had to be on our side.

"Well?" Jeff asked.

"At the other end of the building, just around the corner from the administrative offices, there is a door with a combination lock just below the handle. It resembles the keyboard of a touch-tone phone. That's where the records are."

"How do we get in there, Cynthia?"

She pushed the double doors open with the foot end of the gurney and started to walk on through.

"Cynthia?"

"Dial the clinic, Dr. Brady."

CHAPTER 25

RECORDS

Friday, May 26, 2000

We tried the main nursing-home number listed in the Conroe telephone directory, which we found in the receptionist's desk in the lobby. That seven-digit number did not open the magic door.

"She said the clinic, didn't she? Dial the clinic?"

"Yes, Jeff, but I don't know what clinic she was talking about. Try the other numbers."

We entered seven-digit numbers for administration, physical therapy, the business office, and the east and the west wings of the nursing home's patient care areas, all to no avail. We even tried Frazier's number, listed as the Director's Office in the phone book, but nothing.

"Give me the phone book, Jeff. We have tried every number listed under Pleasant View. It has to be listed under Frazier's old clinic numbers."

I turned to the Yellow Page section of the directory, went to the PHYSICIANS section, and found the listing for Dr. Theodore Frazier. There were three numbers: home, his administrative office at Pleasant View, and . . . Geriatric Clinic. Bingo. The Geriatric Clinic was listed at an address that corresponded to the nursing home's address. I read the number to Jeff, he dialed it, and presto! The door snapped open.

The small, windowless office had a desk and chair in the center of the room. The walls were lined with medical charts, reference journals, and books. We prowled the shelves, stacked from the floor to about a foot over my head.

"*International Journal of Neurology, American Journal of Neurosurgery, Annals of Endocrinology, Brain.* What the hell is Frazier, a GP, doing with all these specialty periodicals, unless he's doing his own patient experimentation?" Jeff said. "This stuff's going to fry his ass, Jim Bob. I think we've got him!"

"We don't have anything, Jeff, unless these medical charts reveal something to incriminate him. For all we know, he's a legitimate practitioner with an interest in neurology. Let's keep moving. I was supposed to be at the beach thirty minutes ago. Mary Louise's going to be worried sick."

"So shut up and start looking. Quit wasting time flapping your jaws. Hey, look at this book," he said, still rifling through Frazier's copious reference literature. "*Neuron Growth Factor: Experiments in Mus Musculus,* written by your friend."

"Who?"

"Rheinhold Bonhoffer. The copyright is 1985."

"You're kidding," I said, walking to him in the cramped little room that couldn't have been larger than twelve by twelve. "What's mus musculus?"

"I can tell you haven't done much research. A mouse. Look at this," he said. "This is published data on his studies where he injected NGF into mice. He was doing that fifteen years ago. I can't believe it. He had several experiments going and reports on each one separately in different chapters. There's one on spinal cord injuries, one on median nerve injuries—to a front paw, I guess—and here's one on the effects of NGF on brain-cell regeneration.

"Why are you just standing there, Brady? Are you enjoying watching me work? Start going through the charts. See what you can find out."

"I want to see how he created brain-cell damage, in order to try NGF on the mice. Unless mice develop dementia naturally, but then, how would you know?" I asked.

Jeff just shook his head, continued to thumb through the pages of the small book, which appeared to have been self-published, similar to those theses and dissertations that bestow graduate degrees from diploma mills. I watched Jeff read as he moved his lips in silence. He stopped, looked at me.

"Well?" I asked.

"I'll be damned."

"What, Jeff?"

"Thyroidectomies. He took their fucking thyroid glands out."

We hurriedly perused the medical charts, checking out patient names and dates of treatment. There were hundreds of charts, too many to study in detail with what limited time we had. The charts were organized in alphabetical order. We selected five patient's names that we knew about—Beatrice Adams, Mildred Bland, Agnes Cutkelvin, Rufus Jeffries, and Charles Pullig—and pulled each from the stack.

"Look at this, Brady. Beatrice Adams's records go back to the 1970s. Frazier's got handwritten notes about blood pressure levels, urinalysis results, EKG tracings, the works."

"Look for a note about her thyroidectomy."

"Okay, okay," Jeff said, studying the notes carefully while I reviewed Rufus Jeffries's chart. His medical records also went back to the 1970s. I learned that Ted Frazier was a meticulous man, carefully documenting even mild maladies, such as seasonal influenza. In the 1980s, the notes were still handwritten. Frazier was probably the only doctor in the world who didn't dictate office notes through a handheld recorder for a transcriptionist to decipher.

"I've got it, Brady. Thyroidectomy done here in Conroe by a local surgeon in 1982. Frazier writes he has her on Synthroid daily. He saw her about once a month," Jeff said, following the records in sequence, turning the pages as he read. "A notation in 1993 reads, 'Patient will be followed at PVNH.' Pleasant View. That's when he came here, right?"

"I think he said six or seven years ago, so that was right about when he moved."

"He continued to see her every month in his clinic here after he moved to the nursing home. He wrote down how she's doing, what meds she's taking, same old shit until '94, when he noted that she's getting some early Alzheimer's signs."

"That's all?"

"That's all I see. What about you?"

"Jeffries's chart is similar, except that he had the thyroidectomy in 1978. Frazier had him on Synthroid, just like Adams. A notation reads that he'll be followed up at PVNH, just like Mrs. Adams. Frazier noted early signs of AD in the patient in 1992, then he was admitted here in 1998. That's all I see. There is nothing further after his admission to Pleasant View. In-patient records must be stored elsewhere. There is not much to incriminate the good doctor, Jeff."

"It's got to be here, Brady. We're just not seeing it."

We reviewed the charts of the other three patients I had treated. Agnes Cutkelvin and Mildred Bland had not had their thyroids removed, at least according to the record, and had been admitted to Pleasant View a couple of years prior.

"I wonder if Pleasant View was built in 1993 and if Frazier came here as its director, or if it's been here for a long time. Do you know, Jeff?"

"I found out from Nurse Guyton, who kindly allowed me to see my 'father' during my earlier ruse, that it was under previous ownership in the late 1980s. It was sold, totally remodeled, and re-opened in 1993 with Frazier as the director. She worked for the prior owners, and said it's run much better, with a higher-income clientele than in the old days. The nursing home was constantly getting cited by the Health Department for one thing or another before Frazier took over. She said he runs a tight ship. The patients are kept clean, the building is kept clean, the food is well above the average, and the medical and nursing care is incomparable. There is a long waiting list for admission, she said."

"God only knows what the monthly fee is, though. If there is even a remote chance of a patient improving, a family is liable to pay anything—"

"We're wasting our time, Brady. What did you find?"

"Dead end on Cutkelvin and Bland. They were admitted '96 and '97, respectively. No thyroid problems are noted. Those two could be genuine Alzheimer's patients."

"What about Pullig?"

"I'm just getting to him," I said, scanning the chart as quickly as I could. It was after ten o'clock. Mary Louise would be starting to get worried. I had to call her, but I was afraid to use a phone in the building. If Jeff and I made it out of the nursing home unscathed, but word got out that two "strangers" had been there, I didn't want the phone company records to lead the authorities, or anyone else for that matter, to either one of our homes. Houston and Galveston were long-distance numbers and easily traceable.

"Let's see, Mr. Pullig's a more-recent patient of Frazier's. He started seeing him in the early '90 s after he moved to Conroe from Beaumont. He'd had a thyroidectomy for cancer before he left Beaumont, and Frazier followed up here. Again, Frazier has had him on Synthroid since '92. He followed Frazier over here in '93, started developing AD symptoms shortly after, and was admitted here in '97. It's a dead end, except we've got the names of three thyroidectomy patients of Frazier's, who are on thyroid replacement, who followed him to his geriatric clinic here at Pleasant View, who got Alzheimer's, who became chronic care patients here, and who died after being transferred to University Hospital for medical problems."

"The Dumond woman said the patients are getting spinals twice a week, followed by ear patches for two days, then they start the cycle all over again. We need the in-patient records."

"Jeff, do you think that those spinals will be documented in the chart? And what about the placement of the scopolamine patches? That has to be in the chart for the JCAH, doesn't it?"

"Don't know, Brady. The Joint Commission for Accreditation of Hospitals is mighty interested in the way the hospitals run, but nursing homes? Especially a private one? God only knows how they are regulated. There must be additional records somewhere. So far, we've got nothing, except for hearsay and innuendo. Unless this bottle of thyroid pills that Mrs. Jeffries gave me turns up something, we've wasted a lot of our time."

"You've still got it, right?"

"Of course, Brady. Right here in my coat pocket," he said, reaching into the left pocket of his new Zegna jacket, which was very wrinkled from all the sitting and sweating he had done that day. Jeff removed the pill bottle, leaned back from his position at the desktop, and started tossing the bottle up into the air and catching it.

Just as I was going to tell him he was irritating me beyond description, that I was tired and wanted to leave, and what a shitty idea it had been for us to spend what seemed like my whole life in this building, I started thinking about those pills.

"Jeff. Jeff!"

"What?" he said, turning to me as I sat in Frazier's chair behind the desk. He stopped the pill-bottle-throwing distraction.

"What's the dose on the Synthroid?"

"Huh?"

"The pill bottle in your hand. What's the dose on the prescription?"

He looked at the bottle, thought for a minute. "Looks like 25-microgram tablets. The instructions are to take one daily."

"What's the standard daily dose of thyroid to replace production after a total thyroidectomy?"

"Well, it depends on the body weight. The older synthetic drugs came in milligrams. These new ones are derivatives of levothyroxine and are in micrograms. To be honest with you, I don't know."

"Can't we look it up?"

"Well, if Frazier's got a current medical text, we can," he said, standing and again combing the shelves for reference material. "He has *Harrison's Principals of Internal Medicine*, last year's edition. Let's see what we have here."

I leaned back in the chair, picked up the pill bottle, and started tossing it. I began to understand the therapeutic value of the maneuver. It was like playing with a Slinky.

"Okay, it says here that the dose is based on kilograms of weight. Based on the average 70-kilogram person, the dose is 25 micrograms a day."

"Huh. Too bad. I was hoping—"

"To start," he said, staring at me.

"What?" That got me out of the chair.

"You start the patient on 25, then slowly increase the dose, so that you don't overdose the patient on thyroid. It needs to be up to 100 to 125 micrograms per day to maintain levels of—do you know what this means, you incredibly smart son of a bitch? It means that sly old Frazier has been massively underdosing his patients on thyroid hormone, so that they slowly but gradually develop dementia from thyroid deficiency."

"Which looks like Alzheimer's disease, which—"

"Gives him more patients to admit to his nursing home for his experiments!" Jeff said, dropping the book and hugging me. We danced around the room and laughed like a couple of kids, until we heard the key lock buzzer sound, saw the door open, then crash against the wall.

"I'll take that pill bottle, gentlemen."

CHAPTER 26

FRAZIER

Friday, May 26, 2000

Dr. Theodore Frazier, general practitioner, medical director of an exclusive nursing home, upstanding member of the medical community, and swearer of the Hippocratic Oath, stood in the doorway of his private inner sanctum, which Jeff Clarke and I had invaded, holding a twelve-gauge shotgun with sawed-off barrels. He held it in his right hand, pointed at us, his colleagues in the healing arts.

"You couldn't leave well enough alone, could you, Brady? You just had to keep pushing. Give me that bottle," he demanded.

I handed him our evidence, which Frazier grasped with his empty left hand and carefully shoved it into the left pocket of an expensive tuxedo jacket.

"Thank you very much, Doctors. I've been worried about those pills for quite some time. All of my other patients' families have been kind enough to bring along all their medications, as instructed, when their loved ones were admitted to this facility. Stella Jeffries, however, kept forgetting, or so she said. However, persistence paid off, and once again I'm in the driver's seat, as I should be. Cynthia?"

I was shocked, dismayed, and disappointed to see my friend and Brady-anointed nurse extraordinaire, Cynthia Dumond, step into the room.

"Cynthia? Please tell me you're not in on all this, are you? You said you were—"

"Dr. Brady, I'm not 'in' on anything. Dr. Frazier has been involved in some very important work here. I couldn't let you interfere with it. I'm very sorry."

"But he's been tampering with people's lives, depriving them of medication in order to create an Alzheimer's-like state of dementia, so that he could experiment with unauthorized treatments. Surely you can't—"

"Enough, Brady," Frazier said. "I've been testing a medication that could change the face of the planet. There would be no more brain deterioration, and no more senility. A few more years of study, and I can make people more productive, for longer periods of time. Those people in their seventies, eighties, and nineties who would former-ly have been wasting away due to decreased mental faculties could continue to work and be creative. They would no longer be a bur-den to society. Don't you realize that nursing homes throughout the country are full of people who, if not for diminished cerebral func-tion, could make incredible discoveries and advances in our society? Discover new medical therapies, new engineering techniques, new vaccines, new solar systems? And all because of my research, Brady. Because I had the courage and the insight and the foresight to take a chance and try a therapeutic technique that's been forestalled by the governmental bureaucracy that's keeping the scientists of today from truly advancing our society."

"Frazier," Jeff interjected, "you've been creating dementia in order to experiment with a cure for a disease that seems to be ram-pant already. Why create more? That's illegal, unethical, and morally unconscionable. We have laws to prevent egotistical maniacs like you from—"

"Shut up! You don't have the foggiest idea what you're talking about. What I've done is genius. Sheer genius! The entire world will applaud my efforts when I've perfected the infusion technique. And the treatment is not just for Alzheimer's patients. I've proven clearly that it works just as well for metabolically induced dementia patients, like in hypothyroidism. And think of the paraplegics and quadriplegics, trapped in a wheelchair world with no leg function, or no arm function. I can repair all that!"

"Ted," I said, "let me try to be the voice of reason here. I can understand, I truly can, trying experimental medication on Alzheimer's patients to see if it would make them better. Nothing has seemed to work with these people, and I doubt that what you've been doing would make their brain function any worse. But underdosing thyroid-deficient patients and creating a myxedema dementia that looks superficially like Alzheimer's disease? These people might have otherwise led perfectly normal lives if you had left them alone.

"And what about the patients who died at University Hospital due to bradycardia and heart block? Those patients would have died eventually of some disorder or another, but you caused their deaths prematurely. And how? By withholding their scopolamine treatments after you infused the acetylcholinesterase inhibitor via the spinal tap, scopolamine which you knew damn good and well they needed. Without it, their heart rates would mysteriously plunge after admission. How could you possibly justify that? You, a doctor, who many years ago pledged to uphold the principles of our profession!"

"For the greater good, Brady. There must be sacrifices along the way. Those patients weren't making any progress with the therapy. They were of no use to me or anyone else. Vegetables, they were, a drain on society's resources and the resources of this institution. I needed more room to bring in patients whom I could potentially improve. For two or three years, I had given those others a chance. They didn't get better, so I made a decision to replace them with ones that might get better. It's all very reasonable and logical, you see."

"But couldn't you have just stuck to your project with the Alzheimer's patients? That could have been excused, understood even," I said. "Weren't there enough people to experiment on without creating even more demented patients by depriving them of thyroid hormone?"

"No. I'm not that young anymore, Brady. I needed to work as fast as possible to achieve my goals. Waiting around for natural dementia patients to show up would have taken too long. You can't tell the difference clinically between AD patients and dementia patients from other causes. Plus, I had my own controlled study. I could create dementia, then see if I could cure dementia. It was perfect until you two started nosing around.

"Fortunately for me, Cynthia here has been an invaluable ally, working as she does on the medical floor at University Hospital where the transfer patients from here are admitted. She's good with the little touches, like removing residue from the scopolamine patches upon the patient's admission to the hospital and making sure they were getting the normal dose of thyroid medicine when their health failed, so as not to arouse suspicion.

"She's also the one that personally goes down to pathology and gets the autopsy reports and makes copies of the slides. I like to see those slides myself and determine if there's any pathological evidence of nerve regeneration, even in the clinical-treatment failures. Of course, not everyone gets a brain study, which is unfortunate.

"Cynthia was sharp enough to get copies of the biochemical studies which you, Dr. Clarke, performed on those four fatalities of Dr. Brady's, the results of which you were trying to keep secret. I was quite pleased to discover high levels of acetylcholine in the brain tissue, as well as evidence of neuron regeneration on electron microscopy. And those four had a marginal clinical response to treatment. Adams improved, but not adequately, in my opinion. It's too bad you ran those acetylcholinesterase inhibitor levels, and very unfortunate you noticed the absence of tangles on the brain biopsies of Bland and Cutkelvin. I have to hand it to you, Clarke, you're sharp. I regret you feel the need to waste those incredible talents of yours as a pathologist. I could use someone like you on my end of this study."

"So, what's next, Ted? How are you going to keep your little project secret now?" Jeff retorted. "Are you going to add two more to your list of murders, namely Dr. Brady and me?"

Frazier stepped forward and turned the shotgun around. I saw the stock headed toward Jeff's head, but he dodged too late. The butt of the weapon struck him in the cheek. The loud crack of his cheek bones breaking preceded his crumpling to the floor in a heap.

"My God!" I kneeled down at Jeff's side, felt his pulse, and put my ear next to his nostrils, making sure he wasn't dead. The left side of his face was caved in. He had a broken mandible and maxilla, at least, with a four-inch laceration at the strike point. He was out cold, but he was breathing.

"Get him up! Cynthia, get his feet. Brady, get his head. We're out of here!"

"But Dr. Frazier—"

"Cynthia, this is no time to play Florence Nightingale. We have a mission to complete. Sometimes, the great stars of history have to perform unpleasant tasks. You'll have to trust me," he said, backing up to stand aside Nurse Dumond. Tenderly, he put his available hand on her shoulder, keeping the shotgun trained on me. "It's for your mother, dear, and all the mothers of our future generations."

She nodded and bent down at Jeff Clarke's feet. "Dr. Brady?"

I stared at her for a moment, then gently picked up Jeff's limp head and slid my arms under his shoulders. Cynthia and I hoisted him and stood.

"Where's your car, Brady?"

I gazed at Frazier, the hatred in my heart building. "Parking lot."

"Let's go, then." He stepped out the door backward, holding the shotgun in my general direction as Cynthia and I struggled with 250 pounds of unconscious pathologist.

We walked toward the emergency-exit door, with me in the lead, walking backward. Frazier stepped around me, entered a code on the keypad adjacent to the door, and shoved open the door. As Cynthia,

Jeff's unconscious body, and I navigated the door, Frazier shoved the muzzle of the shotgun up against my chest. That was the closest I had ever been to the business end of a loaded shotgun.

I backed out the door carefully and stepped onto the sidewalk. I walked backward toward the parking lot, with Frazier walking in the grass between Cynthia and me. At the car, Frazier grabbed the keys from my jacket pocket. He unlocked the trunk, then instructed us to put Jeff inside, which we did.

"Now you."

"What?"

"Do you want what he got?" he asked, bringing the shotgun closer to my face.

I shook my head.

"Then climb in, Brady."

I couldn't remember ever having been in a locked car trunk before, not even playing around as a kid. I had seen the maneuver hundreds of times on television shows and in the movies. It had never looked pleasant, and it wasn't, especially with the shallow breathing of my cohort. His face was turned toward the back seat of the car, mine toward the rear bumper. We were cheek to cheek, so to speak.

I heard muffled conversation outside. Then, the car door opened, and the ignition started. I smelled exhaust fumes and wondered how long it would be before Jeff and I suffocated from carbon monoxide poisoning and lack of oxygen.

I felt the car shift into gear, followed by slow movement through the parking lot. I had known—or felt—that Frazier had been up to no good. He had admitted that. Well, he hadn't admitted that he had been up to "no good." He had admitted that he had been experimenting with the lives of people who were, in his opinion, no longer useful. And he felt justified to use them to try and help others with his maniacal ideas. Ego had guided his modus operandi.

What I had seen, though, was the death of four patients from complications of his "treatment." Two, Bland and Cutkelvin, were legitimate AD patients. Two, Adams and Jeffries, had artificially induced states of dementia through purposeful underdosing of thyroid medication, both of whom might have been perfectly normal otherwise. Charles Pullig, also a victim of thyroid dosage manipulation, survived only because he already had a pacemaker inserted. And God only knew how many other thyroid deficiencies Frazier had created over the years in order to expand his "series" of Alzheimer's cases, in order to ply his revolutionary treatment that would, in his opinion, make him famous—not to mention wealthy, which had to be a major motive in and of itself.

What really turned my stomach, in addition to the gasoline fumes permeating the trunk, was that Cynthia Dumond, a woman whom I had trusted and respected, was involved. Jimmy Morgenstern had told me some weeks before that she was incompetent. I had disagreed with him vehemently. I would still argue her competency, but what she was getting out of Frazier's conspiracy and what her true motivations were, I did not know. Hadn't Frazier said something about her mother? And wasn't I supposed to have seen the mother in my office for some kind of arthritic problem?

The Lincoln stopped again, then moved. We went over a few speed bumps, turned, and the velocity increased. I heard the noises of other automobiles and assumed we were headed toward the freeway, Interstate 45, approaching it from the east on Highway 105.

We stopped again, and I presumed we were at the traffic light at the entry point to the interstate. I frantically pushed on the trunk lid, but to no avail. I repositioned myself onto my back and tried in vain to force the trunk open with my knees. In the relative quiet of what I thought was the intersection, I heard Jeff groan.

"Jeff? Are you okay? Jeff?"

While I was waiting for a response, the car jerked, and I felt a left turn. The car accelerated again, that time quickly, and I discerned we were traveling up an incline. We had to be headed north on the interstate, but where? Huntsville? Madisonville? Dallas?

I began to resign myself to dying. I started to pray for Mary Louise. She was probably in Galveston, trying to keep her worry contained, but thinking I might have had a wreck. I had not told her what all I was going to be doing that Friday, except to go and see Mrs. Jeffries and to go see Frazier at the nursing home. I chastised myself for not keeping in better contact with her about my comings and goings. If she had known where I was supposed to be, then she might have had a chance to find me. As it was, she was down at the beach waiting to hear from me. But it was all pointless, anyway, and I felt myself losing hope.

I damned myself for the foolish investigative work I'd been doing with Jeff. It was going to get us both killed. And for what? What had I really accomplished? Not a damn thing. Frazier was going to remain in business, and his little research project was going to proceed as before. Clarke and Brady were going to be deceased-and-mourned doctors, lying on cold slabs at the University Hospital morgue. And it would all be the fault of my stupid, unrelenting curiosity.

CHAPTER 27

PRISONER

Friday, May 26, 2000

After about half an hour, the car went down an incline, made a sharp left turn, accelerated, then went up another incline. The acceleration continued again for a short time, then slowed, then stopped. The motor kept running for a few seconds, then stopped.

The trunk opened.

"Get out, Brady," Frazier said, still maintaining his superiority via his weapon. I wanted to grab the shotgun and beat him into hell with it.

I climbed out of the trunk and saw that we were on the right shoulder of Interstate 45 on the southbound side. We had apparently traveled north, made a U-turn under the freeway, gotten back on the southbound side, and were now pointed in the direction of Houston. I glanced at my watch and saw that it was close to eleven o'clock, which explained the sparse traffic. I thought of all the comfortably tucked-in people, in warm beds at that hour of a Friday night. And of the revelers at a late-night dinner at Anthony's or the Grotto eating some of the best Italian food in the country. And of the patrons at a private party at Rockefeller's club, listening to the sounds of Bobby "Blue" Bland or Dr. John. And of the couples engaged in mad, passionate love all over the planet.

And then I thought of myself, standing on a highway sixty miles north of Houston, Texas, separated from my bride, about to become another one of Frazier's statistics in his diabolical scheme to change the world. I thought of Attila the Hun, Adolph Hitler, Joseph Stalin, and Charles Manson. And now, Ted Frazier would be added to the list of society's all-too-clever products, deviously trying to alter the natural ways of the world. He would be another of those miscreants who cuts corners and runs roughshod over those he deems less important in a quest for a misdirected goal. In other words, another sociopath or psychopath on the loose.

I stood next to the trunk and saw Cynthia Dumond walking toward us from Frazier's car. Apparently she'd followed us on this little adventure, continuing to assist Frazier by bringing his car along. She walked to the rear of the Lincoln and stood next to Frazier.

"Help Dr. Brady get the pathologist out of the trunk, dear," he said kindly.

"But what are—"

"Don't worry about that right now, Cynthia. Let's get Dr. Clarke some fresh air."

I gently picked up Jeff's head and torso and slid him closer to the edge of the trunk. Cynthia grabbed his feet, and we lifted him from the trunk and rested his feet on the asphalt shoulder. I stood him up with her help and we each put an arm around him. I stared at the passing cars, thinking surely someone would stop, or at least call 911. My God, a man was being lifted out of a trunk! Surely some alert driver witnessed that. I prayed for a Conroe Police car or a Montgomery County Sheriff's SUV. Anyone. Even a Fuller Brush salesman. Hell, I didn't know if they even made Fuller brushes anymore.

"Put him in the passenger seat," Frazier instructed.

He followed us to the front of the car and opened the door, never taking his eyes off me, and never releasing his hold on the twelve-gauge.

"Now, buckle him in."

I looked at Frazier with no small degree of confusion.

"I said, buckle him in, Brady!" he screamed. He looked as though he might be losing whatever self-control he still possessed.

"I don't know what you think you're going to do with us, Ted, but there are people who know we've been up here today. They'll come looking for us, and—"

He lifted his weapon and pushed the barrels into my stomach.

"Buckle him in, and get in the driver's seat, Brady!"

After buckling Jeff into his seat, I walked around the rear of the car, closed the trunk, opened the driver's door, and got in. I harnessed myself in with my seat belt and waited.

"Do Clarke first," Frazier said to Cynthia, who stood next to him by my open door. I thought of shifting the car into gear and taking my chances with any split-second hesitation Frazier might have in using his shotgun. I gazed quickly at the ignition switch. No key. Frazier had removed it before I was allowed to disembark from the trunk.

"Dr. Frazier? I'm worried about all this. It doesn't seem right. Dr. Brady's a wonderful doctor, and—"

"This is no time for hesitation, girl!" he thundered. "We have important work to complete, and these two will prevent it from happening. Who is more important? Them or your mother, and others like her?"

Cynthia hung her head, walked around the front of the car, and leaned into the open doorway on Jeff's side. She took out a small bottle, unscrewed the cap, and suctioned out a full eye dropper.

"What is that?"

"Shut up, Brady," Frazier snapped. "Go ahead, Cynthia."

She pulled back Jeff's upper lid, dropped a few drops into his left eye, then did the same to his right eye. She stepped back, shut the door, and walked around to my side.

"What the hell?" I said, leaning away from her. Frazier reached into the car, grabbed my hair, and pulled my head against the seat.

The cold steel of the double-barrel shotgun was pressed against my neck.

"Cynthia? Do it now."

She leaned around Frazier, half-sat on my hands, pulled my eyelids back one at a time, and put the drops in.

I blinked a few times and noted that immediately my vision clouded. Everything became a blur. I felt my mouth dry up and my pulse start to pick up speed. I started to feel dizzy. And then I knew.

"It's atropine, isn't it?" I asked, starting to panic.

"Very astute, Brady, and a highly concentrated dose. I experimented with it for a while, trying to control the patients' bradycardia. The problem was the eyes dilated excessively and they couldn't see. It made them even more unsteady than usual. Also, its effects were variable. Some were more sensitive to it than others. And it lasts too long. Scopolamine is much more predictable. Besides, when the authorities find you, you'll be dead anyway, so whatever numbskull pathologist does the postmortem on you would expect your eyes to be dilated. Nobody is going to check for belladonna in the blood chemistry tests. A wonderful plan, don't you think?

"Here, Cynthia, keep an eye on Brady," Frazier then said, handing her the gun. "I have one small detail to attend to."

He walked around to the front of the car and opened the hood, blocking my view.

"Cynthia, this is your chance to be a real hero. You have a chance to save Jeff and me from this—this insane man. He cannot let you live either, because you know everything. Surely you're aware of that?"

"I'm so very sorry it came to all this, Dr. Brady. I really am. But I don't want you and Dr. Clarke to interfere with the work Dr. Frazier has been doing. It's so important, for the future of humanity. And there is so much work left to be done. If you only could have just allowed those four patients to die in peace and left well enough alone. Their treatment had not been very successful, even after two years.

Two years! It was their time to go, to make room for new patients who can benefit from his therapy."

"But, Cynthia, what about Beatrice Adams? And Rufus Jeffries? He created their diseases, in order to experiment—"

The hood slammed closed, and Frazier walked back to the driver's door.

"Start the car," he said.

He gave her the keys and she reached in, put the ignition key in position, and turned it. The engine fired up with an incredible roar. It sounded like Frazier had set the idle up higher. Or, he had jammed the carburetor, such that when the car was shifted into gear, it would immediately accelerate to a high rate of . . . oh, shit.

"Now what, Dr. Frazier?" Cynthia asked.

"Go get back into my car, dear," he said.

When she turned to follow his instructions, he lifted the shotgun above his head and cracked her skull with the butt. He caught her before she fell, dragged her to the back door on my side, and shoved her in. He pushed on her buttocks until her head was on the opposite door and her feet were inside the car. He did not buckle her in.

"Been nice knowing you, Brady," he laughed, slamming both car doors. He reached through the driver window and into the car, hammered something, then apparently grabbed the gearshift and shifted into drive. Since I couldn't see, this was my only explanation for the sudden jerk forward.

The Lincoln's acceleration surprised me. I instinctively grabbed the steering wheel, not appreciating the fact that a blind man cannot drive. Not only was I blind, but my head ached, my heart pounded, and I was dizzy, all belladonna effects. I didn't know if I was going to die from atropine poisoning before or after the car crashed into another vehicle or into the concrete median strip. Or maybe the car would run off the shoulder and into the ditch next to the access road, flip, and burn. The safe bet was that death was upon all three of us. How it would happen was the only issue.

I reached for the ignition key, feeling for it first on the dash, then remembered it was on the steering column. It was broken off in the lock. That was the hammering I had heard. I tried the brakes, shoving the pedal to the floor. Nothing. Not even the emergency brake was functional. Frazier had apparently cut the brake lines and set the carburetor to accelerate at full throttle.

So, with an unconscious Jeff Clarke and a silent, concussed Cynthia Dumond, no brakes, a stuck carburetor, a speeding car, and no way to turn off the engine, I did the only thing I knew to do. I tried to steer the vehicle. I felt for the horn, which fortunately was on the pad in the middle of the steering wheel. I activated the horn with my right thumb and tried to feel my way on the interstate. At least I could try to warn other cars that mine was totally out of control.

I didn't know if Frazier had adjusted the wheel, such that the car would enter toward the middle of the road or to one side or the other. I had no idea how fast I was going or where the other cars were. All I knew for sure was that for fifteen or twenty miles, the stretch of Interstate 45 that runs from north of Conroe toward Houston is straight as an arrow. After that, the road starts bending from side to side. If I was lucky, I could live, and perhaps keep my passengers alive, for approximately fifteen more minutes. After that, we would be history.

I kept adjusting the wheel slightly, trying to feel for either shoulder or bumps in the road between the lanes, but nothing registered other than my fright. I had never been so scared. My window was still down, and the night air blew into the car like a high-powered ceiling fan.

I heard a car horn to my left erupt, causing me to turn the wheel toward the right slightly.

I felt some gravel—the right shoulder—and turned the wheel back to the left. I heard another desperate car horn. I felt the presence of road traffic and began to worry about the people I was going to kill when I crashed into another automobile at the high rate of speed I must be traveling.

I felt a car careen off my left fender. I jerked the Lincoln to the right and heard another, loud, persistent horn. I tried to keep the wheel straight, but I didn't know where straight was. I hoped somebody would call 911, tell the Conroe Police or the Montgomery County Sheriff's Office that a nut was on the loose, southbound on I-45, probably a drunk driver, or a kid on drugs.

But if someone came to my rescue, how would they stop the car? The cops could pull up beside the vehicle, turn on the siren, and yell and scream all they wanted, but I COULD NOT STOP THE CAR. No matter what.

I knew I was a dead man. My passengers were about to be dead. And I would be taking untold numbers of people with me if I crashed into someone on the freeway. I couldn't let that happen.

I decided to pull the car toward the right side of the highway and hope that no one would be in the right lane or on the shoulder. As I remembered, there was an embankment that led to the old Highway 45, a road that was still used as an access road to the freeway. At the right moment, I would steer the car abruptly to the right and take my chances with what I hoped would be a single-car crash. We three in the car would surely die, but I could save innocent people who were minding their own business and driving on the freeway that Friday night.

I said my prayers, remembering Dad's admonition that there are no unbelievers in a foxhole, said goodbye to my wonderful Mary Louise, and made ready. I felt for the window and seat controls on the driver's door panel and lowered all the windows in order to better hear adjacent road traffic. The wind gusted loudly through the car. The cool night air was almost pleasant, like I was floating on a speeding cloud across the heavens. Which I would be doing in about ten seconds.

Except that it was loud. Incredibly loud. In fact, so loud that I couldn't hear myself think. I had never heard wind so loud.

I gathered up all the nerve I had, tried to make sure there were no cars to my right, and inched over as best I could. I felt the texture of the road change and decided I was next to the shoulder. I started the countdown. 10 . . . 9 . . . 8 . . . 7 . . . 6 . . . 5 . . . 4 . . . 3 . . . 2 . . . 1. I turned the wheel as hard to the right as I could. I felt the car dip down, bounce and crash, then rise up. I let go of the steering wheel, leaving my fate to whomever had control of it at that moment. The car rose up into the air, and as it rose, I wondered what it would feel like to crash back down onto the feeder. Would the car flip? Would I feel pain? Would I die instantly? Would the car catch fire, and would I be burned alive?

The car jerked again, like a train being coupled to another set of cars. I felt more disorientation, probably from the effects of the atropine. It seemed the car was still rising. I should have felt the crash onto the feeder road by then. I knew I didn't deserve it, but it looked like God was going to spare all three of us the terrible pain of thousands of pounds of steel as it crushed our bodies. I was flying.

Then, we were ascending into heaven, like the prophets of old. I lay my head back and started to let myself go. I waited for the proverbial white light. I waited to greet my Dad.

CHAPTER 28

RESCUE

Friday, May 26, 2000

I was relaxed. I felt I was having the effect of a drug of some sort. I lay on dampness and imagined a smooth, calm lake, or the Gulf of Mexico on a windless day in August. I was floating on top of the water. Or on a cloud of mist. I opened my eyes. The light was blinding. I squinted, saw some shadowy movement in the light. I was at my destination. It was over. I hadn't felt a thing. I was so thankful, I began to weep.

"Dad? Is that you?"

"Lie still, Dr. Brady. You're okay. Can you hear me? You're o-k-a-y."

"Who's there? I can't see."

"Sheriff Ken Adams, Dr. Brady. We're taking you to County Hospital to get you checked out."

"You mean, I'm not dead?"

"No, sir, you're very much alive."

"You're kidding me, right?"

"No, sir. But it was close. Real close."

✦ ✦ ✦

I felt my body being lifted, then carried, by voices that had no faces. I felt the placement of a portable stretcher onto the track of what I assumed was an emergency vehicle. I felt the inflation of a blood pressure cuff on my arm and the beats of my still-rapid radial pulse being counted by gentle fingers.

"Can you see anything, Doctor?" a woman's voice asked.

"Just bright light, which hurts my eyes. I can't keep them open."

"Keep them closed, then, sir."

After a minute or so, I heard another stretcher lock into a parallel runner, and a grating noise as it slid into position.

"Jeff? Cynthia?"

"The gentleman's unconscious, sir," said the female voice. "Please lie quietly. We'll have you out of here in a sec."

"What about Cynthia? The nurse?"

There was no response.

I heard the ignition turn over, the vehicle accelerate, and a high-pitched siren wail. The rhythmic sounds of the ambulance lulled me to sleep.

I slept most of Saturday. I dreamed of electrodes splayed on my shaved chest. I woke up to runs of tachycardia and irregular heartbeats. I panicked over skipped heartbeats and occasional stoppages. Sweats. The need to urinate, afraid to pee in my pants, then an uncontrollable release.

I finally became awake and alert Sunday morning. My vision was blurred, but I could see colors. And contrasts. It appeared my eyesight was going to be restored. I saw shapes, movement.

The first person I recognized was Mary Louise.

"Is that you?"

"Yes, sweetie. How are you feeling?"

"I'm dizzy, I have a horrible headache, and I can't see clearly. And my neck hurts. And my heart feels like it's been trying to beat its way out of my chest. And I have to pee. What in the hell happened?"

I felt her sit on the edge of the bed and hold my hand.

"You have a catheter. Just let it go."

I did.

"What do you remember?" she asked.

"Well, Frazier caught Jeff and I in his private office, going over the medical records of his patients. We were placed in the trunk of my rental car after he knocked in half of Jeff's face. How is he, by the way?"

"I'll get to that. Just tell me what you remember."

"So, we bounced around in the trunk for a while, got on the freeway, then went under the freeway, and stopped. When he let us out of the trunk, we were on the southbound side of I-45, I think, somewhere north of Conroe. That's when Frazier had Cynthia—how is she?"

"I'll tell you. Finish your story."

"Anyway, Cynthia put those damn drops in Jeff's eyes, then mine. They blinded me almost immediately. Jeff was still unconscious. Then, that son-of-a-bitch Frazier hit Cynthia over the head with the butt of his shotgun and threw her into the back seat. Best I can figure, he jacked around with the carburetor, cut the brake lines, broke the ignition key off in the lock, threw the car into gear, and let her fly.

"I tried to keep the Lincoln on the road, but—do you have any idea how hard it is to drive when you can't see anything? You can hear cars whizzing by, horns honking, but you are totally disoriented. It was horrible. I decided I was going to kill a lot of innocent people if I stayed on the highway, so I tried to pull off to the shoulder on the right side of the road and just let the car go.

"I felt the car go down the embankment, then rise. I waited for the crash onto the feeder road, or whatever field is on the other side of the access road, but we just kept rising. I really thought I had died, and somehow, God spared me the pain of a crash. It felt like I was being pulled up into the clouds. It should have been quiet, but there was like . . . thunder around the car. I had lowered the windows, in order to hear bypassing cars better, to try to avoid hitting anybody. I thought the sound was too loud to be wind, but I didn't know what else it could be."

She patted my hand. "It wasn't wind, Jim Bob. It was Sheriff Adams's people in the Montgomery County Air Rescue helicopter."

"Huh. I've been rescued twice in two weeks by one of those things. Guess I owe Ken Adams a big debt of gratitude."

"Yes, you do."

"So, you want to tell me about it?"

"Are you up for it?"

"I'll stop you if I get confused."

"Okay. Well, you were supposed to be home Friday afternoon and go with me to the beach, or you were to meet me down there around six o'clock. When I didn't hear from you, I got a little worried. Then, when I called home and picked up our messages and heard that you were going to be delayed, I relaxed.

"However, sitting outside at the beach house on the deck with a glass of wine, I began to realize that you and Jeff must be on to something. Because I know, young man, you wouldn't consider missing a minute at the beach unless there was an important reason. Right?"

"Right."

"Of course, I didn't know what you had discovered, or where exactly you had found what you might have been looking for. You see, I really didn't know what you and Jeff were up to. So, I went back over your itinerary as best I could remember it and wrote it down.

"I knew you were going to see a patient's wife, at a synagogue, and meet with a rabbi. I couldn't remember his name, or the patient's name, so I called information in Conroe. Since there were only two synagogues, it wasn't that difficult to get hold of Jake Stern. He told me that you and Jeff had been there and were scheduled to see Ted

Frazier around two o'clock. He also said that you were going to visit the relative of one of your patients who had died, and he thought Jeff had told him that it was someone in the sheriff's department.

"When I inquired about the nature of the visit you and Jeff had with him and he told me about the prescription bottle, I decided that your and Jeff's delay in returning to Houston probably had something to do with that nursing home of Ted Frazier's. And knowing you, the time to check it out would be . . . after hours.

"I started to panic while I was talking to Rabbi Stern. He calmed me down, said he would call the Conroe Police Department and the Montgomery County Sheriff's Office and try to find who it was that you and Jeff had talked to that day.

"Well, I couldn't just sit there in Galveston and worry. So, I hung up the phone, got into the car, and drove to Conroe. Jake had given me directions to his home and said if I was really worried, to come on up. Which I was, and which I did."

"You mean, you've been in Conroe? Since when?"

"I left after I made the call to Jake Stern. With the outbound Friday evening traffic out of Houston, I didn't get here until almost nine."

"Then you were at Jake's house while we were rummaging around at Pleasant View. That is so bizarre. And there I was, worrying about you being all by yourself down at the beach, and you were, what? A few miles away?"

"About three miles down Highway 105. Anyway, once Jake Stern located Sergeant Adams, he was kind enough to join us at the rabbi's house. Once we started talking about the discrepancies you and Jeff had found on Rufus Jeffries and Beatrice Adams, Ken started to get concerned. In fact, he became livid, thinking that there might have been some type of foul play in the death of his sister.

"So, he used his skills as a law-enforcement officer to track down the license plate number on your Lincoln from the rental car agency and put out an APB for your vehicle. Then, he took Jake and me over to Pleasant View."

"I can't believe this! What time were you there?"

"Must have been about ten thirty."

"Unbelievable! Frazier probably had just put us in the trunk and was taking us to the freeway."

"At first, Ken couldn't get any satisfaction from the evening supervisor at the nursing home. He insisted that we be allowed to search the building for you and Jeff. He didn't have a search warrant, but the supervisor didn't know that.

"Dear Mrs. Guyton, bless her heart. Ken stormed onto that second-floor nursing station like a madman, thinking that his sister might have been harmed by Frazier and his purported treatment. He asked all the employees about any visitors they might have seen that evening. She, Mrs. Guyton, explained about Mr. Moore's son and his friend whom she had allowed in after visiting hours. She started to cry, poor thing, thinking she was in trouble. Ken asked for a description of the two visitors. All we had to hear was that one man had flaming-red curly hair and the other had on a fringed leather jacket and wore boots.

"Once we knew you two had been there, Ken called for assistance. The three of us and two deputies combed the clinic and the administrative offices, looking for a clue as to your whereabouts. The door to a private office next to Frazier's office was ajar. We saw all the charts and files scattered around the room and figured you two had been there and had been caught.

"About that time, one of the deputies on patrol radioed Ken. He said that a motorist driving south on I-45 reported seeing someone being pulled out of a trunk of a car, a Lincoln. Ken dispatched two squad cars to the approximate location and called for an air search by his one and only helicopter. We ran out of there and headed your way. Jake and I were in Ken's car, the two other deputies in their car. It would have been exhilarating if I hadn't known was your life was in danger. Lights were flashing, sirens blasting, charging through red lights like in a movie.

"On the way, Ken received another call from the station. A motorist traveling south on I-45 had complained about a drunk driver who had tried to run him off the road. Ken checked the license plate number, and we knew it had to be you.

"The two squad cards that Ken dispatched arrived on the scene just as Frazier was leaving in his car. Frazier had apparently hung around to make sure that you were headed in the right direction, which was away from Frazier and toward the bright lights of Houston. They stopped him for questioning. Ted apparently was freaked out by them, because when the two officers pulled him over, Frazier got out of the car with a shotgun in his hands. One of the deputies told him to drop it. He didn't, and they shot him."

"Was one of the guys named Wally?"

"How did you know?"

"Lucky guess. Anyway, go ahead."

"By the time we arrived at the scene, Frazier was dead. The deputy in the helicopter radioed that they had spotted your car, said that you were weaving from lane to lane. So, Jake and I jumped back into Ken's car and he took off after you. Ken kept in radio contact with the helicopter. Wally and the other deputy stayed with Frazier's body and called the Montgomery County morgue.

"When the chopper first sighted you, the pilot said you were all over the freeway. Since we didn't know what was wrong—I knew you weren't drunk—the chopper hovered over you. The pilot used his megaphone and tried to get you to answer him. He even bumped your roof with his rails once but said you still didn't respond. Fortunately, you had all the windows down, so they threw a ladder down. An officer climbed down the ladder, while another officer handed him two large hooks attached to a steel cable. While he was hanging onto the ladder, above your roof, at a high rate of speed, with the helicopter trying to hold its position above you, Deputy—I forget his name, but he was good—locked a hook as best he could under each open front window, and they hoisted your car off the ground.

"We were watching all this from the rear. Of course, I had no idea you had been blinded with atropine and that Jeff was unconscious, or that there was an injured woman in the car. Once the helicopter had you suspended, the pilot hovered over the access road and held the car just above it while the other officer climbed onto the roof, then onto the ground, opened the hood, disabled the engine, and stopped the car. Then, they lowered the vehicle to the ground.

"By then, there was a full 911 rescue team there. When they unloaded you and laid you on the ground, I was right there with you. You kept saying something about your father."

She patted me. I sighed.

"What about Jeff?"

"He has a broken man—cheekbone? And jawbone?"

"Maxilla and mandible. Is he all right?"

"Yes. He was in surgery for several hours. He might have some damage to his left eye, too. The doctor said he would have to wait for the effects of the atropine to wear off to know for sure. Apparently, you two are lucky you didn't die from side effects of the drug. The doctors said you and Jeff each appeared to have been given an enormous dose. You know, you had heart problems for about twenty-four hours. Rapid beat, slow beat, like that, all day and night."

"So I wasn't dreaming after all. How long did he say it would take for the atropine effects to wear off?"

"One or two weeks."

"What?!" I said, rising from my hospital bed.

"Relax. It may not take that long for you. We'll see, he said."

"I need to get home and see one of the ophthalmologists at University. I've got to get to work next week, for God's sake."

"And then, maybe you won't," Mary Louise responded.

I lay my head back and sighed again.

"What about Cynthia? She okay?"

Nothing.

"Mary Louise?"

"Jim Bob, there was a slight problem when the helicopter picked your car up. On the first attempt, one hook slipped, and the car listed severely to one side. You and Jeff were buckled in, but that poor woman . . ."

"You mean?"

"Yes. She slid out of the rear window on the passenger side before the officer could get the hook repositioned on that side. I'm sorry, but she's dead from a massive head injury and a broken neck."

"My God. I still can't believe Cynthia was involved in all this."

"Who was she, Jim Bob?"

"I don't think I feel like talking any more right now. I'll tell you later. Okay? I'm glad you're here, though," I said, and took her hand, kissing her fingertips.

"I love you," she said.

"And I'm grateful you were there for me."

CHAPTER 29

OTHERS

Late May–Early June, 2000

During the ensuing week, which was blessedly slightly shorter since Monday was Memorial Day, I fumbled around my office, dictated chart notes, signed operative reports, and had telephone fights with insurance company representatives. It took that long for my vision to be clear enough to be able to return to my real job of seeing patients and performing surgery.

Meanwhile, the media had a field day with the dramatic rescue of yours truly on Interstate 45 by the Montgomery County Sheriff's Office. The story, of course, opened the Pandora's box of Pleasant View Nursing Home and made public the escapades of Dr. Theodore Frazier. Mary Louise and I were bombarded with requests, which we politely declined, for interviews from the local and national news media. After all, any attempt to cure a deteriorating brain disease, no matter how disgustingly pathological that treatment might be, is front-page news.

Jeff left the Montgomery County Hospital a few days after his emergency surgery, a little sore and swollen, but with the anticipation of a satisfactory recovery. He and I cooperated with the local and state authorities to the best of our ability. Numerous expert endocrinologists and neurologists were called in to sort out the mess Frazier had created at Pleasant View. The information for which Jeff and I had almost sacrificed our lives became the cornerstone for the exposure of the alleged scheme to cure Alzheimer's disease.

As Jeff and I saw it, and the experts agreed, the most pressing problem at the nursing home was to determine which of the current residents had myxedema dementia from thyroid deprivation, as opposed to those who were true Alzheimer's patients. After a considerable amount of scrutiny of the medical records, it was determined by the experts that twenty-nine of the inpatients (including Beatrice Adams, Rufus Jeffries, and Charles Pullig) had been treated at one time or another with thyroid medication for hypothyroidism. Some had been treated by Dr. Frazier in his private practice, either before or after his move to the nursing home. Some had been treated by other physicians for thyroid deficiency prior to their move to Pleasant View and before they were under Frazier's care. All patients had been deprived of adequate thyroid supplementation through underdosing, once they were under Frazier's care. The chronic deprivation of required thyroid medication either escalated the progression of an already-existing dementia, or it created one. The remaining sixty-seven dementia patients were presumed to have Alzheimer's disease, although absolute documentation of the disease process, through pathological study of the brain tissue at autopsy, could not be determined with absolute certainty until their deaths.

One of the most serious concerns of the consulting endocrinologists and neurologists was in regard to the thyroid-deprived patients who were still alive, and had dementia, at Pleasant View. Was their dementia reversible? Due to the potentially hazardous effects of the sudden influx of thyroid medications, small doses would have to be initiated and increased very slowly, so as not to stimulate the cardiovascular system too quickly. Would the patients respond? How much memory would they regain, if any? And how quickly? It was to be an incredibly valuable research study, but not without extreme hazard.

And what about the current population of the nursing home? Ninety-five patients remained after the four deaths at University Hospital and the fifth patient, Charles Pullig, was transferred by his family to another facility after his discharge from University. Had all the Pleasant View patients been receiving massive amounts of acetylcholinesterase inhibitor through biweekly infusion via spinal tap? And if so, what would its sudden withdrawal do to their mental status? Each patient had to be evaluated thoroughly, then observed carefully over time, to determine changes after the infusion therapy had been discontinued.

And what would be the effects on the patients' cardiovascular systems? What would be their physiological responses to abrupt discontinuation of the scopolamine patches used to mitigate the bradycardia caused by the ACH? Frazier had seemed to, despite his madness, balance the effects of increased acetylcholine in the system and achieve a stable heart rate with the patches. It would become a cardiology nightmare, trying to juggle the concomitant withdrawal of scopolamine and acetylcholine levels in the bloodstream.

Neither the medical nor the legal experts consulted over the Pleasant View fiasco had ever seen such a case of multiple acts of negligence on the part of a single physician. Of course, when the story broke, the families of both the surviving patients and the deceased patients were besieged with solicitors offering to take legal cases on a contingency fee. There were many takers, primarily those families of patients who had been induced into a demented state via thyroid deprivation.

Records revealed that hundreds of patients that had been institutionalized at Pleasant View since 1993, Frazier's inaugural year as director. He accepted patients on a two- to three-year plan. He had infused them, experimented with them, then discharged them, at least the ones he thought had improved. The ones that did not get better with his therapy, he transferred to an acute-care hospital, typically with a diagnosis of dehydration, failure to thrive, and cardiac arrythmia. Most of them died of acute, unexplained bradycardia leading to heart failure, except for those rare patients who either had a pacemaker, like Charles Pullig, or those who were otherwise metabolically blessed. No one had stayed at Pleasant View longer than three years. Patients were either discharged or had died.

Frazier had used the Medical Center in Conroe as a transfer facility for the first few years he was in business. Then, he used St. Paul's Hospital, in the Texas Medical Center in Houston, for the next few. Then, his transfers went to St. John's Hospital, also in Houston. Most recently he had been using University Hospital through Dr. James Morgenstern in an attempt to try and cover his tracks. Too many deaths at the same hospital might have alerted hospital officials, so he kept changing his referral patterns. The experts involved in deciphering the former patients' whereabouts, and their respective medical conditions, stated publicly that it would take months, perhaps even years, to accurately evaluate the patient histories during Frazier's seven years as medical director of Pleasant View Nursing Home.

Probably the most interesting, and yet baffling, aspect of the case was the response of the families of the nursing-home residents who had been discharged. It was presumed by the news media, and by the expert consultants privately, since many of the patients were still alive, that those people had improved with the infusion therapy, at least enough to return to some type of home environment. There were a number of those patients—a large number. In fact, of the several hundred patients that had been residents of Pleasant View from 1993 to 2000, almost 250 had been discharged, and therefore had potentially been aided by Frazier's treatment. And I say potentially, because each and every family member, including the Frazier-treated patients who were still alive, steadfastly refused to speak to anyone—not the press, not the news media, not the medical specialists, not even the attorneys.

The escapades of Dr. Ted Frazier became the object of national news broadcast programs, including *Eye-to-Eye*, *60 Minutes*, and

20/20. All the commentators asked the same questions. Why did he experiment with human lives? Why did he create dementia patients? Weren't there enough folks with debilitating memory loss? Why did he do it? For money? For fame? For the potential improvement of humanity? For the greater good? Or did he simply get carried away due to his excitement over the patients who might have improved? And who exactly had improved? And how much? And in what way? These questions no one outside of the families could answer, and the families would not talk, not even for money. Reports surfaced here and there that families were, on occasion, offered six-figure advances for a story on Frazier's treatment of their loved ones. There were no takers.

My impression of Frazier is simple: He was insane. His treatment was a harebrained idea, conjured up during some late night of drinking, precipitated by his young wife's American Express bill. He needed money, and a lot of it. What better scam than to "cure" Alzheimer's disease? Maybe he had some success; who knows. He definitely developed a severe case of egocentricity. Delusions of grandeur. A God complex. To me, the code of silence—as the tabloids termed it, "Cured Alzheimer's Patients Won't Talk"—adopted by the families of Frazier's former patients was simply their way to avoid the public embarrassment of admitting their subscription to one of the greatest hoaxes in the history of medicine. Even better than the Texas physician who purported curing cancer patients with weekly injections of a revolutionary new drug. Turned out, he was using urine extract, and canine urine, at that. I wouldn't have talked either.

And then, I met a woman in my office some months later, on a clinic day. A charming elderly Black woman came to see me about her hip. She said she had arthritis and quite a bit of pain. I examined her, x-rayed her, and determined that she did, in fact, have severe hip arthritis and needed a joint replacement. I gave her the usual spiel about the operative procedure, its risks and complications, the average recovery time, et cetera. Informed consent, it's called. The information that patients want and need, it is.

When I finished my standard oration, she stared at me for a while, without speaking.

"Mrs. White? Did you hear what I told you? And did you understand everything?"

She nodded.

"Well, is there anything else?"

She nodded again.

"What is it, ma'am?" I said, wondering if this would be the introduction to another medical issue entirely.

"My daughter spoke very highly of you, and all the things she said about you are true. You seem to be a good man and a good doctor."

"Your daughter?"

"Cynthia. Cynthia Dumond."

"Oh, I'm sorry. With the name being different and all, I didn't . . ."

"That's all right, young man," she said, in her crackling voice. She stood up, braced herself on the cane, and got right below my face, since she was just over five feet tall.

"I was there, you know."

"Excuse me?"

"I was there. At Pleasant View. For just shy of two years. I had Alzheimer's so bad I couldn't remember my own name, or so Cynthia told me."

"I'm sorry, but I don't understand. If you had Alzheimer's . . ."

"Doc Frazier cured me. Cynthia could tell you, if she was still with us. She started working weekends there while I was a patient, in order to keep an eye on me. He cured a bunch of us, and a lot of us are still alive, those of us whose hearts haven't tuckered out or who haven't gotten the Big C. We're out there—in the city, in the county, in the state—everywhere. He made sure we all kept in touch with each other after we were discharged from Pleasant View. We've been talking and writing back and forth, the ones of us that are left. We've stuck together, granting no interviews, and nobody has broken ranks to get attention for themselves. Doc would have been pleased."

I stepped back and leaned against the adjacent wall. I felt the blood rushing out of my head, like I was going to faint, and I sat down on a nearby rolling stool.

"People have intimated that there were cures, Mrs. White, or at least improvements. But since none of the former patients, or their families for that matter, have been willing to speak to the media or the investigating doctors, there has been no documentation of these so-called cures. I don't understand. If Frazier's treatment actually worked, why wouldn't you survivors come forward? And why tell me?"

She smiled. "Cynthia would have wanted you to know, Dr. Brady. I admit, Doc Frazier did hurt some people. The ones I've read about in the papers, the ones whose minds he messed up by not giving them their medication, that was bad. But then, a lot of us he helped, and we feel like we owe him."

"I'm afraid you're a little late, Mrs. White."

"Oh, not hardly, young man. We have been waiting for the right time, Dr. Brady. We've only just begun, like the Carpenters song. Our voices will now be heard."

With that, she turned to the examination-room door, opened it, and stepped out into the hallway. She pivoted on her cane and looked at me, now sitting on my stool in a state of shock and trying to comprehend what she had told me.

"What do you mean, Mrs. White? About your voices will now be heard?"

She smiled a gracious smile, nodded her head.

"Dr. Brady, we've decided you're the man to tell our story."

ABOUT THE AUTHOR

Dr. John Bishop has led a triple life. This orthopedic surgeon and keyboard musician has combined two of his talents into a third, as the author of the beloved Doc Brady mystery series. Beyond applying his medical expertise at a relatable and comprehensible level, Dr. Bishop, through his fictional counterpart Doc Brady, also infuses his books with his love of not only Houston and Galveston, Texas, but especially with his love for his adored wife. Bishop's talented Doc Brady is confident yet humble; brilliant, yet a genuinely nice and funny guy who happens to have a knack for solving medical mysteries. Above all, he is the doctor who will cure you of your blues and boredom. Step into his world with the first four books of the series, and you'll be clamoring for more.

CPSIA information can be obtained
at www.ICGtesting.com
Printed in the USA
FSHW012129260321
79897FS